NEW YEAR'S BABIES

Eugenia Riley
"The Confused Stork"

"Eugenia Riley spins a brilliantly woven web, ensnaring readers with her ingenious plot twists, endearing characters and an unforgettable love story."

—*Romantic Times* on *Tempest in Time*

Jennifer Archer
"Blame It on the Baby"

"*Body & Soul* is a fun romp that readers who enjoy an amusing romance with a serious undertone will relish. . . . Jennifer Archer scores a bulls-eye with her warm debut novel."

—*Painted Rock*

Kimberly Raye
"A Little Bit of Magic"

"Ms. Raye always manages to add a unique twist to all her novels. [*Something Wild*] is both exciting and captivating."

—*Romantic Times*

Other anthologies from *Love Spell* and Leisure:
MASQUERADE
PARADISE
THE CAT'S MEOW
SWEPT AWAY
CELEBRATIONS
TRICK OR TREAT
INDULGENCE
MIDSUMMER NIGHT'S MAGIC
LOVESCAPE
CUPID'S KISS
LOVE'S LEGACY
ENCHANTED CROSSINGS

New Year's Babies

EUGENIA RILEY,
JENNIFER ARCHER,
KIMBERLY RAYE

LOVE SPELL BOOKS NEW YORK CITY

LOVE SPELL®

November 1999

Published by

Dorchester Publishing Co., Inc.
276 Fifth Avenue
New York, NY 10001

ISBN 0-505-52345-0

Printed in the United States of America.

The Confused Stork

Eugenia Riley

This novella is dedicated, with love,
to my daughter, Noelle,
and her husband, Paul,
with congratulations on
their marriage, and
the arrival of their own
bundle of joy.

Chapter One

Chicago
The Present

Emma Fairchild awakened with a start. Something was terribly wrong.

Her baby was missing!

She sat up in her hospital bed, only to wince at the slight dizziness she felt, and grimace at the pain of her stitches. Her breasts felt strangely heavy, very full and tender. Then she pressed her hand to her stomach and gasped at its flatness. Yes, she had definitely delivered her child. After carrying her baby for nine months, feeling its absence was both awesome and frightening.

Where was her baby now?

She glanced frantically about the stark hospital room, its grimness relieved only by the flutter of the snow falling outside her window. It was a chilly November day in Chicago, and she was utterly alone. She guessed by the few muted rays of light piercing the grayness outside that it must be late afternoon.

Late afternoon . . . How odd. Her last memories had been of early evening. Almost twenty-four hours must have passed.

Emma desperately searched her memory, struggling to recall her last few conscious moments in the delivery room. She remembered the doctor had urged her to push, the excruciating pain, and the drugs that had left her drifting in and out of consciousness. Then, most bizarre, she had heard the fluttering of a very large bird's wings, followed by gasps of shock and panic all around her. And something else. . . .

Good heavens! Had someone yelled, "Holy cow, there's a *stork* in this delivery room!"?

A half-hysterical giggle escaped Emma at the prospect. A stork in the delivery room? That was absurd, impossible. She was in a hospital, not some demented Mother Goose nursery rhyme. Surely the drugs they'd given her had made her hallucinate and dream of storks . . . and babies arriving in neat little kerchiefs.

But one thing she did remember: the plaintive

sound of a baby's cry—*her* baby's cry. The memory of the poignant whimper filled her heart with sheer joy and stark longing, even as the thought brought tears to her eyes. Her baby had been there, this she was certain of. Her arms had ached to hold the wonder of new life. She had fought so hard to awaken, had struggled to speak, to beg the doctor to bring her child to her.

But even as the clamor about her had continued, Emma had sunk deeper and deeper into a dark fog, until unconsciousness had at last overtaken her.

Where was her baby now, and was her child all right?

Emma found the call button for the nurse on her pillow and quickly pressed it. Within a minute, a middle-aged, plump woman in green uniform appeared. Expression wary, she crept inside the room, pausing a few feet away from Emma's bed, as if the sight of her patient intimidated her.

"May I help you?" she asked tentatively.

"Yes," Emma answered anxiously, her fingers clutching the sheet. "I want my baby. Can you bring her—or him—to me?"

The nurse went pale. "I'm afraid that's not possible yet, Mrs. Fairchild."

Panic seized Emma. "Not possible! What do you mean? Is my baby all right?"

The woman coughed. "There's been . . . well, a complication."

"Complication? What?"

"I'm afraid I'm not free to say. If you'll wait a moment, I'll get—"

"*What*?" Emma cried. "What on earth are you talking about? I have every right to see my child, and I insist you bring him—or her—here to me right this minute!"

The nurse wrung her hands. "I'm afraid . . . Well, we may have misplaced—"

"Misplaced?" Emma shrieked.

The woman grimaced at Emma's sharp tone. "I should get the doctor. Is there someone I can call for you?"

Emma was swept by a chill. "I just knew it. Something is wrong!"

"I . . . I'll go get someone to speak with you."

As the woman hurried off, Emma cried, "Wait!"

The woman turned and regarded Emma tensely. "Yes?"

"Can you even tell me if my child is a boy or a girl?"

Looking miserable, the woman stared at her feet. "I'm afraid I can't, ma'am."

"You don't know?"

"I'm sorry, but I can't tell you anymore right now. I'll get someone to explain the, um, situation."

Watching the woman turn, Emma again cried, "Stop!" As the nurse complied, Emma said fretfully, "There's something very strange going on here. I seem to recall. . . . Tell me, was there a stork in the delivery room?"

The nurse gasped and fell back a step. "A s-stork?" she stammered. "Why, that's the silliest notion I've ever heard."

But the shrill way the woman spoke, her utter lack of conviction, filled Emma with dread. Watching the nurse turn again and all but run from the room, she was swamped by a sick feeling.

Tears burned her eyes and anguish throbbed in her throat. Why wouldn't the nurse tell her what was going on? Had her baby come to harm? Oh, this was a nightmare! It was bad enough that Steve had deserted her seven months ago. Emma's attorney ex-husband had informed her he was sleeping with a female client soon after Emma had announced she was pregnant. In a truly cruel and ironic twist, her husband had even bragged that he was expecting *another* child . . . with his mistress! They'd gotten a divorce and Steve had promptly married Shelly, showing no interest in his ex-wife's coming baby, as if he hadn't fathered the child.

Although Emma intended to force Steve to pay child support, she knew her ex was too immature and self-centered to ever become a good father.

Too bad she'd been fooled by his charm, falling in love with a man who could never commit to her or return her feelings.

So here she was, a twenty-seven-year-old divorcée, all alone in the world, with her newborn child missing. There was no one she could call. She'd only been in Chicago for eighteen months, and she'd been so plagued with morning sickness during her pregnancy that she'd only done a little temp work as a secretary. She had no real friends here. Her parents had retired to Mexico and her nearest relative was her grandmother in Nashville. Dear Gran. Although she was too old and frail to come to Chicago for the birth, she'd sent Emma the beautiful bouquet of roses on her bedside table, and the nightgown and robe in the box on her chair.

Inhaling the sweet aroma of the flowers, Emma felt somehow comforted by Gran's presence. Eyeing the lingerie, she glanced down at her unattractive, green-and-white-checked cotton hospital gown. Suddenly she wanted nothing to do with this awful institution; instead she would put on her grandmother's gift, so she could feel closer to her loved one. Maybe she'd feel stronger when someone from the hospital at last brought news of her baby.

Gingerly, Emma got out of the bed, wincing at the pain and wooziness that swamped her. She stepped into her slippers and, breathing raggedly, managed to grab the box and stagger into the bathroom.

Ten minutes later she emerged with her long blond hair combed, wearing the ankle-length blue gown and coordinating velour, princess-style robe. She had just managed to sit back down on the bed when she heard a throat being cleared. She turned to view an older, gray-haired gentleman in an expensive suit standing inside the doorway.

"Yes?" she called.

The man stepped into the room. Tall, thin, and tired-looking, he flashed her a strained smile. "Mrs. Fairchild?"

"Yes?"

"I'm George Peabody, the hospital legal counsel."

"Legal counsel?" Emma didn't like the sound of that at all.

Solemnly, he replied, "I've come to speak with you about your child."

Alarm tingled along Emma's spine. "I knew it! What happened to my baby?"

He flashed her a regretful look. "Although I cannot tell you much, something unfortunate did seem to occur in the delivery room. Now we have every reason to believe your infant is fine, but—"

"But?" Emma echoed frantically.

"There was . . . well, an intrusion in the delivery room."

"I knew it! There was a stork, right?"

The man turned the same sickening shade of white that had paled the nurse. "What makes you ask that?"

Shaking her head, Emma felt intensely confused. "Well, as bizarre as it sounds, I heard wings. The flapping of a very large bird's wings, as a matter of fact. Although I was drugged at the time—"

"Yes, you were," he put in tactfully, "which makes anything you might remember suspect."

"Then I didn't hear a stork?"

He coughed. "That's not what I said."

Emma pounded a fist on the mattress. "What *are* you saying?"

The man appeared so wretchedly ill-at-ease that Emma almost felt sorry for him. "Well, there was an intrusion, and some person—or entity—unknown to us seems to have absconded with your child."

"My God!" Emma's words were a hoarse whisper.

He stepped forward and spoke in a rush. "You must understand, of course, that the hospital cannot be held liable—"

"You can't?" she all but screamed. "It's *your* hospital, damn it. Oh my God, you've lost my child! And if you're not responsible, who is?"

"The person—or entity—that stole your baby," he went on haltingly. "You must know we're doing everything in our power to solve the mystery and find your baby. We've notified the police and the FBI, and they'll be in shortly to question you."

"Question *me*? What about you?"

He avoided her eye. "That's all I'm free to tell you for now, I'm afraid."

Emma's panic was rapidly being overcome with anger. "That's all? You let someone steal my child, and that's all? You bring me my baby, right this instant, you stuffed shirt, or I'm going to start screaming bloody murder!"

"Mrs. Fairchild, please, becoming hysterical will get you nowhere—"

"Want to bet?"

Emma was true to her word. She ranted. She raved. She screamed loud enough to wake the dead. She demanded that her baby be brought to her instantly. Or else.

All to no avail. Within a minute, a doctor and a gaggle of nurses rushed in, held her down, gave her a shot, and unconsciousness sucked her under once again.

Gradually, Emma sensed men and women moving in and out of her room, speaking in muffled voices that filtered through her foggy mind. "She's out cold, thank heaven. We just don't know what to tell her. . . ." "Sorry, Agent Murphy, you can't question Mrs. Fairchild right now. She's been hysterical, you see. Perhaps in a few hours. . . ." "What on earth do you suppose *really* happened in that delivery room?"

Emma struggled to awaken, moaning softly, calling for her baby. Panic clung to her like a dull ache. Her arms were empty, her heart was broken, and she knew she must get up and go find her poor, lost child—the baby whom Steve had never wanted, but *she* wanted so badly.

Still, her heavy eyelids refused to budge.

Then at last she heard a strange shuffling sound and stirred slightly. Just managing to peak through her eyelids, she spotted a gentleman walking into her room, a peculiar, bent-over old fellow wearing an old-fashioned black uniform with brass buttons and a matching black cap with a gold-trimmed visor. He paused next to her bed, then laid a large white envelope near her hand. Smiling at her and tipping his cap, he turned and shuffled out of the room.

At last Emma awakened, alone. She spotted the large official-looking parchment envelope by her hand, blinked at it, and picked it up.

So she hadn't dreamed the strange old man. Its return address read simply "Dispatcher of New Souls." It was addressed in elegant script to "Mrs. Fairchild." On the back, a gold seal was emblazoned with a single word: Heaven.

What on earth? First the stork, now the "Dispatcher of New Souls?" What was this, *Grimm's Fairy Tales*? How many more outlandish things would happen to her today?

Quickly she opened the envelope, scanning the strange though official-looking letterhead that also read, "Dispatcher of New Souls—Heaven."

Emma blinked in perplexity. This was nuts. Nonetheless, she quickly read the letter.

My dear Mrs. Fairchild:

I am writing, with regret, to inform you of a most lamentable occurrence with respect to your newborn child, dispatched to you at 7:05 P.M. yesterday. It seems we should have trusted your baby to more reliable hands. Unfortunately, Ralph the Stork is in his dotage, and after he arrived at the hospital, he became quite confused at the resulting chaos in the delivery room.

By now, you're surely wondering what must have happened to your infant. I fear there's no delicate way to put this. Given the chaos among the hospital staff when Ralph appeared, the poor befuddled bird utterly panicked and flew out of the hospital with your little bundle of joy. Ralph promptly took a wrong turn in time. I'm afraid he mistakenly delivered your child to the stoop of a rogue, a most disreputable fellow, who resides in Victorian England.

We apologize for the mistake and any resulting inconvenience it may have caused you, and trust this matter shall shortly be rectified. Enclosed please find one "Ticket through Time," and best of luck reclaiming your lost child.

Sincerely,
I. M. Bearing
Dispatcher of New Souls

Enclosure

Emma finished the letter, only to shake her head in stupefaction. This *must* be a joke. She wasn't in a hospital but some sort of lunatic asylum. It was totally deranged to expect her to believe that not only had a *stork* delivered her baby, it had delivered it to the wrong century! Perhaps the hospital legal counsel had sent her this crazy missive to confuse her further—which was pretty darned easy to do at the moment.

But as Emma refolded the bizarre letter, a small card fell out. She stared flabbergasted at the elegant writing, which read, "Ticket through Time." The ticket was divided down the center by a dotted line, with smaller print on one side.

She turned the card sideways, squinted, and carefully read, "Tear here and hold onto your stomach."

Emma was stunned. This was ridiculous! Had she not been ready to cry, she would have laughed out loud. Her baby was missing, the hospital staff refused to tell her anything, much less help her find her child, and now someone had left her this demented letter.

Again she stared at the ticket. "Tear here and hold onto your stomach." What harm could it do to tear up the ticket? Afterward, she would rip the silly letter into a thousand shreds as well and find out what exactly was going on here.

Gingerly Emma got out of bed and stepped into her slippers. She held up the ticket and shook her head. "Here goes nothing," she muttered.

Emma tore the ticket straight down the dotted line and held the pieces to her stomach. Then, to her horror, she began to spin. . . .

Chapter Two

London
The Past

"Now Celeste, love, be a dear and come inside. I promise I shall make it worth your while."

"Oh, Matthew, you're being tiresome. You know I must go home straightaway."

Matthew Weymouth, earl of Worthing, was quite frustrated sitting in the cab of his brougham, parked before his Warwick Square townhouse, with his recalcitrant mistress by his side. He and the voluptuous middle-aged matron had shared an intimate dinner at a discreet little restaurant off St. James's Place. Now she was balking at sharing his bed—and it was freezing cold outside!

"What is this about your needing to go home straightaway?" he mocked, greedily eyeing the swell of her bosom, the blush on her cheeks, the thickness of the ebony hair piled high on her head. "You titillate me at dinner with coy repartée, you tease me mercilessly with the batting of your eyelashes, you allow me to tempt you with lobster and the finest French champagne, and now that it is time to pay the piper, you try to shirk your wanton promise?"

Lady Celeste tossed her curls. "You were flirting with the serving girl, you rake."

Righteous indignation rose up in Matthew. "I was not."

"Don't deny it," she scolded. "Besides, I made you no promises about how this evening would end."

Feigning a wounded air, Matthew lifted her hand and slowly, sensuously kissed each soft finger. Smugly pleased to hear her unwitting moan of pleasure, he coaxed, "Have you tired of me so quickly, my love?"

"Why, that is not the case at all."

"Then why are you spurning me?"

She sighed tragically. "Because my husband, Dagmar, has become suspicious of our little trysts."

"Suspicious of us?" laughed Matthew. "Dagmar? Why, the man is older than Wellington."

"The Duke of Wellington is long dead, my dear."

"My point precisely," Matthew responded wryly.

Celeste rolled her eyes. "Ancient or not, my husband has begun questioning my frequent nocturnal absences. I do believe Dagmar suspects I am cheating on him."

Matthew chuckled deep in his throat. "Then if he has already convicted us, why not enjoy the forbidden fruits we so richly deserve?"

"Matthew, you are twisting my words and being unfair," Celeste protested, shivering. "You are not the one with a husband."

"Thank heaven," he drawled.

"Oh, hush."

Frowning, Matthew tried a different tack. He reached out to toy with one of Celeste's ebony curls, feeling a rush of self-satisfaction as she quivered in pleasure. "My love, be charitable. Why, we're within six weeks of Christmas, and I've a present for you inside," he added suggestively.

She harrumphed. "Knowing your predilections, Matthew, I shall be the one doing the giving."

"And you grant your favors so well."

"Matthew, you are incorrigible. Pray, go inside so your driver may take me home. I am freezing."

"Come inside and I shall warm you," he coaxed huskily.

"Matthew—"

Matthew silenced the maddening woman with a kiss, slowly, ardently claiming her until she softened to his practiced wooing and kissed him back. He slipped his hand inside her carriage cloak, stroking her lush, full breast through the silk of her gown. He smiled at her whimper of pleasure and felt her arching shamelessly into his touch, opening her mouth to the brazen thrust of his tongue.

"Oh, Matthew," she panted, sounding suitably debauched.

" 'Tis your choice, fair Celeste," he rasped back, stroking her more boldly. "Stay here, argue, and freeze. Or come inside . . . and be warmed."

She groaned. "I should have known there was no arguing with you, you incorrigible rogue."

"Aye, love, you should have known." He claimed her lips in another leisurely kiss.

Brimming with triumph, Matthew opened the carriage door and stepped outside. Stamping his booted feet to stave off the cold, he gestured gracefully for Celeste to join him on the stone walkway. Casting him a haughty look, she accepted his hand and emerged from the carriage in a rustle of bustled skirts. Their figures backlit by pale gaslight along the cobbled street, their mingled breaths forming white puffs of air, the two approached the front steps of Matthew's pillared Georgian home.

"What will that nosy housekeeper of yours have to say?" Celeste inquired.

"Not to fear, love, Mrs. O'Leery is sound asleep by now."

"As she was the last time you brought me here?"

"So she spied us kissing on the landing," Matthew replied with a shrug. "She's far too loyal to ever stoop to gossip. Besides, 'twas I who reaped the wrath of her lecture in the morning, not you."

"Aye, but when I left, the miserable creature gave me a look foul enough to curdle milk. It mystifies me why you endure her tyrannical harangues."

Matthew chuckled. "I promised my dear departed mother that Hettie and her husband, James, would always have a home with me. Besides, I've need of a domestic couple to help keep my life in order. The two are family treasures."

"Ah, yes. Far be it from your mistress to criticize your choice of servants."

"Celeste, please." Matthew was growing annoyed with her petty complaints. Invariably difficult and high-strung, Lady Celeste was presently being so tiresome that he was actually questioning the wisdom of trying to seduce her tonight. Perhaps the impertinent creature was more trouble than she was worth.

The two paused before the darkened townhouse. "Matthew, I cannot even see the steps," she whined.

"Just clutch my hand, dear, and you shall be fine," he reassured her. But as they started up the steps, he paused at a low whimper. "Do you hear that?"

Celeste had also paused. "Aye. It sounds almost like a cat—and it's coming from your door."

"Aye. Wait where you are." Matthew climbed to the top of the stoop and recoiled slightly as his toe bumped a solid object that was parked to the right of the front door. He heard another low mewling sound. "Has someone left us a basket of kittens?"

He opened the front door, and the light spilling out illuminated a large basket. He gazed down at the wondrous sight and cried, "Great Scot, what is this?"

Celeste had arrived at his side, only to gasp in horror. "My goodness! A baby!"

"Aye," Matthew replied, hunkering down for a better look.

At first he almost couldn't believe his eyes, but yes, it was definitely a child swaddled in a blanket inside the basket. The infant was tiny, with a round, angelic face. Although the child's eyes were closed, its small fists were working helplessly against its face, and its little legs thrashed at its covering.

Matthew shook his head. "What in God's name is a baby doing here—and this one surely no more than a day old?"

He heard Celeste's sound of contempt. "I can answer that."

Alarm seized Matthew, and he popped to his feet. "Oh, can you? Whatever are you implying, my dear? Pray, enlighten me."

Celeste's lovely features clenched in rage. "You cad!" she cried, and soundly slapped Matthew's face.

Matthew recoiled, all but spinning. It wasn't until Celeste stormed down the steps that the full impact of her words sank in. He rushed after her. "Celeste, my God, you cannot think—"

She whirled about and glared at him. "Scoundrel! Don't you dare try to worm your way out of this predicament. That . . . that *foundling* is surely your offspring with some trollop."

"*My* offspring? That's absurd. Damn it, I'm telling the truth!"

She spat at his feet. "Bastard!" And she charged off again.

For a moment Matthew was too flabbergasted to react. By the time he rushed after her, Celeste had already clambered back inside his carriage, and was shouting at the driver to take her home, leaving Matthew to stare in consternation at the departing coach.

Then he remembered the baby on his stoop.

Shaking his head, he hurried back toward the townhouse. What on earth was the child doing there?

Suddenly his thoughts scattered as he felt a chilling burst of wind. He clutched his greatcoat about him as the blast continued to pummel his body and bits of debris swirled about him. Then, just as abruptly, the gust abated and a young woman in a long, flowing gown appeared before him. Eyes gleaming with anger, hair whipping about her head in a golden cloud, she was a starkly beautiful, avenging angel.

"You!" she cried. "Are you the one? What have you done with my baby?"

What was this? *Another* furious woman charging up to confront him about the foundling? Matthew stared flabbergasted at the wrathful seraph quickly approaching him in her long velvet dressing gown. Was he delusional? Who was this creature who seemed to have materialized from thin air, wearing such an outlandish costume?

"Madam, I know not who you are," he replied, gesturing toward his stoop, "but if you are the person who just abandoned this infant on my stair, you must surely be a Jezebel or a trollop. I can only ask, have you no shame?"

His visitor went white. "My baby is on your stair?" she repeated in a hoarse, desperate whisper. Not waiting for him to respond, she brushed past him and climbed the stoop, wobbling as she went. "Ah!" she cried, sinking to her knees. "Thank God! There you are, darling!"

Matthew heard the infant coo as the woman picked it up. He raced up the steps after her. "This child is yours?"

The young woman clutched the infant to her breast, and trembled there on her knees, eyes tightly closed. Empathy rose in Matthew as he noted the wench's teeth were chattering and she was shivering in the cold. In the pale light spilling from the doorway he could see the expression of sublime happiness on her beautiful face.

At last, she spoke convulsively. "Yes, the baby is mine. And he—or she—is soaking wet."

Despite stirrings of sympathy toward his strange guest, Matthew was at once rendered indignant. "You claim the child is yours, madam, yet you know not whether the babe is male or female? What manner of wanton are you?"

Under the circumstances, Matthew thought his questions eminently reasonable. But when he saw the look of anguished helplessness that rushed to the young woman's face in the wake of his harsh words, he regretted them at once. She appeared to be on the verge of tears.

Before he could contemplate the matter further, his plump Scottish housekeeper abruptly lumbered out onto the stoop ensconced in a voluminous wrapper and a nightcap. "By the saints, milord, are you trying to wake the dead?" Hettie

O'Leery demanded in her thick brogue. She caught sight of the woman and babe, and her wrinkled hands flew to her sagging cheeks. "What manner of mischief is going on here?"

Matthew groaned. Now there would be the devil to pay. "Perhaps you might tell me, Mrs. O'Leery," he responded with ill-humor, gesturing toward the young woman holding the child. "This young—er—*woman* evidently abandoned her babe on our stoop, then had second thoughts."

Even as Mrs. O'Leery gasped and crossed herself, the young woman hurled Matthew a haughty look and spoke through chattering teeth. "I d-did not abandon my ch-child. How dare you even imply such a h-horrible thing!"

Before Matthew could reply, his housekeeper harrumphed loudly, planted her hands on her hips, and spoke to the woman. "Aye, young lady, 'tis most apparent to me what the lay of the land is here. Lord Matthew, how could you have done such a despicable thing?"

Again Matthew was stunned. "Me? Why is it every woman I come across tonight assumes I'm some sort of hopeless reprobate? I'll have you know I didn't—"

The housekeeper quelled his protestations with a wave of her plump hand. "Oh, spare me your nonsense, your lordship, and let us get the wench and her child inside, before the both of them freeze to death—or cause a most lamentable scandal."

Matthew was stunned. His housekeeper wanted him to take this chippy and her babe inside his home? "Mrs. O'Leery, have you taken leave of your senses? My heaven, we cannot—"

Ignoring him, Mrs. O'Leery leaned toward the girl. "Hand me that babe, now, girl." As the young woman hesitated, she coaxed, "Don't be afraid, child, I'll not hurt your wee one. Your babe will be safe in Hettie O'Leery's loving arms. And you cannot leave your wee bairn here to freeze in the cold."

Though she still appeared wary, the young woman handed over her infant to the housekeeper.

The Scottish woman clutched the babe to her breast, rocking it gently in her arms. "Ah, wet and shivering you be, poor mite. We'll fix that now." Heading inside, she called over her shoulder, "God's teeth, your lordship, don't stand there like a blabbering idiot. Give the poor woman a hand, will you? She's pale and trembling, and has surely just come from the childbed. And bring along the basket for the wee one."

Thoroughly exasperated but also recognizing defeat, Matthew picked up the basket, then extended his free hand to the woman. "Come along now, madam."

She hesitated. "But we really cannot—"

Matthew clasped her hand and tugged her to her feet. Her hand felt soft and cool, and was shivering in his. It struck him how confused and helpless she must feel in her current plight, no matter who she was. Whatever horrible circumstance had prompted her to abandon her newborn child on his stoop, she was clearly shaken and defenseless. Shame arose in him that he would have denied her and her babe shelter from the cold on this wretched night.

"Come along now," he repeated more gently. " 'Tis freezing, and you'll soon learn there is no arguing with my housekeeper."

Matthew all but pulled the skittish young woman inside his door, feeling taken aback as he noted how truly lovely—and pale—she was. Her hair, blond and thick, fell in soft, glistening waves to her shoulders. Her profile was just as exquisite as he'd first thought: firm chin, full lips, beautifully etched nose, striking blue eyes, and finely arched brows. She was taller than most women, and slender, despite having recently given birth.

But of all her attributes, the mixture of vulnerability and awe on her stark face drew him to her most. As they headed for the stairs, following Mrs. O'Leery and the babe, the young woman wavered slightly on her feet, causing Matthew to instinctively grip her about her waist. A little gasp escaped her and she cast him a startled look, but otherwise didn't resist his touch. He felt warm, womanly curves nestled against him, felt her leaning on him, could even smell the sweet lavender scent of her hair, and was swept by an unaccustomed tenderness. . . .

Even as the strange, quaint Englishman helped her toward the stairs, Emma Fairchild felt weak as a kitten. Swamped by feelings of confusion and unreality, she remembered receiving the bizarre letter back at the hospital, telling her she must retrieve her lost baby from the doorstep of a rogue in Victorian England.

But that couldn't be possible. After she tore the ticket and began to spin, she had suddenly been plunged into a whirling abyss, landing on this dark, cold, cobbled street, lined with townhouses. The fog had swirled about her, and an elegant gaslight blinked on a distant corner. She had spotted this bizarre though handsome man in an old-fashioned greatcoat and top hat, and in a quaint, English-accented voice, he had mentioned the baby. . . .

And when she had found her child on his darkened stoop, raw joy had seared. She had held her infant for a brief moment, had felt him, or her, warm, wet and alive in her arms. A blinding exultation had filled her. Despite all her confusion, never in her entire life had anything felt so sublimely *right*.

Then the housekeeper had taken charge of things, taken her child, and now. . . .

Where *was* she?

The bizarre man had led her inside an old townhouse that smelled of mustiness and antiques. Marble floors rolled past her feet; gaslight hummed in chandeliers overhead; gilded mirrors and velvet-upholstered chairs lined the long corridor.

She climbed the massive, exquisitely sculpted mahogany staircase with the man's help. Above her a vast cascade of carved plaster fretwork painted shades of oyster and pale gold was etched on the high ceiling. On the staircase landing loomed a huge painting of an English landscape that she suspected might be an original Constable.

Who was this man, so real, leading her upward? His arm supporting her waist was warm and strong, and she could feel the hard muscles of his thighs moving in concert with her own. She smelled the spicy scent of his hair. She took in his profile, the strong jaw, full, sensuous lips, noble nose, the dark, deep-set eyes, dark brown, shiny hair. Was he the "rogue" mentioned in her missive from the "Dispatcher of New Souls"?

At the top of the stairs, she caught sight of the magnificent furnishings on the second floor—priceless paintings, marquetry hall tables, Louis XIV chairs—and followed the housekeeper down a wide corridor into a darkened bedroom. Thanks to the gaslight spilling in from the hallway, Emma could just make out the impressive lines of a four-poster bed and massive dresser.

Emma's eyes were drawn to her child as the housekeeper laid the tiny bundle on the bed, and shuffled off to the dresser to light an oil lamp. Quickly Emma crossed over and stared down at her baby wrapped in its pink blanket. She knew at once what the color meant. She gazed at her child's adorable, round face as the newborn baby squinted at her, and tears filled her eyes.

"A girl," she murmured, her voice catching as she stroked the baby's soft, warm cheek.

The housekeeper was moving toward the door. "Now you mind her, lass, whilst I find something dry for the wee bairn to wear."

She lumbered out of the room, and Emma continued to regard the child in wonder. The baby was whimpering slightly and flailing her little hands. Emma touched a tiny fist, and the baby quieted as she clutched her mother's finger tightly with her own, staring at her prize and blowing out bubbles. A knot of tenderness formed in Emma's throat.

"I had a girl," she murmured.

The rogue set the basket down on a chair, removed his coat and hat, then strode over to join her. "You've remembered now?"

Emma glanced up at him, noting again how

dashingly handsome he was, how dark and intense his eyes were—and his puzzled expression. She shook her head. "No. The pink blanket."

"Ah," he murmured, though he appeared bemused. "If I may ask, just how did your child come to be on my stoop, madam? Did you abandon her there?"

"Certainly not!" Emma shot back indignantly.

"Then what happened?"

Emma felt confused helplessness washing over her. "I . . . apparently, someone stole my child and I have come to rescue her."

"Stole your child? But how could—"

Emma shook her head. "Frankly, I don't know."

He blinked at her in perplexity. "My heavens, madam, you seem befuddled. Can you even tell me your name?"

"Yes. Mrs. Emma Fairchild."

"You're an American, Mrs. Fairchild?"

"Yes."

He slanted her a chiding glance. "Well, I must say you're about the most astounding visitor I've ever had the dubious pleasure of meeting."

Emma couldn't resist a smile. "Thank you . . . I think. You are—"

He dipped into a bow. "Matthew Weymouth at your service."

"Mr. Weymouth."

He stiffened his spine. "Lord Worthing is my customary manner of address."

"Worthing," Emma muttered. "Ah, so you must be aristocracy, like a baron or—"

"An earl," he provided.

"Ah."

He coughed. "Since you do at least know your name, may I be so bold as to ask, where is Mr. Fairchild?"

Emma's expression darkened. "He's in America. And we're divorced."

The man appeared scandalized. "Divorced! God in heaven! Is that the way of it in the Colonies these days?"

Emma laughed nervously at his quaint speech. She was not getting a good feeling from this conversation. "Yes, I suppose."

"But, whatever are you doing here in London, all alone with your child?"

Bewilderment swamped Emma. "I . . . I wish I could tell you. But I'm not really sure myself."

He grew increasingly alarmed. "Madam, are you ill? Did having the child somehow damage your mental faculties?"

Emma bit her lip. "I don't think so."

"Then what?"

The man appeared so mystified, Emma flashed him an apologetic smile. "Look, Lord Worthing, it was kind of you to take us in, and I'm sorry for inconveniencing you. As soon as I can get my bearings a bit, we'll be on our way, okay?"

"Okay?" he repeated in mystification.

"We'll be leaving," she clarified.

He gave an incredulous laugh. "You and the babe, fleeing in the dead cold of night? Granted, I've been called a scoundrel, but I am not without some scruples." He nodded toward the baby. "Moreover, clearly someone needs to keep an eye on you before you abandon that poor child again."

Outraged, Emma shot back, "How dare you! I didn't abandon her! In fact, you've no idea what I went through to find her."

Though he glowered at her, he didn't argue the point. "Furthermore, my housekeeper would see me boiled in my own juices if I allowed you and the child to leave this house tonight."

Emma hesitated. "But, from what she said, wouldn't my appearance here cause a scandal?"

He smiled ironically, and Emma found herself feeling unexpectedly disarmed. "Not to fear, young woman. Scandal and I are hardly passing acquaintances."

Before Emma could ponder this odd remark, the housekeeper reentered the room with a stack of cloths and towels. "Sorry that we have no baby clothes, but these should suffice to keep the bairn warm and dry for now." She leveled a stern glance at Matthew. "My lord, you may be on your way whilst I see to your wench and her bairn. We can straighten out this muddle on the morrow."

Matthew appeared flabbergasted. "But she's not my—"

"Now don't make it worse by lying," the housekeeper scolded her employer with a wag of her finger.

"He's not lying," Emma put in. As the housekeeper turned to her with an expression of amazement, she added firmly, "He is not the father of my child."

The woman gasped. " 'Tis a foundling, then?"

Emma lifted her chin. "No, the child has a father. But it is not Mr. . . . er, Lord Worthing."

The housekeeper harrumphed. "Well, I suppose you're the woman to know," she muttered without conviction, then shooed Matthew toward the door. "Be gone, my lord, and leave us women to our work."

"As you wish." He bowed briefly. "Goodnight ladies."

"Goodnight," Emma called back.

Gathering his coat and hat and wearing a frown of utter confusion, Matthew Weymouth quietly slipped from the room.

Chapter Three

"My heaven, what is this?" Mrs. O'Leery gasped.

Emma sat on the bed, struggling to recover her composure while Mrs. O'Leery undressed her tiny newborn. She glanced down at her precious child, who lay flailing her tiny arms and legs. It was hard for her to believe any human being could be so small and delicate. Then her gaze paused on the child's diaper.

"It's a disposable diaper," Emma explained.

"Disposable?" gasped Mrs. O'Leery. "Why, I've never heard of such a thing." Crinkling the outside covering between her fingers, she flinched. "What is this strange material?"

"Plastic."

The woman crossed herself. "By the saints! How does one remove this contraption?"

Emma demonstrated for the housekeeper. "You just pull back the tapes."

"My land. Well, the nappie is wet, all right." The housekeeper removed the soiled diaper, gently lifted the baby's hips, and laid a folded, sparkling white linen hand towel beneath her. Efficiently she wrapped the makeshift diaper about the baby's tiny thighs and tied the corners in place. Then she wrapped the little girl in a soft gray shawl and handed her to Emma.

"There. 'Tis the best I can do for now," the housekeeper fretted. "We have no clothing for infants in this house. Nor a cradle, I fear."

"Oh, I think you've done a fine job. Thank you," Emma replied, cuddling her baby close.

The housekeeper nodded toward the basket Matthew had placed on the chair. "I can line the basket with fresh blankets for you, to make her a bed for the night."

Emma recoiled at the thought of her child being even a few feet away from her. They had already been apart for far too long. "Thanks, but I'd prefer to have the baby on the bed with me. She's far too young to turn over or roll off."

"Aye, from the look of her she's just been born."

"Yes." Emma choked back emotion. "She's just a day old."

The woman went wide-eyed. "Then how did

the two of you appear here, pray tell? You say Lord Matthew is not responsible—"

"He is not."

The woman cast her a chiding glance. "Then what has brought you here in the cold of the night?"

Emma sighed. "Please, may we discuss this tomorrow? I've . . ." She gave an ironic laugh. "I've had a rather long and strange night . . . and my baby and I need some rest."

"Of course, dearie." Gathering up the wet diaper, the woman moved to the foot of the bed, unfolded a quilt and draped it over Emma and her child. "You two just cuddle up here and I'll bring some nice hot chocolate to warm you."

"Thank you. That sounds lovely."

Glancing meaningfully in the direction of Emma's bosom, she added, "If the mite gets hungry, you'll be able to handle it, then?"

Emma was overwhelmed by the question. Fervently she replied, "Heavens, I hope so."

The woman started toward the door. "And there's a water closet at the end of the hallway should you be needing it. Is there anything else you'll want for the night?"

Emma flashed the woman a wan smile. "No, thanks. As you can see, I'm already dressed for bed."

"Aye, lass, I can see."

After the woman left, Emma clutched her baby

close and observed her surroundings. She was clearly in a nineteenth-century English bedroom. She sat on a carved cherry four-poster, with a purple taffeta bedspread and a canopy draped with pale green fabric. The dresser and wardrobe were also of cherry. The fireplace was sculpted black and white marble, with a handsome gold clock resting on the mantel above. Rich lengths of brocaded satin in vivid hues of purple and green swagged the windows. Gold tassels and a gilded drapery rod added regal touches to the decor. The wallpaper was a flocked gold floral pattern, and along one wall stretched a magnificent chaise lounge with carved, scrolled ends and purple and green velvet upholstery.

Heavens, was she in the middle of a dream? Or had she really taken the bizarre flight dictated by the Dispatcher of New Souls? And how had a stork delivered her child to the wrong century?

Again she remembered being back in the hospital, receiving the outlandish letter, tearing up her ticket, starting to spin, and spiraling through some sort of vortex. She'd lost the shreds of her ticket along the way, and had nothing left of her twentieth-century existence.

Except for her child. She gazed again at the precious baby now dozing in her arms, and shuddered with emotion. Whatever magic and madness had brought her and her child here tonight, thank God they were together now.

Her throat tightened as she stroked the downy gold hair on her baby's head and touched her incredibly soft pink cheek. Her girl bore no resemblance to the husband who had deserted her—Steve with his dark, good looks and his eye for women.

In some ways Matthew Weymouth reminded her of Steve. Both men were darkly handsome, and if what Mrs. O'Leery had hinted at was true, Matthew also had a roving eye. Perhaps it would be best to get away from him. But where would she go? She didn't even know where she was—or *when* she was . . . let alone how to get back to her own time.

"Here we are, lass." Emma's thoughts scattered as Mrs. O'Leery stepped back inside the room with a steaming china cup on a saucer. The smell of the rich chocolate filled her senses. She flashed the woman a wan smile. "Thank you. That smells marvelous."

Setting the chocolate down on Emma's bedside table, the woman replied, "You're welcome, lass. Drink up, now, and we'll see you both in the morning."

"I will. And goodnight to you."

Once the door was closed, Emma carefully shifted the baby in her arms and drank the rich chocolate, its warmth and sweetness soothing her and calming her nerves. She had just set down the empty cup and was feeling drowsy, even somewhat content, when the small bundle in her arms began to squirm. She looked down to see her daughter's tiny mouth screwed into a pout . . . and the infant began to whimper, then wail. The child's spine stiffened, and she kicked her arms and legs.

Panic engulfed Emma. She frantically tried to soothe her child, rocking her and clucking to her, wondering what was wrong. She felt the baby's diaper, which remained dry.

She must be hungry. A glance at her baby's mouth, working frantically as if to seek nourishment, confirmed this thought.

Emma planned to breast-feed her baby, and even as the child continued to squirm and cry, she could feel her tender breasts aching and swelling in response. She unbuttoned her robe, untied one ribbon strap on her nylon nightgown and pulled the fabric down away from her breast. Carefully she lifted the baby toward her nipple. The infant rooted about hungrily, then latched on. Emma's eyes widened in wonder, the sight of her baby suckling bringing a rush of joyous tears to her eyes.

But a moment later the baby cried out and pulled away, her little face almost purple. Anguish and confusion assailed Emma. What was wrong now?

Instinctively, she knew: Even though her breasts had swelled with milk, none was actually coming out yet. She couldn't feed her baby! Helpless tears filled her eyes.

What was she to do? This was, of course, her first experience nursing. Perhaps her milk supply wasn't even fully in yet. When she was in labor, the nurse had told her that new mothers often had difficultly nursing the first few times, and a lactation expert was available at the hospital. But who could she call on here? She had landed in some bizarre distant world, and had no idea how else she might feed her child. She couldn't let her baby starve.

Desperate tears streamed down Emma's cheeks.

This was quite a turn of events, Matthew Weymouth mused.

In the small sitting room adjoining his bedroom, he paced in his dressing gown, thinking about the strange, beautiful woman who had arrived that night to claim the equally astounding baby on his stoop. Who was the woman and whence had she and her child come? Had she abandoned the child, then come after her? Or had some bizarre thief really stolen the infant as she'd claimed? These questions bedeviled him.

She was so obviously an American. Had she emmigrated here, only to become ruined, abandoned, her child a bastard? Thank heaven she hadn't accused him of being the father. Nonetheless, he felt strangely responsible for her.

Funny that only an hour ago his main thought had been of seducing his reluctant mistress. Now he had much more pressing matters on his mind, and he felt oddly obligated toward the young mother and child. The woman was quite lovely with her lush blond hair and her huge, bewildered blue eyes. Her vulnerability, and that of her child, had touched a responsive chord somewhere deep inside his jaded heart.

He smiled to himself. Matthew Weymouth wasn't accustomed to feeling gallant toward the opposite sex. He considered himself a connoisseur of fine ladies, and like every epicurean, he craved a feast of delights. His spoiled palette kept him flitting from woman to woman just as a banquet guest might sample each and every dish. But what was it about this forlorn young woman that urged him to linger . . . and perhaps someday partake of a twelve-course meal?

Suddenly his thoughts were interrupted by the sound of a baby's high-pitched wail. The infant was clearly in distress. The sound propelled him into the hallway, up to his guests's door, where he paused as new sounds of lamentation were added to the chorus.

Good heaven, *she* was weeping as well, weeping as if her very heart had been ripped out.

The anguished sound brought Matthew to the brink of panic. As a typically masterful male, he was unaccustomed to this feeling of helplessness. Without even thinking, he flung open her door, stepped inside, and demanded, "What is wrong?"

The sight of her stopped him dead in his tracks. Emma sat upright on the bed, her golden hair falling in a cloud about her shoulders, her beautiful face streaked with tears, one lovely full breast bared naked to his scrutiny. And the tiny babe was flailing about beneath her breast, wailing in a fury, as if the most terrific insult had been afforded her.

Matthew was rooted to the spot, uncertain what to say or do. For the first time in memory, he felt hot color flood his face.

She spoke, momentarily relieving him of his obligation to comment. "I can't feed her," she wailed, hiccuping.

Sympathy for her surged within him, but his sense of affronted decorum overrode his more tender instincts. "Madam, you . . . are . . ." he stammered. "You will cover yourself, pray."

"But that won't help me feed her," she sobbed.

Appalled as he was by her words and her state of undress, Matthew couldn't resist a smile. She was right. Covering that delectable breast would hardly quiet her squalling infant. But this woman who thought nothing of his seeing her naked breast was obviously a tawdry creature accustomed to male scrutiny.

Or one so innocent she thought not to protect herself from a libertine such as himself?

Whatever her true nature, Matthew found the sight of her in such seductive dishabille inflamed his senses to a degree that shamed him. She should know better than to trust herself alone with a man this way. And even a rake should know better than to think to take advantage of a woman in her delicate position.

"My apologies, madam," he stated. "I shall leave you now."

"No," she protested, voice almost hoarse with desperation. "I need your help."

Stunned, Matthew could barely speak. "You . . . what?"

"Didn't you hear me?" she sobbed. "I can't feed my baby."

As the infant continued to add to the cacophony, he held up a hand. "Please, calm yourself. I'll go fetch Mrs. O'Leery."

"No. I want you."

Matthew felt as if a great fist had punched him square in the gut. Stunned, he repeated, "You . . . want . . . me?"

"I need your help with this baby please," she reiterated.

The woman was amazing—either the most skilled courtesan or the most naive innocent he had ever met. "And you think *I'm* the one to assist you?" he inquired in disbelief. "Have you even considered the propriety of being alone with a man in your current, scandalous state?"

She gasped, an expression of horror contorting her lovely features. "You are thinking *sexual* thoughts at a time like this?"

Matthew winced at her accusatory tone and frank speech. "Forgive me, madam, but I *am* a man."

"Well, I won't forgive you," she scolded. "How can you possibly think of . . . of *that* at a time like this. You're as bad as my ex."

"Ex?" he repeated, scowling.

She raised her chin, her lovely eyes flashing angrily at him. "Will you kindly quit obsessing about your own needs and start thinking about my poor baby? What if I can't feed her? She could starve," she sobbed.

Realizing he might soon have an hysterical woman on his hands, Matthew crossed to her side, patted her shoulder, and struggled to keep his gaze from straying to the most perfect breast in memory. Thank heaven, the infant had quieted a bit now.

"Calm yourself, my dear, there's no need for panic."

"No need?" she cried. "How else can I feed her?"

Matthew raked his fingers through his hair. He could not believe he was having such an indecent conversation with this incredible woman. "Well,

I don't know. Having never born any children myself, thank heaven, I'm quite unfamiliar with the process. However, wouldn't it help if you relaxed?"

"How?" she cried.

Feeling almost frantic, he replied, "I have no idea. I suppose we'll have to find a wet nurse—though it won't be easy at this ungodly hour."

Now she appeared on the verge of tears again. "Oh, this is terrible. It's bad enough I've been cast to God-knows-where with my baby. Now I can't feed her, and there's no lactation expert, and . . . damn, my stitches are killing me."

"Stitches?" Matthew asked.

She didn't answer, only began to weep again, the baby whimpering in accompaniment. Matthew patted her arm. "There, there. It can't be that bad. Please, Mrs. Fairchild, you must calm yourself. You must—"

She looked up at him, her expression so stark, so rent with torment and confusion, that Matthew could not help himself. He leaned over and tenderly kissed her. For the first time in his life, he kissed a woman not to slake his own lust, but out of a genuine desire to comfort her.

Yet the sweet trembling of her soft lips beneath his own fired Matthew's passions in a way he hadn't reckoned on. She was so delicious, so soft, her mouth meeting his so trustingly. The lingering kiss seemed to go on forever, until Matthew realized the room had grown silent. He broke away and both of them looked down in amazement to see that the babe was now happily suckling at her breast.

Emma's gaze, bright with joy and tears, met his. "You helped me," she declared raptly. "She's nursing now. Oh, I can feel it! Thank you, Matthew."

Speech was, by now, totally beyond Matthew. He stood trembling, shaken to the core, watching Emma nurse her child. His emotions were in chaos. What had just transpired between him and this woman would be deemed outrageous and unspeakable by society, and yet he felt awed, humbled, as if they both had not only witnessed but had *created* the greatest miracle together.

At last he managed to clear his throat and murmured, "I must leave, now, Mrs. Fairchild."

"No, please stay for just a moment. To be sure."

To be sure? Matthew went lightheaded at the implication of *that*.

Still, he found he couldn't resist the woman's heartfelt plea. But he retreated to a wing chair a safe distance away from her, the one where he'd laid down the basket. Setting it on the floor and settling into the chair, he crossed his long legs and assumed what he hoped was a nonchalant air, while again trying his damndest not to stare at her lovely breast and the precious infant suckling there—a cozy scene that incited thoughts that were far from domestic.

He shifted uneasily in his chair. "Now that things are, well, a bit calmer, can you tell me where you come from and why you left your baby on my stoop tonight?"

"I'm from Chicago," she replied. "But I didn't leave my child—"

"Ah, yes," he cut in cynically. "You say your baby was stolen?"

"Well . . . she was misplaced."

"And how might *that* have happened?"

She appeared mystified by the question. "I really have no idea. It's very complicated."

"No doubt," Matthew muttered. "Tell me, madam, have you no conception of answering a simple, direct question?"

She regarded him lamely. "I can try."

"Can you tell me, for example, how you got here to England? Did you simply sprout wings and fly?"

He watched a slight smile curve her lush lips. "Perhaps in a manner of speaking, I did."

Matthew groaned.

"I'm sorry," she said sincerely. "You know, I'm really not up to answering your questions right now. I'm quite exhausted. Perhaps I can better explain things in the morning."

"Doubtless so. Ah, yes, the morning." Welcoming her cue like a drowning man accepting a life-preserver, he stood to leave.

She flashed him a grateful look. "I do appreciate your taking us in."

"You're welcome. Besides, 'tis the season, is it not?"

She paled. "Can you tell me the date?"

"Why, 'tis November 15."

"And the year?" she pursued anxiously.

Matthew squinted at her, taken aback. Didn't the befuddled creature even know the year? "Why, 'tis 1869, of course."

"Of course," she repeated woodenly, turning white as death. Her voice faded to a reedy whisper. "Would you mind saying goodnight, then? It is rather late."

Puzzled by her strange response, but grateful to be released from the purgatory of staring at her delightful person, he nodded. "Certainly. We'll discuss the rest tomorrow."

"Yes, tomorrow."

Matthew bowed. "Goodnight, Mrs. Fairchild."

"Goodnight, Lord Worthing."

After he slipped out, Emma sat in a state of shock. She momentarily forgot her host's unexpected, stirring kiss, and her own amazing response. Instead her mind was riveted on Matthew Weymouth's last words.

If he had spoken the truth it really was the year

1869 and she and her child had actually been sent to Victorian London.

Then Ralph the Stork and her missive from the Dispatcher of New Souls must have been real. In a bizarre way, it all made sense—and was scary as hell!

A strange, sinking feeling engulfed Emma. She shivered and clutched her baby closer, thankful that her child was nursing, but also terribly shaken.

1869! What were she and her baby to do?

Chapter Four

Morning found Matthew pacing the small kitchen of his townhouse as he sipped hot tea.

At the room's small table sat his housekeeper, Hettie O'Leery, and her husband, James, the house butler. James was an ashen-faced, gaunt old soul who appeared as if he'd lingered on this earth a few years past his own death. The man seldom spoke, and went about his duties with the soundless solemnity of a ghost. His outspoken wife more than compensated for his taciturn nature. At the moment, however, both O'Leerys were busy eating porridge and drinking hot chocolate—acting altogether too calm in light of the present disquieting circumstances.

Matthew didn't ordinarily take his meals with the couple in the kitchen. But this morning he felt the need for human companionship, if not the moral support he knew he'd never get from Hettie or James. A beautiful young woman and her babe lay asleep upstairs in his guest room, and he had no idea what to do about them. Indeed, the dilemma the pair presented—and the memory of kissing Emma's most incredible mouth—had kept Matthew tossing and turning throughout much of the night.

Hettie wiped her mouth on a napkin, heaved herself to her feet, smoothed down her apron, and faced Matthew. "There, milord, I've had my fill. What of our guests? Should I fetch them up a tray?"

Taken aback, Matthew couldn't speak for a moment.

"Your lordship?"

Setting his cup on the sideboard, Matthew pulled his fingers through his hair. "Aye, prepare them a tray. But I shall take it up."

"You?" Hettie protested, aghast. "But you cannot. You're an earl, by Saint Benedict. 'Tis scandalous."

"No more scandalous than having the young woman and her child staying under my roof in the first place," Matthew pointed out irritably.

The housekeeper straightened to her full, menacing height. "Aye, and what are you going to do about that, your lordship?"

"What do you mean?" Matthew demanded.

"The girl is in need of a husband."

"Aye, she is," he concurred dryly.

"Then would you see to it?"

"Me?"

Hettie took a step forward and fixed her master with a suspicious stare. "She came to you in her hour of need, did she not?"

Matthew was flabbergasted. "Yes—but she has already informed you I am not the child's father. Furthermore, she told me that the father resides in America—and the two of them are divorced."

"Divorced? A likely story on all counts." Hettie meaningfully raised an eyebrow. "As far as I'm concerned, the girl's presence here more than speaks for itself."

"Mrs. O'Leery!" Matthew was growing exasperated. "I shall hear no more of this absurd talk. I never laid eyes on Mrs. Fairchild, or her baby, before last night."

Hettie held her peace, though her frown and the tapping of her toe spoke volumes. "Then what do you intend to do about them, milord?"

Matthew waved a hand. "I do not know. Find a suitable situation for her and her child, I suppose."

Hettie gave a shrug. "Aye, cast the chit to a

workhouse, and her babe to a foundling home, why don't you?"

Matthew shook a finger at her. "Quit baiting me, you maddening woman. You know that is not what I meant at all."

Hettie waved a hand. "How should I know what you mean, milord? For all I know, you'd lose no sleep if both of them succumbed in a fever house."

Matthew ground his teeth. "What would you suggest?"

Hettie feigned a look of pious disinterest. " 'Tis your house, milord, and your decision to make."

"One would never know it," Matthew drawled back.

For a moment the two glowered at each other, then amazingly, James spoke up, offering a rare bit of wisdom in his dull, solemn voice. " 'Tis the holidays, milord. Surely you would not cast out the poor wench and her wee one?"

"Of course not," Matthew agreed emphatically. "I'm merely trying to point out the complications, the possible scandal—"

"You barely give a thought to scandal when you bring home your paramours," Hettie put in archly.

Matthew colored, and spoke in trembling tones. "Mrs. O'Leery, as my housekeeper, you will kindly exercise a little restraint and mind your tongue. Moreover, my 'paramours' do not sleep here."

"Ah, so the woman and her babe have dampened your affairs, eh?"

Matthew hurled her a frosty look. "Madam, prepare the tray—and I shall take it upstairs and speak with our guest."

Hettie went wide-eyed. "Your lordship, are you daft? I tell you, you cannot—"

"For the final time, woman, prepare the bloody tray!" Matthew roared.

Hettie recoiled. "Well, you don't have to bless me out like a fishwife." With exaggerated dignity, she curtsied. "As you wish, your lordship."

"Marry the girl. She thinks *I* should marry the girl," Matthew muttered. He climbed the stairs bearing a silver tray lined with a doily and graced with a pot of tea, a cup and saucer, a bowl of steaming porridge, and a napkin. Mrs. O'Leery had even added one of her prized hothouse roses—a mouth-watering, pale-pink maiden's blush—in a crystal bud vase.

God's teeth, it had been a struggle convincing the disagreeable woman to allow him to take the tray upstairs. Of course he was not accustomed to such menial tasks, but he felt compelled to speak with the young woman again . . . or did he feel compelled to *see* her? For that matter, ever since she and the babe had arrived, he'd committed all sorts of impetuous acts—like kissing her last night. That memory sent a tingle down his spine, and his thoughts spun off in a decadent direction he couldn't afford to indulge.

He gently rapped at her door, then paused. No answer came forth. Had she and the child left? Strangely panicked at the prospect, he opened the door and stepped inside.

The woman lay on her side on the bed, her golden hair spread out on the pillow, her fair face angelically peaceful, serenely beautiful in sleep. By her side lay the equally cherubic, sleeping infant swaddled in a soft blanket. The sight of the two of them clutched at Matthew's heart.

Smiling, Matthew strode to the dresser and set down the tray. A rustle drew his attention back to the bed, and he noted she had stirred and was regarding him warily.

When Emma awakened, the first thing she spotted was her baby, sleeping peacefully by her side. She gazed lovingly at her child's pink little face, watched her tiny mouth flutter slightly as she breathed. Joy filled her heart at the knowledge that her child was safe, sound, and where she belonged—by her mother's side.

The sound of dishes being rattled and the scent of hot, spicy tea across the room, drew her attention, and her heart quickened as she spotted Matthew Weymouth standing there clean-shaven and dressed in a single-breasted morning coat with tails and dark trousers. He was even more handsome than she remembered, his eyes so dark and deep-set, his face drawn of strong, classical lines, his dark hair gleaming in the morning light. He smiled at her with a mixture of amusement and tenderness. Her cheeks burned as memories rushed in—of his kissing her and comforting her last night, and of her own appalling response. Even now, at the sight of him, her stomach tightened pleasurably and her breasts swelled, shocking reactions that shamed but also exhilarated her.

What was she doing here with him?

That question brought the reality of her bizarre situation crashing in on her again. She and her baby had truly crossed time—but what were they to do now? Would the man standing across from her afford her any answers?

She wondered what he was thinking. . . .

Spotting Emma gazing at him, Matthew felt oddly warmed. He bowed elegantly. "Good morning, Mrs. Fairchild. I trust you and the babe slept well?"

Emma clutched the covers to her neck. "Just fine, thank you."

"I brought you some breakfast."

"How nice. Thank you."

Matthew picked up the tray, crossed the room

and set it on the bedside table. Gazing at the young woman's flushed, expectant face, and musing to himself that no just-awakened lady had ever looked so beautiful, he cleared a suddenly raspy throat. "You should eat."

"Yes, I suppose so," she murmured. "And afterward . . . Well, I guess the baby and I should go."

"Go?" he repeated tensely.

"You were very kind to take us in last night," she went on. "However, we've imposed on your hospitality long enough."

"But where will you go?" Matthew asked.

She raised her chin, and he could see the pride gleaming in her large blue eyes. "I don't see why that should concern you. Anyway, you've done enough, and we should be on our way."

"On your way where? Have you people here?"

"No." She bit her lip. "As I've explained, my people are back in America." She hesitated. "I think."

He eyed her warily. "You do not know? Well, it's obvious you have no money, no clothing, no means to support yourself or the child."

Pride tightened her features. "Thanks for pointing that out."

Matthew waved a hand. "Young woman, you cannot possibly leave. I must insist you and the child remain under my protection, at least until we can find you a suitable situation."

"I don't need your protection."

"You don't? Woman, it's all but the dead of winter. Why, it's snowing outside. You cannot possibly venture forth without even a coat, and no way to protect yourself—or your child."

She was quiet for a long moment. From her tumultuous expression and the way she kept glancing anxiously at the babe while clutching the sheet, she was obviously struggling within herself. Matthew's heart went out to her. At last she donned her robe, got up gingerly and crept over to the window, staring down at the snowfall, the street below.

Matthew joined her, alarmed at how pale she was. "Mrs. Fairchild, what is wrong? You look as if you've seen a ghost."

"I have," she muttered, still gazing downward. "My God, I still can't believe it really did happen. Look at that!"

"Look at what?" Matthew peered down at the street, which was swarming with people and conveyances, amid a light snowfall. "I see nothing at all unusual. Horses and carriages, an orange woman, a match man, a coal cart, a sausage man, two beggars stopping a passerby."

"I know," she muttered, swaying on her feet. "Oh, my God, look at all those antique spires in the distance."

Worried, Matthew caught her arm. "Antique spires?"

"I'm in another world."

"And you may have a fever."

She glowered at him. "I'm perfectly fit."

"Indeed," he commented, steadying her with a hand at her waist as she wobbled again. "Now back to bed with you. No more arguing."

"Very well," she conceded.

Matthew was pleased when she allowed him to help her settle herself back in bed, close to her sleeping babe. Draping a blanket about the two of them, he sighed. "Mrs. Fairchild, please stay for a time. For the holidays. At least until we can figure something out for you and the child. It would mean so much to Hettie and James."

"Hettie and James?"

"My couple. You met Mrs. O'Leery last night. Her husband, James, is my butler."

"Ah."

"I shall never hear the end of this from her if I let the two of you leave."

"And what of you?" she asked haltingly. "Does it matter to you?"

To his amazement, Matthew was deeply touched by the note of wistfulness in her voice, the vulnerability in her eyes, and his male instincts urged him to reassure her. Gazing at her lovely, expectant face, he spoke, for once, straight from his heart. "Aye, Emma. It matters very much."

She smiled then, a wondrous sight that lit Matthew's soul. "In that case we will accept your kind generosity—for a while."

"For a while," Matthew repeated solemnly.

Emma didn't see Matthew for the remainder of the day, and spent it in her room, resting, recovering her strength, and caring for her baby. Mrs. O'Leery brought her meals up, and she also met Hettie's husband, James, who came up and shyly lit the little coal stove in the corner, making the bedroom toasty warm.

As Emma lay in bed, snuggled up safely with her sleeping baby, hearing sounds drifting up from the busy street below, she struggled to accept the unfathomable: that she and her baby truly had traveled to another time, far away from the world she'd known, the family she loved. The reality was staggering. But she did have a new family now in the form of her daughter. What would the future hold for them here?

She also found herself thinking about Matthew Weymouth, the strange, enigmatic man who had taken her in and insisted they stay. What were his true motives? Was he simply being kind? Why, he'd even brought her up breakfast, and that must be quite odd for the lord of the manor.

Or, given the circumstances of her arrival last night, and how he'd even seen her bare breast, did he presume she was the type of woman who would welcome his bringing a breakfast tray to her room? She just wasn't sure about him. But she couldn't deny how much he intrigued her. . . .

Chapter Five

The following morning, Emma found herself sitting beside Matthew in his old-fashioned carriage, the vehicle clattering down a cobbled street amid an amazing nineteenth-century world outside their windows. London stretched before them, a sprawling maze of ancient church steeples, gothic spires and domes.

Emma felt quite old-fashioned herself, as well as stronger after her day of rest. Matthew had stopped by her room after breakfast, and had insisted he must take her shopping today, to buy clothing and a bed for the baby, as well as a wardrobe for herself. He'd announced that Mrs. O'Leery would watch the child.

At first Emma had resisted leaving her baby behind, secretly afraid her child might disappear again. However, when Mrs. O'Leery had argued that the bairn could take a terrible malady out in the cold, and had promised to watch the infant faithfully, Emma had begun to relent. Since the baby had also nursed well and had gone down for a nap, Emma felt she would be okay for a couple of hours. And she had to admit that Matthew had been right to insist they buy her child some clothes and a proper bed.

Matthew also had asked for Mrs. O'Leery's help in finding something suitable for Emma to wear. Thus, Hettie and James had made a quick trip over to their daughter's home in Chelsea, returning shortly with the outlandish outfit Emma now wore: a high-necked, full-skirted, floor-length blue broadcloth gown; a mauve wool "carriage cloak" with extravagant burgundy fringe; a ribboned bonnet; heeled, black-leather ladies' boots with long laces tied at the ankles and bows on the toes; and black-leather gloves. Although Emma was grateful to be so warmly dressed on a day that was brisk, cold, and smelled of snow, she felt quaint and rather silly dressed as she was.

She stole a glance at Matthew to see him eyeing her with an appreciative gleam in his eyes. He evidently didn't think she appeared the least bit odd. He wore an outfit similar to yesterday's, a dove-gray morning coat and dark trousers, but had added a greatcoat, an elegant top hat and an ebony walking stick. From the slight smile pulling at the corners of his mouth, he seemed to be enjoying their outing.

Emma wished she could share his nonchalant attitude. But, as if their outlandish attire and the whimsical carriage weren't enough to unsettle her, viewing the world outside the carriage windows all but unhinged her. When they had left Matthew's home, it was only to pass endless blocks of stylish Georgian and Palladian townhouses, sidewalks filled with men, women, and children in elegant old-fashioned attire, and cobblestone streets crammed with antique carriages, omnibuses, carts, and drays. They had already seen the magnificence of Buckingham Palace and were now driving beneath the classical splendor of Constitution Arch and entering Piccadilly. Staring at the facades of landmarks such as Apsley House and the Berkeley Hotel, at cozy shops, stately clubs, and sprawling taverns, at citizens cramming the walkways and streets, at street merchants hawking everything from lemonade and ginger beer to hardware and puppies, Emma could only shake her head. She was doubly amazed to spot a placard outside St. James Hall announcing a public reading by none other than Charles Dickens! A chill swept her as she again realized she was stranded in

Dickensian London; indeed, she half-expected to watch Bob Cratchitt stride by with Tiny Tim on his shoulder. She wondered what her host would say if she told him where she was really from—and *when*. The answer to that was simple: He'd cart her off to Bedlam. Wasn't Bedlam supposed to be here in Victorian London?

She heard Matthew chuckle and glanced over to see his expression of wry amusement. "Is something wrong?"

"No—it's just you're gaping at everything with such a sense of amazement. Haven't you ever seen London before?"

"Actually, I haven't," Emma confessed, "and certainly not this London. Tell me, where are we going?"

"To Burlington Arcade. We should be able to get you everything you and the child will need there."

"Really, you're being too generous," Emma scolded, "and so are the O'Leerys and their daughter."

"What else should we do—have you gallivanting about London in your nightclothes?" he teased. "And you still haven't explained to me how you arrived at my townhouse in such a risque state to begin with."

Emma stared solemnly at a pitiful street urchin trying to sell a passing gentleman a small bundle of firewood. Should she try to explain things to Matthew? She instinctively knew he'd never believe her. "I don't think I can explain it."

"Perhaps you fled the hospital without paying your due?" he suggested ruefully.

That comment pulled a smile from Emma. "Now there's an explanation."

Pleasure lit his eyes. "We must keep you safe from the bobbies, then," he laughed.

Emma nodded, and glanced out her window again. She wondered why Matthew was being so kind to her. Perhaps there was a reason she and her baby had been brought here to his door. She wasn't sure why anything happened anymore—why she and her baby had been hurled back in time, or what their futures held. But she did know Matthew Weymouth fascinated her more with each passing moment.

Soon Emma was strolling with Matthew through fabulous Burlington Arcade, her arm linked with his as they passed elegant shops with leaded-glass fronts. Matthew's driver, Crispin, followed them at a discreet distance. As handsomely dressed shoppers milled about them, Emma stared in amazement at the display windows of a china shop with its elegant Meissen and Staffordshire pieces, a haberdashery sporting every kind of old-fashioned men's hat imaginable, from beavers to bowlers to elegant silk; a silversmith displaying elegantly crafted Gloucester pieces; and a bakery with mouth-watering scones and loaves of bread displayed on a rack outside. She breathed deeply, filling her lungs with the delicious scent of the freshly baked bread.

"This is all so charming," she murmured.

He nodded. "Ah, here we are, our first stop. The Nanny's Retreat."

Emma gasped in delight, staring at a gorgeous wicker bassinet just inside the front window of the quaint little shop. "Look, Matthew. Why, I've never seen a prettier bed."

"Then it's yours."

"Oh, you mustn't."

"Don't you want the best for your baby?"

Emma slanted him a reproachful glance; he certainly knew how to coax her cooperation.

Not waiting for her to protest, he opened the door and ushered her inside. A plump older woman in a long woolen gown came forward, and curtsied in greeting. "May I help you and the missus, sir?"

Emma felt herself blushing at the woman's erroneous assumption, although Matthew retained his composure. "Actually, the lady is my distant cousin, a widow from America, here in London with her baby."

"How nice, sir," said the shopwoman.

Emma didn't protest, though she glanced at Matthew in consternation.

"I'm afraid the infant hasn't a suitable bed or

the proper clothing for an English winter," he went on, "so we'll be needing most everything for her."

The shopwoman clapped her hands in glee and turned her shining face to Emma. "How wonderful. So 'tis a girl, eh? What might be her name, madam?"

Emma felt her cheeks heating again. "I . . . actually haven't named her yet."

The woman appeared taken aback. "Well, I suppose there's always time before the christening. Now, what may I show you first?"

Emma selected an entire wardrobe for her daughter—adorable embroidered gowns, crocheted booties, diapers, blankets, cloaks, caps—while Matthew looked on with an indulgant smile and spoke only to urge Emma to buy something if she seemed hesitant. The white wicker bassinet, a carved wooden cradle, and a full supply of bedding were also selected. At the shopwoman's suggestion, Emma chose a few nursing flasks, with a nipple attached to the bottle by a long rubber tube. She was especially touched when Matthew added some rattles and a stuffed doll to the growing collection.

After he paid the bill and asked the shopwoman to have everything delivered to his townhouse, he and Emma continued down the arcade together.

"Thank you for everything, Matthew," she said sincerely.

"You're welcome."

She raised an eyebrow at him. "I'm curious about something. So I'm your cousin now—and a *widow* from America?"

He sighed. "I'm sorry if I seemed presumptuous, Mrs. Fairchild, but the idea you being a divorcée from America, here in London. . . ."

"And staying with you," she finished. "It all seemed too scandalous, eh?"

"Did I offend you?" he asked anxiously.

"No, not at all," she confessed. "In fact, I found it all rather old-fashioned and chivalrous."

Emma was charmed to note color shooting up Matthew's face, and she felt a secret thrill that she'd managed to rattle him a bit. They continued walking in amiable silence.

"I might as well be a widow," she remarked after a moment.

"How so?" he asked.

Emma's expression was turbulent. "My ex-husband showed no interest in the baby. It was as if she didn't even exist."

Indignation flared in his eyes. "Then he's the worst sort of cad."

"I agree," Emma stated, flashing Matthew a grateful look. "He may as well not exist to me and my daughter."

Matthew squeezed Emma's hand and regarded

her with keen compassion. He ran his thumb over her gloved fingers, and she frowned in confusion.

"Matthew, what are you doing?"

A distracted expression crossed his face, and he turned and began pulling her in the opposite direction. "I've just had a thought."

"Matthew!"

He now paused by the front window of a jewelry store. "Wait right here. I shan't be long."

Watching him dash inside the shop, Emma was too perplexed to respond. True to his word, Matthew reappeared within a few minutes, holding up a simple gold wedding band.

"To keep up the illusion," he explained awkwardly, nodding toward her hand, "for the child's sake. I mean, I noticed you're wearing no wedding ring."

"I'm divorced," Emma reminded. But she acknowledged his point with a rueful smile. "Still, I agree it's probably best that I wear a ring."

"Good," he said, sounding relieved.

Emma removed her glove and was about to reach for the ring, when Matthew took her hand, slipped the ring on her third finger, and winked solemnly. She was stunned by the unaccountable thrill that swept her at his touch.

A moment later, Matthew nudged her to a stop before an elegant *couturière* shop with French puffed curtains in the front window. "Now for you," he explained, opening the door and ushering her inside to the accompaniment of a jangling bell.

"You've done enough already," she protested.

Inside, the little shop was posh, with velvet-upholstered Victorian furniture, a vivid blue and gold oriental rug on the floor, and mouth-watering silk and satin gowns on display.

A tall, pretty strawberry-blond woman in lacy blouse and long skirt emerged from the back of the shop and came forward, smiling at the sight of Matthew. She spoke in a cultured voice with a slight French accent. "Why, Matthew, darling, what a wonderful surprise."

"Claudette." Matthew took the woman's slim hand and kissed its back, then turned to Emma. "May I present my cousin, Mrs. Fairchild, a widow from America."

Lips twitching at Matthew's announcement, the woman curtsied. "Mrs. Fairchild. I'm Claudette Moreau."

Emma extended her hand. "Pleased to meet you, Ms. Moreau."

The woman frowned, obviously puzzled by Emma's calling her "Ms." Shaking Emma's hand, she said, "Please, you must call me Claudette."

Emma nodded, while Claudette glanced expectantly at Matthew.

Matthew cleared his throat. "Claudette, my dear cousin has just arrived from America with her child, and is in dire need of a complete winter wardrobe. May I count on your assistance?"

Claudette winked at him slyly. "Of course, Matthew. As always."

As Emma wondered what she meant by the phrase "as always," Matthew cast the dressmaker a chiding look. "How long will this take?"

"Why, it could be an hour or two, for measurements and such."

"I see." Matthew dug into his breast pocket, then handed Claudette several gold sovereigns. "If I leave Mrs. Fairchild here with you for a while, may I count on you to take good care of her?"

Claudette grinned first at Matthew, then at Emma. "But of course. Anything for you, Matthew."

"Good. See that you spare no expense in outfitting my cousin."

Claudette looked Emma over speculatively. "Will she be needing gowns for the season, then?"

"Of course. Everything, including formal wear."

Claudette didn't reply, though she raised an eyebrow in obvious amusement.

Just as Emma was about to protest again, Matthew turned to her. "My dear, may I have a word with you?"

"Oh . . . of course."

He glanced meaningfully at Claudette, and she

curtsied and moved off toward the back of the shop.

Matthew leveled a severe glance on Emma. "I can tell you're about to start objecting again. I won't hear of it."

"You're impossible—and spending far too much on us," Emma chided.

"It's my pleasure."

He pulled out an ornate gold pocket watch, flipped it open, and stared at the dial. "However, I do have a bit of business to attend to in my office over at the Exchange. Therefore, if you've no objection, I'll leave you in Claudette's capable hands. Crispin will, of course, remain behind to escort you home. I shall try to return here before you leave, but if not, I'll join you at home later."

"But how will you go about your business if Crispin stays with me?"

"I'll let a hansom cab."

"No, you mustn't," she protested. "You take the carriage. I can take a cab."

He raised an eyebrow. "My dear, really. No gentleman worth his salt would allow a lady to hire a ride on the streets."

Emma smiled despite herself. "You know, Matthew Weymouth, you *are* very old-fashioned and proper."

Emma was surprised by the devilish hint that gleamed in Matthew's dark eyes. "Take care, my dear," he admonished. "When I see you smile that way, I don't feel nearly as proper as I should."

Even as she wondered what his comment meant, he leaned over and briefly, tenderly kissed her cheek. Then he was gone, leaving Emma with her heart giddily racing and a flush of excitement creeping up her cheeks.

Feeling quite rattled, Emma glanced over at Claudette to see her grinning as if she knew the most delectable secret.

Chapter Six

"So—a pretty American cousin in the clutches of Matthew Weymouth," Claudette murmured.

Standing in the back room of the dress shop, wearing the camisole and bloomers lent her by Mrs. O'Leery's daughter, Emma wondered at the woman's rather cynical comment. Emma stood facing the ornate pier mirror, while the dressmaker knelt at her feet, measuring her with a cloth tape.

"Why would you say I'm in Matthew's 'clutches'?" Emma responded rather coolly. "He seems the perfect gentleman."

Claudette trilled a laugh. "My dear, you can't mean to say you're unaware of his reputation with the ladies? Lord Worthing is known to be quite deadly."

Even though Emma's conscience urged her not to participate in gossip, her curiosity won out. "Deadly in what sense?"

Claudette carefully looped the tape around Emma's waist. "Why, Matthew has left a string of broken hearts in his wake. He's notorious for seducing married woman—several have even wanted to leave their husbands for him, but Matthew has managed to end all of his liaisons with no lasting complications like matrimony."

"I see," Emma murmured, frowning. "And is he currently involved?"

Claudette's eyes gleamed merrily. "*Oui*, rumor has him linked with Celeste Manning, wife of the earl of Moorhouse. According to the gossips, Lady Celeste has fallen hard for Matthew, although according to form he's only trifling with her affections. However, rumor also has it that if Lady Celeste cannot win Matthew for herself, she aims to pair him up with her eligible young daughter, Lady Dorcas."

Emma frowned over this. "A mother would want to pair her own daughter up with her lover? A . . ." She struggled to think of a term Claudette would understand. "A rogue?"

Claudette laughed again. "*Oui*, Matthew's reputation is scandalous—and not just with the ladies. Politically he's quite an outspoken liberal in the House of Lords, supporting Gladstone's bill to bring suffrage to the poor, even backing Mill's doomed effort to enfranchise women. Between his radical political beliefs and his dalliances among the fairer sex, Matthew has raised more than a few eyebrows among *le beau monde*. But he is quite powerful, and rich as Midas. The Mannings are land-poor aristocrats and could do worse for their daughter."

"Perhaps," Emma murmured, troubled by Claudette's disclosures about Matthew's reputation with women, but pleased to hear of his liberal politics.

Claudette's expression shone with devilment. "Yet one cannot help but wonder what complications may ensue from the arrival of Matthew's lovely widowed cousin from America."

Emma didn't smile back. "Just what are you implying?"

Claudette blanched. "I didn't mean to cast aspersions, madam. I'm merely offering a friendly word of advice—that Matthew favors women of experience, and knows precisely how to exploit them."

"Are you speaking from your *own* experience?"

Claudette's coy smile gave away that she was. "Just take care, my dear. And please know that if—and when—Matthew does marry, it will no doubt be to a lady who is both highborn and virginal—someone like Dorcas Manning."

"Thanks for the advice," Emma replied stiffly.

Standing, Claudette folded her tape. "If you'll excuse me, madam, I think I have a frock or two that should do for immediate wear. I'll fetch them for you to try on."

"Certainly."

Watching Claudette leave the small room, Emma was lost in thought. She must take great care around Matthew Weymouth. Yes, he had acted kind and gallant toward her and the baby, and perhaps he also supported some noble causes. But Claudette had reminded her of the type of man he really was—just as much of a philanderer as Steve had been. She mustn't let the memory of Matthew's tender kisses sway her. Behind that solicitous facade lay a man who was no doubt every bit as selfish and self-absorbed as her ex.

Matthew sat in his office at the Exchange, rapping a pencil on his desk. He felt little interest in the financial papers scattered before him. Instead, his thoughts were focused on the delightful, mysterious creature who had arrived on his stoop last night with her adorable babe. He still wondered who Emma Fairchild really was and why she and her child had appeared so dramatically at his home.

And, while he still couldn't understand how the child had arrived at his home before she had, he found it increasingly difficult to believe that Emma had abandoned the baby there, for she seemed fiercely protective of, and devoted to, her tiny daughter. Nor could he believe Emma was a trollop, for she was too refined and well-educated. He *could* believe she was a worthwhile young woman of apparently tragic circumstance who desperately needed a husband and a father for her child.

And *that* possibility left him squirming in his chair.

Matthew hasn't anticipated his feelings toward Emma and her child—tenderness, protectiveness. Such softer emotions were supposedly foreign to a profligate such as himself. Yet the woman had a unique way of tugging at his heartstrings—and when he'd kissed her goodbye before leaving her with Claudette, the brief contact of his lips on her soft, warm cheek had stirred him mightily. Where women were concerned, Matthew was totally unaccustomed to feeling tenderness rather than lust, concern rather than self-interest.

What was happening to him? He was thirty-four years old, a man of much experience, and quite jaded regarding matters of the heart. Yet in the few brief hours since they'd intruded on his life, Emma and her child had already managed to warm that cold heart of his.

Looking about at his richly appointed office

with its leather settee, marble-topped tables and mahogany bookcases, he realized his life was quite full of possessions, but bereft of true meaning. His investment banking firm, held in his family for many generations, had financed a good portion of Mayfair, the Piazza, and Regent's Park. His own investments in the East India Company and in African gold mines had reaped a vast harvest of riches. He wasn't just comfortable, but extraordinarily wealthy. And he possessed an able staff who afforded him a fair amount of leisure time.

Time for his other diversions. Women, sport, politics. He eased his conscience by championing the causes of the downtrodden in Parliament, and by contributing generously to worthwhile charities, all the while congratulating himself on his magnanimous nature.

Yet how shallow and artificial his entire life seemed when juxtaposed against the plight of a destitute young woman and her darling babe. . . .

"Sir, may I have a moment?"

Matthew looked up to see his spectacled clerk, Samuel Parsmith, standing in the doorway with an anxious look on his face. Slim and fair, Samuel was a fine-looking gentleman, despite his threadbare brown suit and perpetually anxious expression.

"Yes, Parsmith?"

"Your lordship, have you decided yet what you

will do regarding the request for financing of a new steamer for the Woodrow Line? As I'm sure you'll recall, you were concerned because they experienced that disaster with the *Neptune* off Newfoundland last year."

Matthew leaned back in his leather chair and frowned pensively. "Ah, yes. I think we should give them the benefit of the doubt and assume lightning won't strike twice in the same place. After all, steam travel to America is so popular these days. Tell them we'll extend the requested credit—after all, 'tis the season, is it not?"

Parsmith broke into a grin. "Aye, your lordship. Chairman Gibbons will be pleased."

Nodding, Matthew stood. "You work very hard here, don't you, Parsmith?"

Parsmith appeared taken aback for a moment, then nodded vigorously. "Aye, sir, I try my best."

Matthew stroked his jaw. "I must see about giving you an increase."

Parsmith broke into a rare, boyish grin. "Aye, sir, that would be most welcome. Not that you haven't been entirely generous."

"Aye, but it takes a precious lot to survive these days. Have you a family, Parsmith?"

He shifted from foot to foot. "Nay, your lordship. I haven't had the time as yet."

"Not the time?" Matthew asked. "But you're getting rather long in the tooth, are you not? You must be all of thirty."

"Aye, I'll turn thirty on Boxing Day," Parsmith confided with a rueful grin.

"The day after Christmas?" Matthew pursued eagerly. "Why, you must start thinking about a bride to warm your bosom, and children to scamper about your hearth. Perhaps make your calls to the New Year's Day open houses, and woo all the available young ladies."

Color was steadily moving up Parsmith's face. "Aye, sir."

Matthew struck a thoughtful pose. "As a matter of fact, I have a young, attractive widow staying under my roof at the moment. My cousin from America—she's here with her small babe."

"How lovely, sir," Parsmith replied, clearly puzzled.

"Would you be amenable to meeting Mrs. Fairchild at some point?"

Now the poor clerk blushed to the roots of his hair. "Aye, sir. Certainly. I should be most honored to meet your cousin."

Matthew clapped his hands. "Splendid. We'll have you around for tea soon. And—er—that will be all for now."

Looking supremely grateful, the clerk nodded and all but dashed out the door. Matthew frowned. What on earth had possessed him to think of playing matchmaker?

* * *

When Emma emerged from the shop, the coachman following with a stack of boxes, she spotted Matthew briskly approaching her from down the arcade, his stride long and elegant, his ebony walking stick flashing in the late morning sunshine. Her heart quickening at the sight of him, she smiled in pleasant surprise. "Matthew, you're back."

Arriving at her side, he offered his arm. "I concluded my business earlier than expected and thought I'd come round to escort you home."

"How kind of you."

As they started off, he asked, "So, did you and Claudette plan an extensive wardrobe?"

Emma sighed. "Yes, from what she says, I'll be keeping her busy for some time to come. She wants me back next week for a fitting."

"Of course."

"But I cannot impose on you for that long," she protested.

Matthew raised an eyebrow. "I've already told you, Mrs. Fairchild, that we shall not even discuss your leaving until after the holidays."

"But—"

"I mean it, Emma."

She fell silent, frowning to herself, though secretly thrilled by his calling her "Emma."

Observing her, he gently squeezed her arm. "Are you feeling all right, my dear?"

"Oh, fine," she reassured him with a quick

smile. "I'm just getting a bit anxious over the baby. We must have been gone close to two hours."

"Don't worry, she's in perfectly capable hands with my housekeeper."

Emma nodded. "I know. But I'm also a bit tired."

He glanced at her anxiously. "Ah, yes, how thoughtless of me. I'm forgetting that it hasn't been that long since your . . . er, confinement."

"Oh, I'll be okay, and I did get so much rest yesterday." She forced a brighter expression. "So, tell me, what do you do, Matthew?"

"Do?" he repeated.

"At the Exchange."

"Ah, yes. I run an investment banking firm. Actually, my staff runs it, affording me time to spend with lovely ladies such as yourself."

Emma felt herself blush. "I see."

"Indeed, I was just thanking my clerk, Parsmith, for his devotion and hard work," Matthew continued meaningfully. "A fine young man, Parsmith. I was telling him we must have him around for tea sometime."

Puzzled, Emma murmured, "That sounds nice."

Glancing away rather uneasily, he went on, "I also told him he's of an age where he needs to start thinking about settling down, finding a wife, having a family."

Although perplexed by his train of thought, Emma couldn't resist needling him a bit. "Aren't you of that same age, Lord Worthing?"

He feigned a look of shock. "Me? Why, I'm a hopeless cause already."

Emma gave a discreet cough. "That's pretty much what Claudette was telling me."

He scowled. "Was she telling tales out of school about me?"

"Are they true?" Emma challenged playfully.

Matthew appeared astounded, then laughed. "My, you American ladies are blunt, aren't you?"

Emma faced him down saucily. "You haven't answered my question."

Matthew frowned, gazing ahead. "What else did Claudette tell you?"

Disappointed that he was evidently determined not to answer her, she released a long breath. "Oh, that you're quite a liberal, a champion of the causes of the masses."

He snapped his fingers. "My nobler nature. Now there's a subject I can warm to."

Emma could only shake her head. Matthew Weymouth was a charming rascal.

As they continued on to the carriage, Matthew spoke eagerly of some of his political activities in the House of Lords—how he'd recently helped to elect his friend, William Gladstone, as prime minister, and of his pride in helping Gladstone shepherd through a bill of Irish reforms. Her admiration for him rose when he spoke of how he sincerely believed the underprivileged deserved the same rights as anyone else. When he casually mentioned historical personages such as John Stuart Mill, Benjamin Disraeli, Thomas Carlyle, and even Queen Victoria, Emma could only shake her head in awe, amazed to hear of such famous historical figures spoken of in the present tense.

On the way home, the coachman circled the area before heading back toward Mayfair. Emma delighted at the sight of a train going past on an overhead trestle, whistle blowing and steam billowing from its stack. She thrilled at the gothic splendor of the Royal Courts of Justice, and was amazed by Wren's Renaissance masterpiece, St. Paul's Cathedral. She was enchanted by the view of Monument and the imposing Tower of London. Matthew laughed at her awestruck reactions.

In her mind, she compared the marvels of this nineteenth-century world with the technologically advanced time she'd left behind. It occurred to her that she really hadn't lost a lot, even if she and her baby were stranded here forever as she sensed they might be—although of course she'd miss her family. But something about this place, this time—and, to be honest, this *man*—drew her. She felt at home, as if this were the setting where she and her child were always meant to be.

The carriage wound its way past the pillars of Mansion House and down the Strand. As they rattled by Covent Garden, Emma gasped at the sight of a vendor unloading small, cut evergreens from a dray.

"Christmas trees!" she cried.

"Ah, yes," said Matthew. "The custom made so popular by the Prince Regent, and honored even now, years after his death."

Thinking of the personal significance, Emma wiped away a tear of joy. "You know, it's my baby's first Christmas."

Tenderness shone in Matthew's gaze. "It is, indeed. Shall we get her one, Emma?"

Emma regarded him happily. "Would you?"

"But of course. Anything for your child—and to see you smile that way."

Impulsively, she hugged him. "Oh, thank you, Matthew."

Emotion tugged at his voice as he gazed down at her. "You're most welcome, my dear."

"You know, I think you've given me an idea," she added wistfully.

"Yes?"

Emma smiled dreamily. "I think I'll call my daughter 'Noelle.' For the holidays."

"Lovely," he agreed.

They had great fun picking out a small fir tree. Crispin lashed it to the back of the carriage, then they drove home, passing through Trafalgar Square and Piccadilly Circus. Moments later, laughing, their cheeks bright from the cold, they entered Matthew's townhouse. In the marble-floored foyer, Hettie rushed forward, wringing her hands.

At once anxiety gripped Emma. "Mrs. O'Leery, what is it? Is my baby all right? Oh, I knew I never should have left her!"

Hettie patted Emma's hand. "Not to worry, lass, the wee bairn hasn't stirred at all and is still fast asleep." She cast Matthew a chiding glance. " 'Tis you, sir, who is at sixes and sevens now."

Matthew frowned. "What is wrong?"

Before the housekeeper could answer, a voluptuous middle-aged woman in a rose-colored silk gown emerged from the drawing room. Her stance regal, head held high, the dark-haired beauty smiled frostily at Matthew, then glanced at Emma with disdain. Emma mused that the woman really was quite striking, her high cheekbones and full mouth compensating for a rather pinched expression and sharp nose.

"Why, Matthew," she murmured, stepping forward in a rustle of her skirts, "wherever have you been?" She smiled venomously at Emma. "And with whom?"

Grasping Emma's hand and pulling her along with him, Matthew spoke in a rush. "Lady Celeste, what a pleasant surprise." He gestured to

Emma. "May I present my distant cousin, Mrs. Fairchild, from America."

Although Celeste raised an eyebrow, she possessed enough grace to extend her hand. "Mrs. Fairchild. A pleasure."

"Thank you. Same here," Emma muttered, gritting her teeth at the other woman's noticeably limp handshake.

Matthew turned to Emma. "Emma, dear, this is my old friend, Lady Moorhouse."

Emma nodded. "Good to know you, Lady Moorhouse."

"Indeed," Celeste echoed cynically. "So, Mrs. Fairchild, whence do you hail?"

"Er—from Chicago."

"My, you've traveled such a long distance," she commented. "Is Mr. Fairchild here with you?"

Emma stammered, "I—"

"My cousin is a widow," Matthew cut in firmly. "She's here with her baby."

"Her baby?" gasped Celeste, her cool composure quickly dissolving. "Matthew, you can't mean the one that I . . . that we . . ."

Matthew quelled her with a harsh glance. "Celeste, really."

"Oh." Glancing from Emma to Matthew, Celeste blanched, then flashed Matthew a cold, calculating stare. "I just happen to be very interested in your guest—and her situation."

"Ah, yes, Lady Celeste, you're the soul of kindness, as always." Forcing a pleasant expression, Matthew rubbed his hands together. "Well, shall we all go into the drawing room and have tea?"

"No, I can't stay," Celeste replied irritably. "I just wanted to drop in to make sure you're still planning to attend the tree-trimming celebration and dinner at our home Friday week."

Matthew hesitated. "I'm really not sure—"

"Of course Mrs. Fairchild is welcome, as well," Celeste added with forced courtesy.

Before Matthew could respond, Emma touched his arm. "Please, you mustn't change any plans on my account."

He flashed her a smile, then turned back to Celeste. "We're both delighted to accept."

Celeste smiled back, though her eyes glistened with malice. "Splendid. If you like, Mrs. Fairchild, you may bring a homemade ornament for our tree. That is what the other guests will be doing. Dagmar—that's my husband, Mrs. Fairchild—will be so pleased to know you both will attend." Her gaze shifted meaningfully to Matthew. "So will Dorcas."

"Ah, yes," he murmured. "How is your lovely daughter?"

Celeste's expression was sweetly poisonous. "Actually, the cold weather has gotten her dispirited, but I'm sure she'll perk up once she learns you're attending next week, Matthew."

"We shall look forward to it." Matthew offered his arm. "May I see you out?"

"But of course." Linking her arm through Matthew's, she said frigidly to Emma, "So good to meet you, Mrs. Fairchild."

"And you, Lady Moorhouse," Emma responded in an equally remote tone.

As soon as Matthew and Celeste were out the door, Emma turned to Mrs. O'Leery, who stood in the shadows. "Who *was* that woman?"

The housekeeper merely rolled her eyes. "Hadn't we best check on the wee bairn?"

Emma's hands flew to her face. "Oh, heavens, of course."

Following the housekeeper, Emma hurried toward the stairs.

Chapter Seven

Upstairs, Emma entered her room followed by the housekeeper. Next to the bed, she found her baby still asleep inside the blanket-lined basket where Hettie had placed her. She noted that Crispin had already placed the boxes from the *couturière* on her bed.

Kneeling beside her daughter, stroking her soft, cherubic face, Emma sighed in supreme happiness.

Standing, she touched the housekeeper's arm. "Thank you so much for watching her, Mrs. O'Leery."

Hettie waved her off. "She's no trouble, that one. An angel straight from heaven."

"Nonetheless, I couldn't have gone out today without your help. And you should see all the lovely things Matthew insisted we buy for her—and me. A cradle and bassinet, clothing for us both. Everything we could possibly need. All the baby things will be delivered this afternoon."

Hettie nodded. "Splendid, lass. I'll have everything sent up when the man arrives."

"And you must thank your daughter for lending me this outfit, as well," Emma went on, smoothing down a fold of her skirt.

Hettie chuckled. "Ah, my Moira was more than happy to help, especially as she has no need for what you're wearing at the moment."

"No need?" Emma murmured, confused.

Hettie cupped a hand around her mouth and lowered her voice. "She's quite large with child herself. She and her dear Milton are expecting their first wee one come St. Valentine's Day."

Emma beamed. "How wonderful. So you'll be a grandmother, then?"

"Aye, and your bairn is giving me a fine taste."

As if she'd heard, the bairn began to stir, whimpering, thrashing about, then blinking open her eyes and squinting up at the two women. "Well, look who's awake," declared Emma. Again she hunkered down, letting the baby clutch her finger in a tight little fist. "Hello, sleepyhead."

The infant cooed at her mother, and Emma felt joy welling up inside her. She was grateful that her child was safe, healthy and warm. And there she had to thank Matthew Weymouth and his dear housekeeper.

"I'm sure the mite is starved by now," put in the housekeeper, holding out her arms. "Here, lass, give her to me. I'll change her whilst you prepare to feed her."

By the time Emma had finished nursing Noelle, the delivery man had arrived with the layette and baby furnishings they'd purchased. Emma dressed her infant in an adorable white linen gown with pink embroidered flowers, and placed her in the beautiful white bassinet covered with lace-trimmed silk organza. Emma then lingered in her room for several hours, ate the hearty soup Mrs. O'Leery brought up for lunch, and watched the baby. She busied herself by putting away Noelle's new things, and trying on her own new dresses.

Late that afternoon, while Emma was again nursing the baby, Mrs. O'Leery slipped inside to tell her Matthew had requested that she and the baby come down for supper, and to decorate the tree afterward. Despite all her doubts about Matthew, Emma found anticipation building at the thought of being with him again.

Emma wore one of her new gowns, a high-collared, sapphire-blue silk, down to dinner. When she stepped inside the dining room with the baby, Matthew turned to stare at her appreciatively. He stood next to the sideboard sipping an aperitif. Emma smiled back giddily, for he looked stunningly handsome in his dark suit in the candlelit room.

Before either could speak, Hettie burst in from the kitchen, setting down a pewter tray of mouth-watering baked ham.

"Ah, there you are, lass. Give me the wee one, now. I've set up the cradle for her in the kitchen, and I'll be watching her whilst you eat."

Thanking Mrs. O'Leery, Emma surrendered the baby, and Matthew came forward to pull out her chair. "You look lovely, my dear. May I pour you some wine?"

Emma smiled, breathing in the enticing scent of his bay rum. "Thanks, but I probably shouldn't, as I'm nursing."

Although he appeared bemused by her reference to nursing, he didn't comment as he took his seat. During the meal, Matthew inquired solicitously of her and the child. Emma was fascinated by the magnificent table and its beautiful accoutrements—intricately carved silver candlelabras, breathtaking crystal, gold-trimmed Worcester china, snowy white linens. And the food was like nothing she had ever tasted before—quaint preparations such as tongue with currant sauce, sweetbreads, and whipped syllabub. Everything was incredibly fresh and delicious.

Although the mood at the dinner table was somewhat restrained, liveliness ruled afterward when they all moved into the drawing room to attend to the tree, which Matthew had placed in a rock-lined brass urn in the far corner. Emma strung popcorn and made paper chains, and Matthew carefully draped both on the little fir. The air bore the delicious scents of the evergreen and the wood burning in the grate.

Across from them, Mrs. O'Leery sat on the silk brocade settee facing the crackling fire, her fingers busily knitting a baby blanket, her toe gently rocking the cradle where the baby slept. James had already retired to the room the couple shared at the back of the house. But, seeing the housekeeper there happily sharing their evening, Emma was again reminded of how she'd learned that Matthew Weymouth was an active promoter of the rights of the underprivileged. This knowledge that he might possess more substance than the classic, self-absorbed womanizer further endeared him to her.

Matthew moved back a few paces and scowled at their handiwork. "Well, Emma, the paper chains you suggested are a nice touch, but the tree doesn't look unduly festive with just that and the popcorn string."

She nodded. "The tree needs ornaments, as well. Perhaps we could hang some decorated cookies—"

"And sugarplums," called out Hettie. "We'll need some of those, won't we, your lordship?"

"Certainly," Matthew agreed.

"Shall we have the entire Christmas, your lordship?" Hettie went on eagerly. "Not just the tree, but an Advent wreath and Yule log, the plum pudding, the goose and all?"

Matthew grinned at Emma. "Sounds lovely, don't you think?"

Joining in the spirit, she asked, "Will we celebrate Thanksgiving, as well?"

He laughed. "But that's an American tradition, love."

Emma felt herself blushing at Matthew's endearment, for it had rolled off his tongue in a silken way that rattled and thrilled her. "Of course," she replied, embarrassed. "You're right."

"Well, we'll just have to bake a goose anyway, won't we, milord?" Hettie put in. "In honor of our American guests."

Matthew winked at Emma. "Of course. A splendid idea. For Emma." He glanced tenderly at the cradle. "And her baby."

"Hear! Hear!" seconded the housekeeper.

Abruptly Matthew cleared his throat, and addressed Hettie. "We must also host a traditional open house on New Year's Day, to introduce Mrs. Fairchild to all my friends."

At this, Mrs. O'Leery cast her employer a baleful look and harrumphed loudly.

Matthew clapped his hands. "Well, I'd best fetch some water for the tree."

After he strode out, Emma went to sit beside Hettie. She gazed lovingly at Noelle. "She's so good—she hardly ever cries. All she does is eat and sleep."

"Aye, though the mite will awaken to her new world in due course and put you through your paces, I'm sure," the housekeeper replied, knitting needles clicking.

"May I ask you something?" Emma asked the kindly woman.

"Surely."

"You don't approve of Lord Worthing's hosting a New Year's Day open house?"

Setting down her knitting, Mrs. O'Leery frowned. "My dear, everyone knows such gatherings are staged to show off the eligible young ladies in a household. All the swains in town make their rounds that day. Why, some bachelors are known to leave their calling cards at several dozen fêtes before the sun goes down."

Emma was taken aback. "Why, I had no idea. You think Matthew intends to try to find me a husband?"

Hettie took up her knitting again. "That's the appearance of it."

Emma's brow was furrowed. "You know, today he was praising the attributes of his clerk to me."

The housekeeper snorted derisively. "Well, if

you want my opinion, his lordship should see to his responsibilities himself."

"Mrs. O'Leery, really," Emma admonished. "I told you Matthew is not responsible for my child."

"I know, lass. His lordship told me you're an American—and *divorced.*" But the housekeeper's skeptical look indicated she believed otherwise.

Matthew now reentered the room with a bucket of water. "Mrs. O'Leery, I noticed your hambone boiling rather vigorously out in the kitchen."

With a gasp, Hettie set down her knitting. "Blessed saints, I must tend it or tomorrow's soup will be ruined. And may I bring you folks some wassail and hot chocolate?"

"Sounds lovely," Emma answered.

After she left, Matthew watered the tree, then stood by Emma. After gazing fondly at the sleeping baby, he grasped a poker and began gently stoking the fire. "Penny for your thoughts, Emma."

She smiled dreamily, listening to the crackling sound of the wood, feeling content and toasty warm. "I was thinking about Christmas—past Christmases, that is."

"Are you missing your family?"

Emma's expression grew wistful. "I'm an only child, and my parents have retired to Mexico."

"How unusual," he murmured, sounding baffled. "Tell me about your home. Didn't you say you are from Chicago?"

She laughed. "It's very much as you've heard, I'm sure—cold and windy." Fearing he would question her further, broaching subjects she was unprepared to address, she rushed on, "And what of your family, Matthew?"

He sighed, set aside the poker and sat down beside her. "I've a married younger brother in Kent, and two small nieces. We lost our parents five winters past in a horrible influenza epidemic."

Emma nodded, soberly thinking of how common, even minor, illnesses killed thousands of people in these times. "I'm so sorry, Matthew."

"Thank you."

She eyed him quizzically. "Tell me something."

"Yes?"

"A moment ago, Mrs. O'Leery was making you feel uncomfortable, wasn't she?"

He appeared taken aback by her observation. "Indeed?"

"Isn't that why you maneuvered her out of the room?"

He laughed. "Are my motives that transparent?"

"Yes," she chuckled.

"Perhaps I just wanted to be alone with you," he suggested wickedly.

"Then you're a bad boy, and you'll likely get

ashes in your stocking come Christmas morning," she teased back.

He chuckled, then grew sober, leaning forward to rest his elbows on his knees and lace his fingers beneath his chin. "Truth to tell, my irascible housekeeper doesn't approve of the way I'm treating you."

Emma's lips twitched. "You mean, your plans to marry me off?"

Blanching, he sat bolt upright. "I'll be deuced if you aren't the most outspoken, impertinent woman I've ever met!"

Although humor quirked at Emma's lips, she met his eye gravely. "If you mean I tell the truth and speak my mind, then you're right."

"Heaven help me," he moaned.

"Matthew, your motives are quite transparent," she went on gently. "First you hint to me about your clerk, then you announce the open house on New Year's Day. Your housekeeper explained the significance."

"That interfering woman," he muttered.

"Matthew, my point is, you needn't take responsibility for me and Noelle. I don't need you to find me a husband."

He gazed at the baby for a long moment, his expression softening. "But doesn't she need a father?"

Touched by the note of caring in his voice, Emma nonetheless replied, "If I do decide that,

I'm perfectly capable of finding a father for her on my own."

Admiration shone in his gaze. "My, you're a formidable woman, Mrs. Fairchild."

"And aren't you dodging the real issue?"

"The real issue?"

Emma raised an eyebrow. "Let me take you back to this morning, and a certain lady's visit."

"Ah. That."

"There's obviously something going on between you and Lady Celeste."

His brows rushed together. "What makes you say that?"

She rolled her eyes. "Really. Do you think I'm a fool?"

A chuckle rumbled forth. "Never, my dear."

"The real issue is, the baby and I are cramping your reckless bachelor lifestyle, aren't we?"

That remark left him frowning for a long moment. Then, catching her totally off-guard, he leaned over and tenderly, briefly claimed her lips. His mouth felt warm and delicious on hers; his kiss took her breath away. Emma was overwhelmed by the wave of yearning that swept over her. Matthew's kiss was all the more disarming because it was so sweet, fleeting, and unexpected.

When he pulled back, she eyed him in anticipation as he held her spellbound with a passionate look. His voice was rough. "Now you're the one overlooking the *real* issue, Emma."

Now you're the one overlooking the real *issue, Emma*. On Sunday morning, as Emma sat beside Matthew in St. Margaret's Church, the baby dozing in her arms, she still remembered his provocative statement earlier in the week, and the incredible chemistry that had flared between them the night they had decorated the tree together. Over the remainder of the week, as Emma had continued to adjust to her child, and to the world of 1869 London in which they'd found themselves, an underlying tension had smoldered between her and Matthew, although they hadn't again directly addressed their situation.

This morning was a welcome distraction for her. She felt particularly thrilled that Matthew had invited her to go with him to church. The majestic sanctuary was filled with elegantly dressed lords and ladies, and the scent of pomade and fine French perfume filled the air. Hettie had explained to her that St. Margaret's was the parish church of the House of Commons, and was considered the most prestigious house of worship in London. Indeed, Emma marveled at the grand design of the sanctuary, the Flemish stained-glass panels, the altarpiece featuring the Supper at Emmaus. She also very much enjoyed the service, the beautiful rendition of the *Ave Maria*, the readings, and the sermon.

Afterward, amid a crush of people moving for the doors, Matthew introduced Emma to many of his friends and acquaintances, people she knew were historical personages, such as the two recently retired prime minsters, Lord Derby and Benjamin Disraeli, even the new prime minster, Matthew's friend, William Gladstone. Emma felt totally awed to be in the actual presence of these famous figures who had existed for her only in history books before. And the obvious pride Matthew took in making his introductions warmed her heart.

Then Celeste Manning swept up to them with her sour-faced, elderly husband and a pretty, voluptuous young woman whom Emma guessed was her daughter, in tow.

"Why Matthew, Mrs. Fairchild, what a pleasure to see you again," she murmured.

"Celeste, Dagmar, Dorcas," Matthew rejoined politely.

"Mrs. Fairchild, kindly meet my husband, Lord Moorhouse, and my daughter, Lady Dorcas," Celeste added.

Shifting the baby in her arms, Emma murmured, "How do you do?" and shook hands with them both.

"Pleased to meet you," Dagmar said in a grating voice. "Celeste has told me you will also be joining us for our tree-trimming dinner next week, Mrs. Fairchild."

"I'd be delighted, Lord Moorhouse, if it's not an imposition."

He waved her off. "Certainly not. Cook prepares more than enough for Wellington's army."

Now Dorcas smiled at Matthew, fluttering her eyelashes and speaking in a coy little voice. "I'm pleased you're coming, Lord Worthing. I've wanted for ages to show you the sampler I'm completing. It's quite striking—a view of the ponds at Kensington Gardens."

"It sounds lovely, Dorcas. I should love to see it," Matthew replied.

Dorcas giggled.

"Until Friday then," Celeste added.

As the family moved on, Noelle began to stir and whimper. Matthew glanced at her anxiously. "Is she hungry?"

"Well, we do need to get her home."

He held out his arms. "Let me take her. You've carried her long enough."

"But I mustn't impose—"

"Please, Emma, 'tis no imposition."

She handed over the child, and was at once thrilled by the look of pride on Matthew's face as he gently rocked Noelle in his arms and clucked to her. At once the baby quieted and stared up at him solemnly. She realized in awe that this was the first time Matthew had actually held her child, and he did so with such tenderness and grace, the sight swept her with treacherous excitement.

"Why, Matthew, I must say you seem quite a natural at being a father."

Emma started, turning in the direction of the person who had evidently read her own mind. She watched the grinning vicar step up in his robes.

Matthew, coloring slightly, greeted the clergyman with a nod. "Vicar Posteridge, may I present my cousin, Mrs. Emma Fairchild, from America."

The tall, thin man nodded to Emma. "Mrs. Fairchild."

Emma shook the vicar's hand and smiled. "Good to meet you. I so enjoyed your sermon."

"Thank you. Are you visiting England alone?"

Emma hesitated, glanced at Matthew, then murmured, "I'm a widow."

"Actually, we're glad you've stepped up, vicar," Matthew added. "We need to speak to you about having my cousin's baby christened—er, don't we, Emma?"

Pleasantly surprised, Emma replied, "Of course. What a wonderful idea."

The vicar smiled. "I'd be honored to christen your child."

"Good," said Matthew. "And I shall act as the child's godfather, of course."

Emma eyed him in amazement. Matthew was certainly full of surprises.

"Splendid," the vicar said. "Why don't the two of you come by later this week, and we can set a date. It's always such a thrill when a new baby arrives this time of year, don't you think?"

Glancing at Emma, then back down at the cooing child in his arms, Matthew was positively beaming. "Aye," he murmured.

Late that night, Matthew sat in his study downstairs, sipping brandy, unable to sleep.

He couldn't get the day's events out of his mind. Or the last week's. Slowly but surely, Emma Fairchild and her darling babe were winnowing their way into his jaded heart.

He remembered the joy he'd felt decorating the tree with Emma, the thrill of teasing her, flirting with her, sharing himself with her. He felt so *close* to her. How he admired her spirit, her intelligence, her strength of character, her pride. And that brief, incredible kiss he'd stolen had left him starved for more. She had the face—the mouth—of an angel, and the charming nature of an enchantress.

Today had capped it all off nicely, sending him hurtling toward his own emotional ruin. The very memory made his fingers tremble as he lifted the brandy snifter. Holding her babe for the first time. That precious bit of life in his arms.

Seeing the trust in the dear babe's eyes as she had regarded him so soberly. He couldn't ever adequately describe the tender, stirring emotions that had consumed him then. The desire to protect and cherish Emma and her child forever.

Mercy, was he lost? Whatever had possessed him to volunteer as the child's godfather? Why not go ahead and propose to Emma as well, on the spot? It was all the same brand of sheer lunacy.

He didn't like what the woman's child was doing to him. Or what *she* was doing to him. Good Lord, could he be falling in love? If so, he was appalled with himself, but worried for Emma and the child. He'd never been able to stay with one woman for long. Could he change now? He'd make a wretched father and husband.

He must escape this dilemma before it was too late, before the sweet lair of Emma's smile trapped him forever. And he must find an answer for her and Noelle—and for the moment, Samuel Parsmith seemed the perfect solution.

Chapter Eight

During the week that followed, Emma became even better acclimated to life in the nineteenth-century and continued to regain her physical strength. She was able to pick up some more local customs when she went for fittings at the dressmaker, or shopping with Mrs. O'Leery or the coachman, but mostly she stayed at home and cared for Noelle.

Matthew kept very busy and acted distant and preoccupied, spending much of his time at his office at the Exchange. Emma was not fooled by his remoteness; she wondered if he regretted their kiss the night they'd decorated the tree, and his volunteering to become Noelle's godfather on the Sunday afterward.

Noelle proved a delight, and was thriving on Emma's breast milk. She still did little more than eat or sleep, though sometimes she had brief periods of wakefulness where she would make little sounds, examine her own hands and feet, or stare up at her mother thoughtfully. She was an incredibly placid baby. Emma was supremely grateful to see her child doing so well; she had worried about the baby's catching some dreadful malady here in London. Of course she was very particular about keeping germs away from Noelle, even going so far as to boil the baby's drinking water and all of her diapers, gowns, and blankets.

Although Mrs. O'Leery no doubt thought Emma's extreme fastidiousness odd, she didn't complain.

On Tuesday, three days before Lord and Lady Moorhouse's dinner party, Emma went to the dressmaker for the final fitting of the gown she would wear. When she and the coachman returned an hour and a half later, she found Matthew in the entryway, conversing with an attractive blond man.

Matthew turned to her with a smile. "Ah, Emma, your timing is perfect. My clerk has just come by with some papers for me, and I've been wanting to introduce the two of you."

"How nice," she murmured.

"Mrs. Emma Fairchild, meet Samuel Parsmith," Matthew said.

Emma extended her gloved hand. "How do you do?"

The man grinned shyly, bowed, and shook her hand. "Most pleased to meet you, Mrs. Fairchild."

"Well," said Matthew, rubbing his hands together, "why don't we all have some tea, so the two of you may become better acquainted?"

Bemused, Emma replied, "I really must go check on the baby."

"Ah, yes, Lord Worthing was telling me you have a new child," said Samuel. "Congratulations."

"Thank you."

"Yes, do go check on the baby," Matthew directed. "And why not bring her back down when you're through? I'm sure Samuel would love to see her—wouldn't you, Sam? The mite is just adorable, I must add."

The poor man colored, speaking with excruciating awkwardness. "Of course I'd be honored to see the child—if it's not an imposition, Mrs. Fairchild."

"I'll have to see," Emma hedged, frowning.

"We'll be waiting for you in the drawing room," Matthew added meaningfully.

Emma was tempted to make a face at him as she swept away. Why was Matthew playing up the virtues of his clerk again? Of course, Samuel Parsmith was a fine-looking man, and he seemed polite and pleasant—but he was clearly every bit as put off by Matthew's obvious machinations as Emma was. Besides, she wasn't shopping for a husband. She had enough to contend with—a new baby, *and* a new century!

Yet, if Matthew were pursuing her, would she feel differently? This question left her frowning thoughtfully as she climbed the stairs.

In her room, Noelle was just stirring as Emma came in, and the little girl gurgled up at her mother in recognition. Emma picked up her child and held her close with a sigh, kissing her soft forehead and breathing in her delightful baby scent.

After changing Noelle and spending a leisurely time nursing her, Emma resolved to go downstairs and speak with Matthew. Surely Samuel would have left by now. She wrapped the baby in a blanket and took her along.

But when Emma walked into the drawing room she found both men still there. Standing, Matthew smiled amiably and Samuel grinned awkwardly.

"Ah, there you are," Matthew greeted. "Sam wanted to go back to the office, but I insisted he wait and see the baby."

Casting Matthew a chiding glance, Emma crossed the room. "Here she is."

Samuel gazed down at the child with the awe-struck expression of a bachelor unaccustomed to being around infants. "She's lovely, Mrs. Fairchild."

"Thank you."

"And she appears to be thriving," he added shyly.

"She is."

Matthew indicated a wing chair by the fire. "Emma, do sit down and warm yourself and the babe."

"Thank you." She sat down with the baby, and the men followed suit.

An awkward moment followed, then Samuel coughed. "Mrs. Fairchild, Lord Worthing was telling me you're from America."

"Yes. Chicago."

"So you're quite a long ways from home."

"Indeed," Emma agreed ruefully.

"As a widow with a small child, Emma hopes to start a new life here," Matthew put in helpfully.

Emma glowered at him.

Samuel blushed. "A splendid idea."

Matthew lazily crossed his long legs. "In fact, I was just telling Samuel the other day that he should think about finding a wife. Imagine if he found a child, as well—why, an instant family."

He smiled pensively. "Come to think of it, just look at the three of you. All blond—I'll be deuced if you don't look like a family already. Isn't that so, Sam?"

Reduced to stammering, the clerk replied, "Well . . . I-I suppose—"

"Mr. Parsmith, where are you from?" Emma interrupted sweetly, before tossing Matthew another glare.

He appeared immensely relieved. "From Birmingham, ma'am."

"Do you have family there?"

" 'Fraid my people have mostly passed on."

Matthew elbowed him. "All the more reason to find a family of your own, eh, man?"

As if prodded by a fireplace poker, Samuel popped up from his seat. "Well . . . well, I hate to seem rude, but I really must be going. I've all those accounts left to reconcile at the office, your lordship." He bowed to Emma. "Good to meet you, madam."

"Likewise."

Matthew stood. "I'll see you out," he said wearily.

Once he returned to the room, Emma lit into him. "Matthew, how could you play such a shameless matchmaker! Your poor clerk was miserable!"

Matthew's grin was unrepentant. "My clerk was nothing of the kind. I was only thinking of what was best for you and your child."

Emma was exasperated. "Damn it, I'm perfectly capable of deciding that on my own."

He eyed her cynically. "This from the woman who abandoned her child on my stoop—and hasn't yet told me why?"

Appalled, Emma shot back, "Matthew, that's not fair!"

Instantly contrite, he replied, "You're right. I'm sorry." Distractedly he pulled out his pocket watch. "Look, I've no time to discuss this now. I'm late for an appointment."

"Matthew—"

But the maddening devil merely strode out the door.

Matters remained strained between Emma and Matthew during the remainder of the week. Even when Mrs. O'Leery treated them to the promised Thanksgiving dinner on Thursday night, Matthew was taciturn, his smile forced, his conversation stilted. In fact, he revealed his emotions only once, when Emma tactfully suggested that it might be time for her and Noelle to move on. At that point, he became furious, forbidding Emma to even broach the subject again. Emma was so frustrated with him, she didn't know what to do.

On Friday evening, Hettie offered to watch Noelle while Emma attended the dinner party with Matthew. Actually, she would have preferred to stay at home with Noelle, but Matthew was quite insistent, and promised they wouldn't be gone too long.

Hettie helped her dress in her new gown—a stunning pink velvet confection, with a low, lace-trimmed neck, puffed sleeves, fitted waist, and an extravagant bustled skirt with ruffled underskirts. Hettie pulled Emma's hair back and arranged sausage curls to frame her face.

"Here's a finishing touch," Hettie added, tying a cameo attached to a pink velvet ribbon around Emma's neck. "You look lovely my dear."

"Thank you," Emma said gratefully. "And thanks for watching the baby. Matthew—his lordship—promised we won't stay away long."

Hettie waved her off. "Ah, the mite's no trouble at all."

Hettie helped Emma don her matching cape and gloves. After grabbing the beaded reticule that contained her homemade ornament, Emma went downstairs and found Matthew in the drawing room standing with his back to her, warming his hands by the hearth. He cut a masterful figure in his formal black tailcoat and matching trousers.

Evidently he heard the rustle of her skirts, for he turned to stare at her in awe. He spoke in a husky voice. "Emma! My dear, you're a vision."

Excitement stormed through her at his words,

his appearance. He did look magnificent, cleanly shaven, with his dark hair slicked back, diamond studs gleaming on his sparkling silk shirt. It was such a relief to have him acting warmly toward her again.

"Thank you, Matthew. You look wonderful, as well."

Grinning, he crossed the room. "I'm almost afraid to let you loose around other men tonight." He offered his arm. "Shall we go?"

"Of course."

Emma was almost giddy as they traveled in the coach toward the Manning home in Mayfair. She kept catching Matthew's gaze straying ardently in her direction. It seemed obvious he had eyes only for her tonight.

Moments later, they entered the drawing room of the palatial mansion, the room aglow with soft light from crystal chandeliers, and filled with elegantly dressed lords and ladies swarming about a massive Christmas tree. Emma's spirits fell as she caught sight of Samuel Parsmith standing across the room, looking forlorn in his pedestrian brown suit.

Emma turned to Matthew. "Why is Samuel here?"

He glanced away guiltily. "I believe our hostess is about to explain matters."

Indeed, Emma then spotted Celeste Manning, ensconced in a fabulous bustled gown of gold satin, approaching them. The matron grabbed Samuel's arm en route, and towed him along.

"Well, hello, Matthew, Mrs. Fairchild," Celeste greeted, extending her hand to Matthew.

Matthew took and kissed her hand. "Celeste."

Celeste glanced at Emma. "Mrs. Fairchild, I understand you know Mr. Parsmith." She laughed. "I just loved Matthew's suggestion that I pair up the two of you tonight. The clerk with the little American." Before Emma could respond, she rushed on, "Now, Matthew, darling, you must come with me. Dorcas is just dying to show you her sampler."

Even as Matthew tried to protest, Celeste grabbed his arm and tugged him away.

A miserable silence fell in the wake of their departure. Emma turned to Samuel. "I'm so sorry."

He flashed her a lame smile. "Please, don't be, Mrs. Fairchild. Actually, I'm honored to be invited to a lavish event such as this. See how the other half lives and all that. And in the company of such a beautiful lady."

Emma cast him a chiding glance. "Mr. Parsmith, you don't have to be polite. I could tell how miserable you were the other day when we met."

Surprising her, Samuel shook his head. "Mrs. Fairchild, I assure you I'm not simply being polite. I'm actually quite honored to be with you. And if I seemed miserable the other day, it was only because I was afraid Lord Worthing was—

well, was imposing my presence on you."

"But you weren't any imposition," she protested.

He grinned shyly, and Emma noted he was actually quite handsome with his blue eyes, fair complexion and blond hair. "I'm pleased to hear that, Mrs. Fairchild. May . . . may I fetch you some punch?"

"That sounds lovely," Emma replied. She nodded toward the tree in the corner, where several lords and ladies were milling about, adding on ornaments they'd brought along for the festivities. "But first, I did bring an ornament for the tree."

He offered his arm. "I should be honored to escort you over to place it on a bough."

Across the room, Emma took out her ornament—a colorful paper cornucopia suspended from a red ribbon and filled with candied fruits—and placed it on the tree. Around her, other ornaments hung on the boughs: everything from small cast-iron toys to gingerbread men to beautifully decorated eggshells. Although the attendees were chatting gaily with one another, virtually everyone in the aristocratic group ignored Emma and Samuel.

Once all the ornaments had been placed on the tree, Dagmar Manning came forward, calling for everyone's attention. Then Dagmar had a uniformed footman light the many candles on the tree, while the guests cheered. Afterward Lord Moorhouse led the assembly in a rousing chorus of "We Wish you a Merry Christmas."

Despite the high spirits of the crowd, few made any friendly overtures toward Emma and Samuel. Indeed, when Lord and Lady Moorhouse led the grand procession to the dining room, followed by a giddy Dorcas on Matthew's arm, the footmen deliberately maneuvered the guests into line so that Emma and Samuel were the last to leave the drawing room, and also the last to be seated at the the palatial Jacobean table.

"Well, we're below the salt, all right," Emma muttered as Samuel helped her seat herself.

He flashed her a strained smile but didn't comment.

The feast that followed was incredible, so many courses that Emma lost count: venison soup, curried rabbit and salmon with shrimp sauce, sweetbreads, whole hams and a goose syllabub, jellies and pies. Each course was served with a different wine or liqueur, although Emma was careful to avoid them since she was still nursing. Emma tried to enjoy the dinner, and Samuel was a pleasant companion, but every time her gaze strayed toward Matthew, seated near the head of the table with a blushing Dorcas at his side, she could only see red.

She tried to tell herself she was angry because her escort for the evening had deserted her. But she knew the truth was that she'd fallen hard for Matthew Weymouth, and the sight of him with Dorcas made her insanely jealous. At one point he caught her perusal and flashed her an apologetic smile; she stared back coldly for a moment, then returned her attention to Samuel. Inside, she was growing more and more furious with Matthew, and not just due to jealousy. He had made his feelings clear: She was beneath him. So was dear Samuel, for that matter.

After dinner, the guests sang several Christmas carols as Dorcas accompanied the group on the piano in the drawing room. Emma was surprised when Matthew left his chair after the third song and approached her and Samuel.

"Is it time for us to leave?" he inquired tensely.

She regarded him proudly. "Yes. I need to get back to Noelle."

Matthew nodded, reached out and shook hands with Samuel. "Good to see you, Sam."

"Aye. And you, your lordship."

Matthew offered his arm to Emma. "Shall we bid our hostess goodnight?"

As he led her away, she offered him a honeyed smile, whispering between gritted teeth, "You mean you can tear yourself away from Dorcas?"

Matthew shot her a reproachful glance. "One reason I want to leave is her mother's shameless matchmaking tonight."

Emma laughed. "That's ironic. Now *you* know how it feels."

He cast her a surly look but didn't comment.

After hearing numerous protests from Dorcas and her mother because Matthew was leaving so early, they finally made their way out the door and proceeded home in silence.

Inside the front door of the townhouse, Emma could not wait to get away from Matthew, if only to go upstairs and sob in anger and frustration. It was hell trying to keep her emotions in check, especially when she caught him staring at her intently.

After he helped her out of her cloak and hung it on a hall tree, she muttered, "Thank you, Matthew, and goodnight," then rushed off for the stairs.

But he hurried after her, catching her arm. "Wait."

Fighting the treacherous excitement stirred by his fingers on her flesh, Emma turned to him defiantly. "Please let go of my arm. I need to go see about Noelle."

At once, he released her. Nonetheless, he pleaded, "Please, Mrs. O'Leery is with her. Wait just a moment, I've something to tell you."

Emma's chin came up. "Yes?"

Matthew's slight smile was miserably penitent. "Emma, what I did tonight . . . I thought I was acting in your best interests."

"Baloney," she said.

He blinked in stupefaction. "What?"

"You're a snob, Matthew."

"I'm what?"

Emma felt angry tears burning her eyes. "Tonight, you decided to show me I'm unworthy of your attentions. So you placed me with Samuel while you flirted with Dorcas."

"Emma, that's not true," he protested.

"It is true, damn it."

"Emma, I felt . . . I meant no disrespect toward you or Samuel, and I'm actually livid at Celeste for treating you both so shabbily."

She gave a bitter laugh. "Sure, I could tell you were livid tonight—the whole time you sat there gaily laughing with Dorcas."

He pulled his fingers through his hair. "I thought . . . I thought Samuel would be good for you."

Blinking away tears, she said, "Well, you're right about one thing. He's a better man than you are."

He regarded her helplessly.

"Why did you do it, Matthew?" she demanded.

"Why?" he asked ironically, eyes alive with emotion.

Emma was stunned by what happened next. Matthew hauled her into his arms, crushed her body close to his, and kissed her with desperate passion. This time all restraint dissolved; his hands roved over her body, and his tongue pushed hungrily deep inside her mouth.

And in that moment, desire staggered Emma as well. She could no longer fight her feelings. Anger became passion, pride became need. She moaned in abandon and clung to Matthew, giving herself over to the raw splendor of his kiss. She had waited for a lifetime to feel the wonder of his mouth on hers, the closeness of his hard, magnificent body against her own. It struck her powerfully that this was meant to be, that Matthew Weymouth was indeed the reason she and her baby had journeyed across time. She curled her arms around his neck and feverishly kissed him back.

At last he broke away, breathing harshly, his gaze burning into hers. "Why?" he repeated in a tortured tone. "Do you have any idea what it was like for me tonight, seeing you, so damned beautiful, sitting there with Samuel while I lost my mind with jealousy?"

"Jealousy?" she repeated with an incredulous laugh. "*You* were jealous? But you're the one who urged Celeste to invite him in the first place! Why, Matthew? Why are you pushing me toward him?"

His hands clutched her shoulders. "Because I'd be bad for you, Emma. Very bad. I'm a disaster for any woman, but I'd be especially wrong for you."

He turned and left her there, embroiled in longing and turmoil.

Chapter Nine

In the weeks that lead up to Christmas, Matthew again was a polite stranger toward Emma, forever kind and solicitous, but remote. Their passionate kiss after Lord and Lady Moorhouse's dinner party had definitely put distance between them. Emma didn't doubt that Matthew wanted her in a physical sense, especially when she spied him staring at her in an ardent, even covetous way. He had said he was bad for her. But Emma knew that he obviously didn't care enough for her and the baby to offer them a true commitment.

Indeed, he took to spending evenings away from the townhouse, leaving Emma and little

Noelle with the O'Leerys. When Emma asked Hettie where Matthew was, she shrugged and said he was likely out gambling.

Likely in the arms of some other woman, Emma mused, stunned at the hot torrents of jealousy this possibility brought rushing to her. She wondered how it was that this man had managed to steal her heart so quickly, especially when he so often disregarded her feelings.

Nonetheless, Matthew appeared both proud and full of emotion on the Sunday afternoon of Noelle's christening in a brief, private ritual at St. Margaret's. When the vicar sprinkled holy water on the child's head, Matthew looked on with concern. When she gave a startled cry, he held and soothed her afterward. He solemnly repeated his vows as the child's godfather, and Emma's heart overflowed with love as she looked on.

But Matthew had also invited the O'Leerys and Samuel along for the ceremony, and later as the group left the church together, emerging in the brisk winter air to a stunning view of Parliament and the soaring gothic nave of the Abbey, Matthew maneuvered Emma close to his clerk, and also saw to it that the two sat together when the group stopped off for tea at Simpsons in the Strand.

Samuel became something of a fixture around Matthew's townhouse, frequently stopping in to drop off papers or discuss business with Matthew, and Matthew always saw to it that on those occasions, Emma and Samuel spent time visiting alone. Although it irritated Emma that Matthew was trying to manipulate her this way, she wouldn't be so rude as to snub Samuel, who was really a very nice young man. She felt she had no choice but to chat with him for a few minutes each time he stopped by.

Three days before Christmas, the inevitable occurred. That afternoon, Emma was sitting with Samuel on the settee in the drawing room, when he set down his tea, cleared his throat, and spoke awkwardly. "Emma, there's a subject I've been meaning to broach with you."

Wary of what she knew was coming, Emma's spine stiffened. "Yes?"

He smiled shyly. "I've enjoyed your company tremendously over these past few weeks, and you know I adore Noelle."

"We're both fond of you," Emma replied.

"I'm not a wealthy man, Emma," he continued, eyeing her wistfully. "But I'm hardworking and loyal. I guess what I'm trying to say is, I'd be greatly honored if you would consent to become my wife. And I promise you I'd do everything in my power to be a good father for Noelle."

The silence that followed was acutely strained and painful. Samuel's expectant look. Emma's sad smile. Skirts rustling, she rose and warmed her hands before the crackling fire, taking a long moment to collect her thoughts.

At last she turned, wincing at the look of disappointment in Samuel's eyes. "Samuel, I'm deeply honored. But I can't marry you."

He blanched, standing beside her. "Why not?"

"I don't love you," she confessed miserably.

"But . . . didn't you say you're fond of me? Isn't there hope you would grow to love me . . . if not now, perhaps in time?"

Emma touched his arm. "You're a dear, sweet man, but—"

"Is it because I'm not wealthy, like Lord Worthing?" he cut in with a hurt look.

"No, no of course not," she reassured him. "It's because neither of us feels the passionate affection needed for a lasting marriage."

He swallowed hard. "Aren't there matters more important—like finding a father for your child?"

"My child will be fine. And if you're honest, Samuel, you'll admit you're really doing this at Matthew's urging."

He drew himself up with dignity. "That is not true."

"Isn't it?" she pursued gently. "What if you didn't propose? Wouldn't you expect Matthew to become disappointed with you, perhaps even fire you?"

Samuel clutched her hands in his and spoke earnestly. "Emma, you must understand something. The first time I came here, it was at Lord Worthing's invitation, and I attended the Manning dinner party at his request, as well. But after that, I came here because I wanted to. Lord Worthing has not pressed matters with me."

Emma sighed, lowering her gaze. "I'm so sorry, Samuel. I'm very touched that you asked, but I won't be changing my mind."

He leaned over and briefly kissed her cheek. "I'm afraid you don't feel nearly the regret that I do, dear Emma."

Matthew sat alone at his club on St. James. While all around him, his friends and colleagues were gaily visiting, drinking and smoking, playing faro, hazard or whist or betting on the wheel, he had consigned himself to a corner table, where he nursed his whiskey and thought about Emma.

Today Samuel Parsmith had asked for permission to propose to his "cousin," and although it had killed him, Matthew had politely agreed. At this very moment, Samuel was no doubt sitting in his drawing room pressing his suit with lovely Emma.

The very prospect made black torrents of jealousy roil through Matthew's mind. He wanted nothing more than to race home and claim Emma for himself. The truth was, he didn't trust himself around her anymore, not since their kiss after the Manning dinner party. One taste of her set him on fire, and he had been obsessed with her ever since. With each kiss they shared, his passion for her grew—he couldn't even look at her now without wanting to pull her close again and devour her alive.

It no longer mattered who she was, where she had come from, or how she and Noelle had arrived at his home. He just needed her.

Emma's baby also was slowly stealing her way into Matthew's heart. The christening, and his commitment as the child's godfather, had forged a deep bond between him and Noelle. Every time he looked at the adorable mite, he wanted to hug her, coo to her, make a perfect idiot out of himself.

He wanted them both. But he still felt he'd make a terrible husband and father. He just wasn't ready for that sort of commitment.

He was in hell. Ever since lovely Emma Fairchild and her babe had appeared in his life, he hadn't been able to even look at another woman, much less take his ease with one.

The knowledge that he craved only Emma, only she who could quench the hunger in his ravenous heart, frightened the hell out of him.

Although Noelle slept peacefully, Emma tossed and turned throughout much of the night. She was livid at Matthew, eager to give him a piece of her mind, but he still hadn't come home. How dare he manipulate her and Samuel as he had. She had a feeling the poor man had been genuinely hurt by her refusal to marry him, and this was, of course, entirely Matthew's fault.

By the time the pale, rosy rays of dawn were visible through the curtains, Emma had made her decision. She rose, quickly saw to her toilette and dressed, then began to pack hers and the baby's things in a carpetbag.

When Mrs. O'Leery brought in breakfast, she gasped at the sight of Emma's bed, the half-filled carpetbag, and neat stacks of clothing next to it. Setting down the tray, she asked, "What are you doing, child?"

"I'm packing."

The housekeeper's mouth fell open. "What?"

"Did Matthew ever come home?"

"Aye, in the wee hours, though his lordship is still fast asleep."

Emma harrumphed. "Good. Then we'll be gone by the time he wakes up."

Looking extremely anxious, Hettie stepped closer. "Have you taken leave of your senses, child? Where will you go, alone, penniless, with a wee one, in the dead of winter?"

Emma sniffed, speaking hoarsely. "I don't know. I just can't stay here anymore. He doesn't want us here. You've seen how he's been pushing me toward Samuel."

"Aye," the housekeeper agreed. "So is that the reason you want to go?"

Emma wiped away a tear with her sleeve. "Samuel proposed yesterday, and I said no. I don't love him, but I think he may have fallen in love with me. If his heart is broken, it's Matthew's fault. He tried to engineer all of this."

Hettie nodded, eyes gleaming with righteous indignation. "Aye, the man is a fool. You love him, don't you, lass?"

The color shooting up Emma's face gave away her true feelings. With a sigh, she admitted, "Yes, I suppose I do. But I'm certain he'll never feel the same way about me. Otherwise, he would have stopped this silly matchmaking."

"Oh, child." Clucking softly, Hettie patted her back. "Listen, now, you cannot go. This is madness. You look as though you haven't slept at all."

Emma's voice cracked. "I haven't. But please don't try to stop me."

Hettie hesitated for a long moment. "Very well. If you're determined to leave, I shall help you, lass."

"How?"

Hettie thought fiercely, then snapped her fingers. "I know. You and the bairn can go to my daughter's home in Chelsea for now. She and her husband are expecting a wee one, and already have the nursery all fixed up."

"But I can't intrude on them."

"Nonsense," Hettie replied stoutly. " 'Twas Lord Worthing who bought them their house as a wedding present, so they'd be more than happy to help."

Taken aback, Emma murmured, "My, he can be very generous." *But not with his heart*, she added to herself.

"Will you stay with my Moira for now, till we can figure something out for you?"

Emma flashed Hettie a sad though grateful smile. "Yes, I will. Thanks, Mrs. O'Leery."

When Noelle awakened, Emma fed her and dressed her warmly, then the coachman drove her, Hettie and the child over to the Flanders' townhouse in Chelsea. As the carriage halted before the modest Tudor-style home, Emma spotted a soft glow in the front windows, and snowflakes flitting about.

Hettie patted Emma's gloved hand. "Stay right here, lass. I'll go get help to see the two of you in."

In a gush of cold wind, Hettie lumbered out of the conveyance, returning momentarily with an attractive young couple bundled up against the weather. The woman was obviously about seven months pregnant.

Cheeks bright from the winter air, the woman offered her hand to Emma and spoke in a Scottish brogue similar to her mother's. "Mrs. Fairchild, welcome to our home. I'm Moira Flanders and this is my husband, Milton. We're honored to have you and the wee one here with us."

"Thank you," Emma said, shaking the woman's hand. "We're sorry to intrude."

The woman's gaze was fixed tenderly on Noelle, sound asleep in her mother's arms. "Ah, 'tis no intrusion at all, and your little one's an angel. May I carry her in for you?"

"Yes, thank you, that would be nice."

The group went inside, Moira carrying the baby and Milton Emma's bag. From the tiny foyer they proceed directly into a modestly furnished drawing room with a large stone hearth along one wall and a simple wooden staircase beyond that.

Moira sat down in a Windsor rocker by the fire with Noelle. "Mrs. Fairchild, me mum tells me you are exhausted. I insist you go upstairs to rest, while I rock the wee one."

"You're too kind," Emma said, grateful for an opportunity to rest after a long night. "But you'll call me if she needs me?"

Moira smiled. "Of course."

Hettie motioned toward the stairs. "Come along, now, lass. Milton, lead the way."

Milton led them upstairs into a small but pleasant nursery equipped with both a Jenny Lind crib and a daybed with colorful pillows and quilts.

Emma smiled at Milton. "Why, it's charming."

He grinned awkwardly, setting down her carpetbag. "Thank you, madam. We are pleased to have you and your baby stay with us."

After he shuffled out, Hettie pointed to the daybed. "Now it's down for a nap, missy, and I'll not hear one word of protest. Your wee one will be fine downstairs with my Moira—she welcomes the practice."

Emma flashed her a grateful smile. "Thanks, Mrs. O'Leery."

Emma seated herself on the daybed, removed her cloak and shoes, and lay down. Hettie tucked a quilt around her and headed for the door.

"Sleep, child. We'll figure out the rest later."

Half-asleep already, Emma mumbled a reply. Then she remembered Matthew, and concern washed over her. "Wait!"

"Yes, lass?" Hettie asked, turning.

Emma sat up. "Promise me you won't tell Matthew where we are." Voice breaking over the words, she finished bitterly, "That is, if he even cares."

"Aye, lass. As you wish."

But a secret smile pulled at Hettie O'Leery's mouth as she slipped from the room.

Chapter Ten

In a panic, Matthew Weymouth paced inside the front hallway of his home. When he'd stopped by Emma's room moments earlier, he'd found she and Noelle were gone, along with most of their belongings. Utter dread had seized him, especially at the possibility that she may have eloped with his clerk. Oh, what had he driven her to with his foolish matchmaking?

All at once, the front door swung open with a chill blast of air, and Mrs. O'Leery lumbered inside. Matthew quickly stepped toward her. "Mrs. O'Leery! Where are Emma and the child?"

With a shrug, she removed her gloves, cap, and cape. "They've gone, my lord."

He waved a hand. "I know they're gone. Any simpleton could have figured that out. But *where* have they gone?"

She hung the items on the hall tree, keeping her expression proud. "I don't think you have a right to know that." She started past him, heading for the kitchen.

He caught her arm. "Wait. Did she run off with Samuel?"

"Run off with your clerk?" Hettie asked sardonically.

"Aye. Tell me!"

She shot him a fulminating look and shook off his touch. "I repeat, my lord, that you have no right to know, not after you shamelessly ignored the poor woman and her child—and tried to force her into wedding your clerk."

Despite the housekeeper's stern words, relief swept over Matthew. "Then she did not run off with him?"

"No," Hettie answered coldly.

"Thank heaven. I mean, I knew he planned to propose yesterday. Did it not go well?"

Hettie laughed bitterly. "Now there's an understatement, my lord. She refused him flat."

Matthew broke into a grin. "And did she say why?"

"She doesn't love him."

"Ah."

"As for who she loves . . ." Hettie's gaze swept

her employer contemptuously. "I'd say the unfortunate young woman loves a fool."

For a moment, Matthew was filled with the crazed hope that he might indeed be the "fool" Emma loved. Then, noting his housekeeper's still smoldering expression, he gestured in supplication. "Mrs. O'Leery, I implore you. I only wanted what I thought was best for her."

"Balderdash. You wanted what was best for *yourself.*"

Matthew groaned. "Perhaps you're right. I'll admit I've been a fool—self-absorbed and self-centered, not knowing what was best for me, and allowing two utterly precious human beings to slip through my fingers. But I've come to my senses now, if only you—and Emma—will give me another chance."

Hettie glowered.

"Please, woman, I beseech you. I . . . I think I love her. Where is she?"

Unmoved, Hettie continued to frown and tap her toe, and Matthew fervently hoped she would soon relent. . . .

Emma lay dreaming of Matthew. He was bending over her, tenderly kissing her, then he was snatched away and she was alone, anguished, heartbroken. . . .

With a gasp, she sat up in bed to see him sitting across from her in a ladder-back chair, regarding her with so much longing, so much tenderness, that the sight of him took her breath away. Then she remembered how much he had hurt her, and pain tightened in her throat.

"Matthew! What are you doing here?"

He spoke with a telltale huskiness. "I've come to take you home, my love."

Emma started to protest, then realized he called her "my love." Joy, warring with pride, almost choked off her next words. "How did you know where to find us?"

He rose and crossed over to the daybed, sitting down beside her. She would have scooted away, but he caught her hand. "No, Emma," he said firmly. "We've avoided this long enough."

Still struggling to hold her ground, even as the heat and strength of his hand on hers warmed her to the core, she proudly met his ardent gaze.

He smiled wistfully. "As to how I found you, I prevailed upon Hettie O'Leery to tell me."

"But she promised she wouldn't!" Emma blurted out.

Matthew reached out and smoothed down Emma's mussed hair. "Oh, my love, don't you know no promise could keep me away from you?"

Cheeks burning, Emma didn't know what to say. Matthew was now gazing at her so intently she feared he might devour her alive. She wanted to throw her arms around him and kiss him insensible, but she still hurt too much.

"Nonetheless, it wasn't easy getting her to tell me," he went on. "Nor was it easy convincing Milton and Moira to let me come up here. That leaves just you, my love." He stroked her cheek. "After all I've endured to find you, I'm truly hoping you'll be more biddable."

Slowly dying inside, Emma pulled away from his touch. "Matthew, please go. I can't go back with you."

"But why not? Don't you know I care for you?"

Emma almost started crying. "Yes, you *care* for me, but not in the way that really counts."

"You're wrong, Emma."

She blinked away hot tears. "I'm not wrong. I made a fool of myself once with a man who was afraid of commitment. I'll never do that again. I deserve more than that for a husband—and Noelle deserves more for a father."

"I agree," he replied passionately, clutching her hands. "That's why I want you to marry me, darling."

"What?" Despite a flood of joy at his words, Emma could not believe what she was hearing. "You ignore me for weeks on end, and now you want to marry me?"

Anguish and regret shone in his eyes. "Emma, you must understand that I've been an idiot. Ever since we kissed that first night, I've been fighting what I feel for you. Yes, I feared I couldn't commit to one woman for a lifetime. You were entirely right about that. When I stayed away, I told myself I was doing what was best for you and the baby. But it was all to no avail, for I was only punishing myself. I was miserable every minute without you. Everywhere I went, I found myself looking for you or Noelle. What I felt for you was simply too strong to be denied."

Emma stared, desperately wanting to believe him, but still not sure she could fully trust him again.

"I was wrong to push you toward Samuel, too. Today, when I found you were gone, my first thought was that you might have run off to marry him. It all but drove me mad." He squeezed her hands. "Now, I can only pray that you'll forgive me, that I haven't destroyed our chances, that you might feel even a little of what I feel."

Emma was almost to the breaking point, for the look in his eyes was tearing her apart. "What do you feel, Matthew?"

"I love you with all my heart."

"Oh, Matthew." Trembling, Emma fell into his arms. "I love you, too. But I didn't think you could ever—"

"Hush, now, darling," he whispered back, his mouth crushing hungrily over hers.

Passion inflamed them both. Matthew kissed Emma with a desire and a tenderness that left her melting inside. She kissed him back, mating her tongue with his, thrilling to the rumble of his groan. When he gently stroked her breasts, she thought she might die of the pleasure. She drew him back onto the bed with her, held him close and kissed him without restraint, feeling the hardness of his desire rising between them.

"I'm so sorry I hurt you," he murmured, kissing away her tears. "So very sorry."

"You're with me now—and I want you so, I could die," she whispered back.

He pulled back, gazing into her eyes, his own burning with need. "Emma, darling, we mustn't."

She grinned. "The baby is still downstairs with Moira."

An agonized moan escaped him. "I know, darling, but it wouldn't be right." He trailed his lips over her mouth, her warm cheek, and his voice was thick with longing and frustration. "Soon, love, I promise. When you're my bride."

She hugged him tightly. "Yes, soon."

He took her hand and solemnly kissed it. "Will you do me the honor of becoming my bride, Emma? If so, I swear I shall pledge my heart, my loyalty, my love, to you forever. And I shall endeavor to be the best possible father for Noelle."

"Oh, yes, Matthew, yes."

He clutched her close. "Then come home, my love, and let us celebrate Christmas together."

* * *

They rushed home with the baby and announced their good news to the O'Leerys, sharing a cordial with the couple in the drawing room. In a rare, effusive moment, James grinned and pounded Matthew across the back. Hettie couldn't stop wiping away tears or hugging Emma and Noelle.

The balance of the day was spent in last-minute preparations for Christmas. Mrs. O'Leery watched the baby while Emma went shopping for a present for Matthew.

On Christmas Eve, they burned the Yule log and ate Mrs. O'Leery's fabulous Christmas dinner, complete with baked goose and plum pudding. Then on Christmas morning as they knelt beside the tree with the baby asleep in a cradle nearby, Matthew solemnly handed Emma a small, gift-wrapped box. She opened it to find a gorgeous sapphire and carved-silver ring inside.

"Oh, Matthew!" she cried, "you shouldn't have. It's beautiful."

He solemnly took out the ring and placed it on the third finger of her right hand. "To celebrate our betrothal, my love—albeit a short one."

Emma threw her arms around Matthew and kissed him for so long, she almost forgot to give him her present, a gold and ivory pen and letter-opener set. When he finally did open his gift, the sight of it brought a delighted smile to his eyes.

The days following Christmas were busy, filled

with preparations for the wedding. Since Emma was ostensibly still a widow, she had the dressmaker make her a tasteful ivory silk gown. At home, Matthew insisted Hettie and Emma should transform his sitting room into a nursery for Noelle, to be occupied as soon as Matthew and Emma were married.

Matthew secured a special license from the archbishop and they married on the morning of New Year's Eve. Two dozen or so of Matthew's best friends gathered in the sun-splashed sanctuary. The O'Leerys sat on the front row, Hettie holding Noelle and wiping away tears.

As she pronounced her vows, Emma felt love welling inside her, especially as she glimpsed the answering love in Matthew's eyes. Suddenly she felt an overwhelming sense of peace, of belonging. Ralph the Stork had made a wonderful mistake dropping Noelle at the doorstep of a rogue—her rogue. She and Noelle definitely belonged here with Matthew. She would miss her family and the world she'd left behind, but she and her baby were meant to share their lives with Matthew, in this time. One day she would explain all of this to him—and she thought he would understand.

When Matthew kissed her, she *knew* he would understand.

After the service, the entire group shared a wedding breakfast at the elegant Café Royal on

Regent Street. The vicar led a toast to the bride and groom; Mathew again kissed Emma while the guests cheered.

That night after putting Noelle down in the new nursery adjoining Matthew's bedroom, Emma joined her bridegroom. Her pulse quickened at the sight of him, standing near the bed in his gold brocade dressing gown. He eyed her eagerly in her old-fashioned white, lace-trimmed linen gown.

"Is the babe asleep?"

"Yes," Emma smiled at her husband.

"Then come have some champagne with me by the fire, Lady Worthing."

Emma was thrilled to hear her new married name. "My, how can I resist when you call me that? But just a little, I'm still nursing."

They settled close together on the loveseat facing the fire, sipping champagne and kissing. Matthew raised his glass. "To us, my love. To our happy future together."

"To us." Emma gazed raptly at him. "Oh, Matthew, this is so wonderful. Being so warm—and so close to you."

"I agree." He curled an arm around her waist and nuzzled her cheek with his lips. "Ah, you smell so delicious and you're heavenly soft. But are you disappointed that I didn't whisk you off to some exotic locale?"

"Never!" she denied. "There's no better place

on earth to be than here with you and Noelle."

He pressed his mouth to her hair. "In the late spring, we'll plan a proper honeymoon—perhaps to Paris or Venice."

"We'll take Noelle along?"

"Of course. And likely Hettie and James, as well."

Emma smiled dreamily, then frowned and bit her lip. "Matthew, there's something I've been meaning to tell you."

"Yes?"

"About my past and where I *really* come from," she said soberly.

"You're from America."

She laughed ruefully. "I'm from a place that seems so much farther away than America, my love. And there's so much to explain." Laughing, she added, "Why, there was even a stork."

"A stork, eh?" With a smile of amused indulgence, Matthew took his bride's half-empty champagne glass and set it with his on the floor. "No more champagne for you tonight."

"Matthew! Why, I only had two sips—and I do have *much* to tell you."

He chuckled. "My love, we shall have all the time in the world to discuss it. What matters to me tonight, Lady Worthing, is not your past but our future together." He stood and offered his hand. "Come here, my love."

Emma eagerly let Matthew pull her up into his

arms. She kissed him with all the love brimming in her heart.

Though his arms trembled with passion about her, he pulled back to regard her soberly. "Is it too soon, my love? I mean, after having the child, and all?"

She shook her head. "It's been six weeks. I'm sure I'll be fine."

His smile lit her soul and he led her to the bed. He swept her up into his arms and laid her down on the striking, gold silk jacquard counterpane. "Do you have any idea how beautiful you are, or how long I've wanted you?"

Emma eyed him covetously, brushing her fingers against the crisp dark curls peeking out from the V of his dressing gown. "I want you, too, darling. And love you even more."

"I love you so much my heart is bursting." Glancing downward, he ruefully added, "And perhaps something else."

Chuckling, Emma glanced in the same direction and saw what Matthew meant. Unabashed, she reached out and undid his sash, smiling at his raised eyebrow. "Please, I want to see you."

"My, I've unleased a temptress," he murmured, but at once he complied, standing proudly naked before her.

Emma swept her gaze over her husband's glorious body and the hard rise of his desire. "You're beautiful, too, my lord."

Passion flared in his eyes, then he lay on the bed beside her, kissed her deeply, roving his hands over her body. Within seconds he raised her gown, and she eagerly helped him. Her nakedness was bared to his scrutiny, and he gazed down upon her with incredible tenderness. His finger reached out to touch a swollen nipple, and she gasped in ecstasy.

"Look at me, Emma."

She met his gaze.

Matthew spoke with such devotion, he imprinted the words on his bride's heart. "My darling, I've made love to many women over my lifetime. But never have I wanted to be one with a woman—truly *one*—as I do with you tonight."

"Oh, Matthew." Emma held him close, reveling in the feel of his hard, warm, naked body on hers. She spoke through tears, "Make us one. Please, darling, make us one."

She could no longer speak, for Matthew's ravenous mouth took hers, possessing her utterly. His skilled lips slid down her throat to her breasts. When he sucked her nipple into his warm mouth, Emma cried out in rapture and clutched his shoulders, urging him on with words of love. His hand reached down, his fingers boldly parting and stroking her. Emma writhed at the sweet, shattering sensation.

"Yes," she whispered. "Oh, I love that."

Her words were exquisite torture to Matthew,

especially as his bride ran her soft hands over his body, caressing, stroking, even touching his aching member, driving him insane. He tried to hold back, tried to stoke his bride's passions slowly, enduring the frustration for as long as he could. But her moans aroused him until he could bear no more. Feeling he might indeed burst with his need of her, he slid up her body and smiled down into her eyes as he positioned himself between her spread thighs. He claimed her, felt her exquisite warm wetness clutching him, then paused, though it was agony, when she winced slightly.

"Too soon, my love?" he repeated anxiously.

She shook her head. "My doctor—was a perfectionist. Perhaps he overdid the stitches."

Matthew could only raise an eyebrow at that. He was amused, perplexed, but also dying, his bride's frank words and the exquisite feel of her flesh only further inflaming his desires. "I . . . I'm grateful for the man," he managed at last.

Then he was lost in her, forging deep until he came to rest inside her, and he knew her hoarse cry was of joy, not pain. Her hot flesh held his so tightly that he never wanted to leave her, yet the urge to possess her, to bond the two of them utterly, overcame him. She shuddered so sweetly against him he thought he might expire then and there, for heaven could be no finer.

"Is it all right for you, darling?" he whispered.

"Yes, oh yes," she murmured, raising her hips to meet him.

Matthew's control broke at her trusting surrender. He clutched Emma's slender body close and moved without restraint, quickening his pace when she moved with him. His mouth ravished hers as he devoured his bride with his love.

Beneath her husband, Emma knew the overpowering ecstasy of being joined, body and soul, with the man she loved. She could barely breathe, her heart was pounding with such fierce joy. Pleasure shook her in staggering waves as she clung to Matthew, secure in his love. His forever.

They awakened at midnight to the sounds of firecrackers. Simultaneously, Noelle began to whimper in the next room.

Even as Emma stirred, Matthew touched his bride's arm. "No, let me get her, love."

Emma flashed him a grateful smile.

Putting on his dressing gown, Matthew strode into the nursery. Noelle was awake in her bassinet, and spotting Matthew, she grunted.

Grinning, he lifted the child into his arms, cherishing the feel of her tiny warm body against his shoulder. "It's all right, angel, just a little New Year's celebration."

The baby cooed, and Matthew smiled.

"Ah, that's better," he murmured, patting her

back. "Tell me, will you call me 'Papa' one day, little one? I shall try my best to be worthy of such an exalted title. You must know I love you every bit as much as I love your mother."

The baby gurgled and nestled her soft cheek against Matthew's throat, as if she understood. Exultant tears burned his eyes and he felt supremely grateful for the wondrous gift of mother and child that he'd been granted.

When he returned to the bedroom with Noelle, he spotted Emma standing at the window in her nightgown, her exquisite form outlined in moonlight, with fireworks bursting beyond her. Matthew's heart ached with love for her and the babe.

Emma turned to smile at him. "Is she all right?"

"Yes, love. Likely just a bit startled by the fireworks." Moving over to join her, he gestured outside, where Roman candles were exploding in showers of radiance across the night skies. "Look, my love. A new year. A new decade." He glanced down at the babe. "A new beginning for us, with our new child."

"Yes, *our* child," Emma agreed hoarsely. She gazed down at Noelle, then cried out in joy. "Look, Matthew! She's smiling at us. She's happy we're a family."

Matthew glanced down, heart warmed as he observed the babe's toothless grin. "Aye, love, she is." He wrapped his free arm about Emma's waist and kissed her cheek. "How blessed we are, Emma. How blessed *I* am."

"I know, darling." With a lump in her throat, Emma thought of the miracle she, Matthew, and Noelle had been granted, how the fates—and a confused stork—had reached across time to pull together a loving family for a precious, needy child.

The young family stood cuddled together at the window, staring at the fireworks, bathed in the promise of the new year, on the brink of their glorious future together.

Dear Reader:

I wish to take this opportunity to wish you a happy New Year, a happy Millennium, and to thank you for your continuing support of my career.

I do hope you enjoyed "The Confused Stork," and would love to hear what you think of it. And please watch for my year 2000 releases. In April as part of the new The Time of Your Life series, Love Spell will publish my *Lovers and Other Lunatics*, a fun, sexy contemporary romp set in the Houston/Galveston region. Also watch for *Embers of Time*, a haunting, emotional time-travel romance set in Charleston, South

Carolina, tentatively scheduled for release by Love Spell in the fall of 2000.

Still available from Love Spell is my June 1999 release, *Bushwhacked Bride*, a hilarious western time-travel romance in the Wink & Kiss special series. If you haven't read *Bushwhacked Bride*, I do hope you'll order it from Love Spell or your favorite bookseller.

I did want to let you know that my author bio was mistakenly omitted from *Bushwhacked Bride*, and to assure you that I welcome your feedback on all of my projects. Indeed, I still have plenty of my most recent free bookmarks and newsletters available, so please do get in touch if you'd like to receive these.

You can reach me via e-mail at eugenia@eugeniariley.com, visit my website at http://www.eugeniariley.com, or you can write to me at the address listed below (long SASE appreciated). Thanks and best wishes!

Eugenia Riley
P.O. Box 840526
Houston, TX 77284-0526

Blame It on the Baby

Jennifer Archer

This story is dedicated to Mom and Dad with love and appreciation for filling our home with babies and giving me the joy and aggravation of family.

Also, thanks to Kimberly Willis Holt, Connee McAnear, Jodi Koumalats and Ronda Thompson for sharing their editing skills and their suggestions.

Chapter One

Christmas-weary diners crowded the tables at Confucius Says. Tory Beecham-Todd leaned back in her chair and linked her hands across her rounded belly. The baby was restless tonight—kicking, twisting and turning like an acrobat. She'd swear the kid had just done a back flip. At least *someone* at the table had energy to spare.

Across from her, Tory's husband, Dillon, worked his way to the last grain of rice on his plate. She wondered how he could always eat so much, yet stay so thin? Too thin, she realized with a jolt, wondering when he'd dropped so much weight. He looked as if he'd lost every pound she'd gained in the past eight months. And she'd gained plenty, despite her faithful exercise routine.

With tired eyes, Tory studied Dillon more closely. Not only was he thinner than normal, his olive skin seemed to have paled a shade. And his typically sleepy-looking eyes looked sleepier than usual. Two and a half years ago, when their daughter Kayla was born, he'd cut off his shoulder-length black hair. Short as it was, though, tonight even his cropped locks looked droopy—as droopy as Tory felt.

When her vision blurred, Tory gave in to fatigue, closed her eyes and sighed. The only thing keeping her going was the news that had arrived in the mail today—a letter that was, right this minute, tucked safely away in the pocket of her coat, which lay folded on the chair beside her. As soon as Dillon finished eating, she'd share the surprise, but for now, silly as it might be, she liked savoring the secret, being stingy with it, keeping it all to herself.

"Babe?"

"Hmmm?" Tory answered.

"You're not gonna fall asleep on me, are you?" he asked with the lazy drawl she'd always loved.

"No, I'm going to fall asleep on this chair."

"I'm not sure I can carry you outta here."

She opened one eye. "Are you saying I'm too fat?"

"No." The corner of Dillon's mouth lifted. "I'm saying I'm too weak."

Tory opened her other eye. "It was nice of Lisa and Michael to give us a night out." As a Christmas gift, Dillon's boss, Lisa O'Conner, and her husband, Michael, who was Tory's boss, had given them a gift certificate for dinner at Confucius Says, tickets to a movie, and their services as sitters for Kayla tonight. "Too bad I'm too tired to enjoy it," Tory added, yawning.

"Yeah, me too." Dillon yawned back. "Wanna skip the movie?"

She nodded. "Look at us." Tory fought her stomach to sit up straight, then gave up the futile battle and slumped back in her chair. "You'd think we were an old married couple."

"We are an old married couple."

"No, we're not. We just feel old. And if we're this boring after only three years of marriage, no one will be able to stand us after ten. How long has it been since we've had a night out together, just the two of us?"

Dillon shrugged. "How old's Kayla? Two and a half?"

"See? After two and a half years we finally get some time alone and all we really want to do is go home and go to bed."

Dillon wiggled his brows. "Sounds great to me," he said, his voice low and suggestive.

Tory made a face. "I meant to sleep. If you haven't noticed, I'm pregnant."

With his dark eyes holding steady on her face, Dillon shoved his plate aside. "So?"

"So, I'm a *lot* pregnant."

"So?"

"So, I'm exhausted. You are, too. Admit it."

He reached across the table for her hand. "We deserve to be exhausted. Think of all we've been through since we got married. Kayla's birth, both of us working and going to school at the same time, trying to make ends meet. Now, another baby on the way." He squeezed her fingers. "At least the load got a little lighter after I graduated last semester."

For you, maybe, Tory thought, but refrained from voicing the words. After finishing college, Dillon merely increased his hours at Wishful Thinking, the restaurant he managed, while she'd continued the long, slow trek toward earning her own degree. Tory worked three mornings a week at a law firm and attended classes the other two mornings. Occasionally, she'd taken a night class and had even picked up three credits in an Internet online program approved by the university.

"Now that you've graduated, too," Dillon continued, "things are bound to get easier for us. Less stressful."

The people at the next table laughed at some

comment Tory hadn't heard. She felt like laughing too as she glanced down at her stomach, then scowled across at Dillon. "Our little unexpected addition to the family is due to arrive in a month. Things aren't going to get any easier. Not for a long, long time."

Grinning, he lowered his gaze to her belly, apparently unfazed by the pessimistic tone of her voice. "One of these days we're gonna figure out how that keeps happening."

"Oh, I *know* how it happened. *You* were in too big a rush to postpone things and go make a purchase at the drug store."

Dillon's expression shifted from amusement to defensiveness in the space of a second. He released her hand, lifted his own to idly scratch one sideburn, a habit he'd acquired since cutting his hair. "When a guy finally gets a green light after six weeks of waiting, he doesn't want to waste time taking a detour."

"I'd been studying for finals," Tory snapped.

"So had I."

"Kayla had a stomach virus. I was up to my knees in dirty diapers. But you wouldn't remember, because you were never home."

Dillon's eyes went cold. The veins in his neck bulged. "Well, pardon Kayla for putting you out. I was working a full-time job and carrying a full load in school. You're the one who only works part-time. I can't be with Kayla as much as you can. I wish I could."

Tory bristled. He'd flipped the wrong switch. The guilt switch. She had always known having a baby would change her life, but until Kayla's birth, she'd never imagined the joy a child would bring . . . or the amount of stamina-draining work. "I have news for you, Dillon Todd. Kayla *is* a full-time job."

"If you want to accuse me of causing all your problems, that's fine. But no way am I gonna sit here and listen to you blame Kayla. Our daughter's not a job." His eyes narrowed. "I can't believe you'd say that, Tory. I guess next you'll be blaming the baby, too."

Tory's throat constricted. Dillon might as well have slapped her. The restaurant's clamor suddenly seemed louder than before. "I'm a good mother," she said in a strained voice. "Don't you dare say I'm not. I love Kayla, and I love this baby, too. They're my first priorities. I'm just. . . ." She crossed her arms and looked away from him.

Across the restaurant, back toward the kitchen, an old Chinese man stood behind the counter, his shrewd eyes steady upon her. A chill prickled Tory's skin as she met his piercing gaze. And all at once, she felt herself being drawn into a vacuum where only she and the shriveled old man existed . . . away from the noise of the restaurant . . . away from her worries . . . away from Dillon. She shivered; it was as if the tiny man was probing her mind.

Dillon huffed a breath and broke the spell. "I'm sorry, Babe."

With a shudder, Tory pulled her attention away from the elderly gentleman.

"I shouldn't have said what I did," Dillon continued. "I know Kayla and this baby weren't in our plans; they came along before we were ready. But everything will work out. I promise you." He cocked his head, smiled at her. The tiny silver loop in his left ear caught a ray of light and sparkled like a holiday decoration. "Know how I'm so sure?"

Tory sniffed back tears. "How?"

"Because I have a surprise for you. This night out isn't the only Christmas present Lisa gave us."

Wiping her eyes with a napkin, Tory sat a little straighter. "You got a bonus?" After the holidays, they could use the extra cash.

He shook his head, his black eyes shining with excitement. "It's better than a bonus. Lisa's expanding. She's ready to open another restaurant, and when it gets going, she's considering a third one."

Dread spread through Tory like spilled milk across a counter. "Here in Oklahoma City?"

"No, the first one will be in Norman. Close to

the university. She wants me to manage it, but that's not all."

Dillon leaned forward, his gaze scanning her face, his expression so filled with anxious hope that she instantly felt pressured to respond positively to whatever he was preparing to tell her.

"Lisa made me an offer to buy in," he said quickly. "To be her partner."

Tory wanted to be fair about this, told herself she should be fair. Nevertheless, she felt the walls going up around her mind, could hear the door slamming shut on Lisa's offer and Dillon's obvious desire to accept it. "Buy in with what?"

Dillon swallowed, licked his lips. His gaze shifted down, then up again, and Tory glimpsed a flash of fear behind the excitement in his eyes. Fear, she guessed, of what her reaction to his next words might be. "It won't cost much," he said. "I won't be a full partner. If Dad co-signs I can get a loan. I've checked with the bank. I've talked to Dad, too."

"You've already looked into everything? Without even discussing it with me first?"

"I didn't want you to have to worry about anything. It's all set." The legs on his chair squeaked as Dillon scooted closer to the table. "You don't have to do a thing."

"We'll have another payment to make every month, right?"

"We've put away some savings. We can fall

back on that at first if we have to. This is our future, Babe. It's a great opportunity for us . . . for our kids." He lifted a hand, stroked his sideburn with fidgeting fingers. "I'll get a share of the restaurant's profit. And that's *in addition* to my salary. Think of it, Tory. After the restaurant takes off and the money's coming in, we could afford to finally get out of the apartment. Buy a little house with a back yard for Kayla and the baby to play in."

"That's *if* the restaurant takes off. It could just as easily bomb. Then what? I mean, how will we pay off the loan then?" She shook her head. "This is the wrong time, Dillon. You're moving too fast. We're not ready. We don't have enough money to pay another loan, and there's too much else going on in our lives. What about your hours?"

"I'll have to put in some extra time for at least the first year. Launching a new restaurant isn't easy, you know that. But—"

"But you already work ten-hour days." A flush of heat climbed Tory's neck. Across the table, Dillon became tensely quiet. She turned her head, stared out the window into the snowy night where twinkling Christmas lights were scattered like party confetti. "I have a surprise, too, Dillon."

No longer feeling the joy and anticipation the letter had initially caused, she reached for her coat, pulled an envelope from the pocket and handed it to him.

* * *

Dillon studied the return address on the envelope, then slipped the letter out. After reading it slowly, he lowered the paper to the table and stared down at it. "You've been accepted to law school."

"For the fall semester."

He looked up at her, so beautiful sitting across from him, her huge, hazel eyes brimming with distress. The smooth, pale skin beneath those eyes was smudged by dark rings of fatigue. Dillon remembered a time not so long ago when Tory had all but sizzled with energy and life. He couldn't stand to see her so exhausted. It hurt him, made him feel guilty, like he'd failed her. "I didn't even know you'd applied," he said quietly.

"I told you all along I'd apply when I graduated. I guess you just weren't listening."

"I heard you. But, I thought. . . ." He traced his finger along the edge of the letter. "Never mind what I thought. Congratulations. You've worked hard for this."

"I have worked hard," Tory said defensively, her nostrils flaring slightly as they always did when she was angry. "You don't sound very sincere. I mean, you don't seem happy for me."

"You're wrong. I'm proud of you." How could he *not* be proud? Not only was his wife beautiful, she was smart and so very capable. She deserved a hell of a lot more than he had given her so far.

Tory shot him a skeptical look. "You knew this was what I wanted, what I planned to do. You knew when you married me. Did you or did you not encourage me? You told me to 'go for it.' Were those just words, Dillon? Did you think it would never really happen, so it was safe for you to pretend to stand behind me?"

He looked down at his hands as he folded the letter and returned it to the envelope. "I wasn't pretending. I just didn't expect this so soon. I . . . I guess I thought you'd wait a while. Until Kayla was older. And now, with the baby coming—"

"With the baby coming, I'll need your support more than ever. I can't do this if you're working fourteen hours a day, seven days a week. It's not fair. And our savings . . . I can get a student loan for my school expenses. But I thought we'd agreed to use our savings to fall back on for personal expenses when I quit my job."

Dillon's head came up quickly. They'd discussed a leave of absence after the baby came, but he'd thought she'd go back to work within a couple of months. Since she'd graduated, she could work every morning and still have the afternoons free for the children. And then, when the restaurant got going, she could quit altogether.

"I'll have to quit my job," Tory said with conviction. "I can't work and go to law school and take care of the kids, too. It's too much."

"It *is* too much. You could wait to go to law school. Kayla needs you. The baby—"

"They need *you*, too. Don't try to lay a guilt trip on me, Dillon. You're only twenty-four years old. You have plenty of time ahead to have your own restaurant. But I've been accepted to law school for the fall semester. If I pass up this chance, who's to say I'll ever get a second one?"

She glanced down at her lap. "Sometimes . . . I have this dream. I'm on a train that's leaving the station. And there's another me standing there, watching the train pull away. I reach out to her when she starts running after it. But she can't keep up, and she starts to fade away." Tory met his gaze again. "This has always been my goal. Dillon. I've been straight about it with you. Ever since we met. That other me at the station . . . she's the person I've always dreamed I'd be, and now she's finally caught up to the train. If I don't grab hold of her hand now, I'm scared to death she'll disappear."

"You shouldn't be afraid. You—"

"Don't tell me how I should feel," Tory interrupted, nostrils flaring.

"Things happen." Baffled by the wounded look in her eyes, Dillon shook his head, wondering how she could be so unreasonable. "Things change. We have two kids to think about now."

"I *am* thinking about them. My going to law school is every bit as important to their future as your restaurant. This isn't the 1950s. I'm not the little woman tucked away at home, waiting for her man to provide for her and the kids. I mean, I know our lives have changed in ways we never expected." She blinked, looked away from him. "Sometimes I feel so alone. Like we're miles apart. Like we don't even know each other anymore. I don't have a clue what you're thinking . . . how you feel about us, or anything."

Dillon ran his fingers across the short spikes of his hair, wishing he could run them through her hair instead; those wild curls that fell around her shoulders like flickers of fire. She was the one pulling away. Just like in her dream. He felt it as surely as he felt the winter chill in his bones. He would never be enough for her . . . he and the children.

Worried and confused, Dillon shifted to stare out the window. The frosty night looked bleak and miserably bitter. "Our lives may have changed, Tory, but I haven't. I still feel the same way about us as I always have. You're right about one thing, though. I don't get you. No way do I get you at all. If our kids come first—"

"Well, that makes two of us, because I don't get you, either."

From the corner of his eye, he saw her prop her elbow on the table, her chin in her palm. After a few silent minutes, the waitress came with the bill. It sat on a small black tray topped by two fortune cookies. Dillon glanced over at the woman.

"Can I bring you anything else?" she asked in a lilting voice.

"No, thanks." As he watched her leave, an icy chill lifted the hair on his forearms . . . as if someone had opened the restaurant door, letting the wind in to swirl snow around him. His gaze strayed to the kitchen area where an old Chinese guy leaned against a counter studying them openly, apparently unconcerned by the fact that he'd been caught staring. With a nod of his head, the old man turned, walked to the kitchen door, pushed it open, and disappeared.

The muscles in Dillon's arms and legs tensed, quivered. With a sense of wariness that had little to do with his argument with Tory, he faced her again. "So . . . what's the solution to all this?"

She picked up the fortune cookie closest to her and cracked it open. "I don't know. I really don't." After pulling the tiny slip of curling white paper from inside the cookie, Tory read the fortune aloud. "A new beginning awaits you if you'll speak your heart's desire." No humor graced the sound of her chuckle. "My heart's desire . . . you know what that is?"

More sad and dejected than he could ever recall feeling, Dillon shook his head.

"I wish we could start the new year with a better understanding of each other. I wish you could know what it's like for me, day in, day out."

"That goes both ways. I wish you could know what it's like for me, too."

Tory sniffed. "I just want all this resentment we have toward one another to be replaced by a little compassion. Is that so much to ask?"

Darkness . . . silence. Then Tory was swirling . . . swirling, faster and faster, around and around and around, caught in a giant whirlpool that swept up color and light and sound with each rotation, a dizzying blur of weightless sensation that seemed oddly familiar in a vague, distant part of her mind.

She had no sense of time, but at some point the spinning slowed. The streaking colors separated, congealed into shapes. The garbled sounds crystallized, formed distinct words. . . .

"Ma'am? Are you okay? Can I get you some water?"

Recognizing the waitress's lyrical voice, Tory pressed her fingers against her closed eyes. Her head throbbed, her mouth was dry as desert sand. "Yes . . . some water . . . please. I . . . I'm a little dizzy," she answered. But it was a man's voice she heard, not her own. Confused, Tory opened her eyes to see the waitress blinking down at her, frowning.

"Sir? Is something wrong? Are you and your wife ill?"

"My wife?" Tory drew in a sharp breath. *She* had spoken the words, hadn't she? Yet, her voice was a low, drawling rumble; a male voice. Dillon's voice.

She glanced across the table, and her heart collided against her chest. It seemed she was looking into a mirror at her own reflection, yet there was no mirror on the wall across from her, or anywhere in sight.

"Babe?" the reflection said in a shaky voice . . . *her* voice. "What's happening?"

Blood rushed to Tory's head and pounded like a crazed drummer as she gazed in disbelief at her pregnant clone—a woman with curly, copper-colored hair and horrified, wide hazel eyes.

The clone's throat bobbed convulsively. She glanced down at her rounded belly, then touched it. "No way. This can't be real. It's a dream." The woman lifted a hand to the copper curls, scratched the side of her cheek—like Dillon always scratched at his sideburns. "Please tell me this is just a crazy dream."

Chapter Two

Tory's hands trembled as she lifted them, palms out, in front of her face. Only they weren't her hands at all. They were the hands of a musician, the fingers long and elegantly masculine, with large, weather-roughened knuckles, and short, rectangular nails. As she turned them over, Tory stared in amazement at the pads of each callused finger, toughened from Dillon's years of plucking guitar strings.

"I'll bring you some water," the waitress said, sounding apprehensive as she backed away from the table.

"I don't believe this. No way do I believe this!"

Lowering her masculine hands, Tory glanced

up again and across the table at the source of the panicked declaration. Not only did the woman's voice sound exactly like her own, the woman *looked* exactly like her, too. With eerie certainty, Tory knew Dillon was inside that woman's body—*her* body—staring back at her through her own green eyes. "D—Dillon?"

"Are you seeing what I'm seeing?" he asked.

"I—" Tory moistened her lips, swallowed. "When I look at you, I see me, and when I talk . . . I hear you."

Dillon shifted his gaze slowly down to his protruding belly. He placed his palms against it, spreading his fingers wide. "Oh, God, I . . . I'm pregnant," he said, his now feminine voice rising on a wave of hysteria. His hands slid slowly up his rib cage, paused beneath his full breasts. "I'm a woman. I'm a pregnant woman!"

Trembling uncontrollably, Tory touched her nose, her cheeks, her chin, amazed and horrified by the familiar face she felt beneath her fingertips. Dillon's face, not her own.

"It's a nightmare," Dillon said shakily, shoving his fingers through the mop of long, red curls atop his head. "It must be. Whichever one of us is having it will wake up in a minute. Let's just calm down, close our eyes and wait for that to happen. Okay?"

Tory couldn't force herself to answer, but when Dillon closed his eyes, she leaned back in her chair and closed hers, too. She listened to the sounds of the restaurant . . . the din of conversations . . . the rattle and clink of dishes . . . the delicate twang of Oriental music in the air. And above it all, the frantic pounding of her own heart . . . or Dillon's, she wasn't sure which.

"Here is your water, sir."

Opening her eyes, Tory saw that the waitress had returned. The young woman placed two glasses on the table. Tory peeked across at Dillon. He still looked like her.

"Nobody's waking up," he said, his words clipped, frantic. "It must be the food. Yeah, that's it. They put something in the food that's making us hallucinate." He grabbed hold of the waitress's wrist and looked up at her with wild eyes. "Tell me what they did to our food!"

The waitress jerked her arm from his grasp and staggered back. "Please, ma'am, let me call a doctor for you. I think you are not well."

"He'll be fine," Tory said.

The waitress's forehead wrinkled. "He?"

"My hus—I mean, my wife will be fine. He, I mean *she* is just a little stressed out." Tory forced a smile. "Here. . . ." She searched the adjacent chair for her purse, realized it was on the other side of the table next to Dillon, then reached into her back pocket and pulled out his wallet. "Let me pay you." She handed the waitress the gift certificate. "You can keep the change. Give us a few minutes and we'll be out of here."

As the waitress left the table, Tory returned her attention to Dillon. Though she felt on the verge of a nervous breakdown, she guessed she'd have to postpone it until he got over his. One of them had to keep a level head, and she could see it wasn't going to be Dillon. He had turned to the window and was studying his female reflection in the glass, touching the face that had once been hers, leaning in closer, whimpering. He looked as if he might run screaming from the restaurant at any second.

"Oh, please, Dillon. *Please* don't freak out on me now." She choked down her own hysteria as she caught sight of her image in the window. "We've got to get a grip." When he didn't respond, just kept staring at the window with shocked eyes, she grabbed his arm and tugged until he faced her. "We've got to get a grip, do you hear me?"

"You're *me*," Dillon whispered. "Look at yourself." His voice rose. "You're *me*!" He bit his quivering lower lip and grimaced. "What's going on? *What are we gonna do*?"

Tory closed her eyes. "I don't know. I . . . I can't think when I look at you and it's me who's staring back." Slowly, dreading what she knew she'd see, Tory opened her eyes again. "I need to get away from you for a minute to clear my head." When his panicked look intensified, she added, "Just for a minute. I'll be right back. I—I'm going to the restroom. Just stay right here, okay?"

Dillon didn't answer. Instead, he scratched his cheek, then patted it, as if feeling for beard stubble.

Tory stood and started for the restroom, her mind racing. She recalled the old Chinese man and the unsettling way he'd made her feel . . . her argument with Dillon . . . the fortune cookie.

She pushed open the restroom door and walked inside. *The fortune cookie.* What did the fortune say?

Headed for the stalls, she passed a gray-haired woman washing her hands at one sink in a row of three. The woman glanced up . . . and gasped.

"Hello," Tory said, the sound of her baritone voice sending her heart to the floor. She stopped walking, twisted around, and caught sight of her own reflection in the mirror . . . *Dillon's* reflection.

The elderly woman didn't bother to turn off the faucet. With her frightened eyes glued to Tory, she grabbed her purse from the floor with one wet hand, clutched her other hand to her chest, then backed toward the exit.

"I'm, uh, sorry," Tory stammered. "I, uh, forgot I was a man. I mean . . . I thought I was a woman."

The lady froze.

Mortified by the delirious laughter that gurgled from her own throat, Tory stepped closer to the woman. "Don't be afraid. It's just . . . I, uh, haven't been a man long . . . I—"

In a swift move that defied her years, the woman lunged at Tory, purse swinging. "Stay away from me, you pervert!"

The first blow hit Tory on the side of the face. She lifted her hands to ward off the second. Instead of delivering a third, the woman turned, pushed open the door, and ran.

Dillon felt numb all over—his mind, his body, his emotions. He stared at the broken fortune cookie on the table in front of him, then slowly lifted the curling slip of paper. "Your heart's desire. . . ."

Light-headed, he reached for the second cookie, cracked it open, and silently read the fortune inside.

"These sound more like riddles than fortunes," Dillon mumbled. He started to stuff both slips of paper into the pocket of his jeans, then realized he no longer wore jeans and that Tory's maternity dress had no pocket. Reaching for her coat, he tucked the fortunes inside that pocket instead.

As he sat back to wait for Tory, Dillon felt strangely detached from everything around him. He focused his attention on the bathroom door. An old woman bounded out. She seemed distressed as she hurried toward the front counter. Not more than five seconds later, Tory followed, and the brief, blessed numbness that had temporarily held Dillon's sanity intact was replaced by pulsating anxiety. Certain he was trapped in an old episode of the Twilight Zone, he watched his own body quickly approach the table.

When Tory came alongside him, she reached out a hand that had once been his and snatched up the law school letter. She stuffed it quickly into a jeans pocket that had, only moments before, belonged to him, too. Her gaze darted toward the gray-haired woman who was talking to the old Chinese man behind the front counter.

"I'll use the bathroom at home," Tory said. "Let's get out of here. Hurry."

Dillon tried to stand, but his stomach got in the way.

"Here." Tory offered him a hand.

Minutes later, Dillon drove his Jeep down the highway, trying to ignore the sickening sight of his pink, polished fingernails against the steering wheel. "What happened to your cheek?" he asked Tory, noticing a big, red welt on the side of her face.

"That lady in the restroom hit me. I forgot I belonged in the men's room instead of the women's."

He cringed. "What are we gonna do, Babe? We can't go home." He lowered his gaze to his breasts. "Not like this."

When Tory didn't answer, he shot a quick look

across the seat. She had flipped down the visor and was gazing into the mirror. Quickly, he shifted his attention back to the road. "I can't even stand to look at you. I . . . I think I'm gonna throw up." He swallowed. "If we go home, what will we tell the O'Conners? They'll know something's wrong. And Kayla . . . what about her?"

"We won't tell them anything. I mean, why should we? We're going to go home, go to bed, and in the morning when we wake up, this will all be over. One of us will be telling the other about a crazy nightmare."

"And if that doesn't happen?"

"Then—"

"Jeez!" Dillon swerved the Jeep across the white line.

"What's wrong?"

"Something just . . . ow!" He swerved again.

Tory reached for the wheel. "Get off at the next exit."

Dillon exited, then pulled into a service station parking lot. "Something's wrong. Something stabbed me in the ribs. Twice. My stomach . . . it feels like it's turning inside out. I—"

"It's the baby kicking you . . . moving around." Tory lifted her masculine hand and placed it against his bulging stomach. "The little thing's been active all day."

For several moments, Dillon couldn't speak as

he concentrated on the disturbing movements beneath his dress. "I have a *baby* inside of me," he said, aware of the frantic hitch in his voice, but unable to control it.

Tory touched his arm. "Dillon—"

"This is wrong. I'm not supposed to know how this feels. I'm a *man*, for God's sake."

"Not anymore."

"I don't care what I look like. *I'm a man.*"

Some time during the night, Tory stirred from a deep sleep to the sound of a woman's voice calling her name. She pulled the covers more tightly around her shoulders. "Let me sleep a little longer, Mom," she mumbled. "Please—" A thought drifted through her mind . . . she must have laryngitis. Her voice sounded deep, croaky.

"Babe," the woman whispered. "It's me, Dillon."

Tory blinked awake, squinted up at the silhouette looming over her. She jumped, and her heart jumped with her. "What? Who . . . ?"

"It's five o'clock in the morning, and I'm still you and you're still me, and the whole world is totally and completely screwed up! I can't stay like this. I'm serious, Tory, I'm gonna go crazy if I don't get back inside my own body soon."

It all came back to her, hit her head on, like walking into a wall. Tory sat up and turned on the bedside lamp. Beside her, Dillon sat wearing boxer shorts and his biggest T-shirt. It wasn't big enough, though. The garment stretched tight across his full breasts and abdomen, so tight she could see his belly button jutting against the fabric. Earlier, he'd absolutely refused to wear one of her nightgowns, protesting that it didn't matter if he was in her body or not, he'd feel like a cross-dresser.

Tory scrubbed a hand across her face, trying to wake up. Dear God, she had beard stubble on her cheeks and chin! "I can't believe this," she moaned. "I mean, I really thought it must be a dream."

"How can you sleep at a time like this?" Dillon asked, sounding miserable.

"I was exhausted. In fact, I wish you hadn't bothered me. That's the best sleep I've had in eight months."

He crossed his arms beneath his enlarged bosom and scowled at her. "Well, I haven't slept at all. In addition to worrying about this predicament we're in, my back is killing me and I have the worst case of indigestion you can imagine. Not to mention your snoring. I'm surprised you haven't blown the roof off the house."

Tory raised a brow. "Well, well, well. Now you know why I've been sleeping on the couch for the past few weeks."

"Okay, okay, this isn't the time for I-told-you-so. I think I'm about to lose it. We have to figure out how to switch back." Dillon peered down at himself, and when he spoke again, he sounded as if he might cry. "I can't go on being you. I've never been to the bathroom so much in my life."

Fighting down another deranged giggle, Tory reached up to rub his back. She couldn't count the number of uncomfortable nights she'd lain awake between trips to the toilet listening to him snore, wishing that for just one hour he could feel her pain, so to speak. But now, in spite of herself, she felt sorry for him.

"I did some thinking before I fell asleep," she said. "I decided that if this isn't a dream, then there must be a reason it happened. I mean, maybe we're supposed to learn something from the whole experience."

Dillon pulled back his long, red hair, and held it together at the nape of his neck. "You know I don't believe in all of that . . . things happening for a reason and everything."

"How can you sit there in that body, looking at me in this body and still have such a closed mind? If you never believed in magic or miracles or *anything* before, surely you do now."

He puffed out his cheeks, exhaled. "You have a point there."

"I was thinking about that fortune cookie. What did it say? Something about a new beginning if I'd state my heart's desire?"

Dillon stood. "I put the fortune in your coat

pocket before we left the restaurant. I'll get it."

Tory watched him waddle across the room to the closet with one hand pressed to the small of his back. He opened the door, reached inside, located the coat, and pulled a strip of paper from the pocket. Returning to the bed, he sat, then read the fortune aloud. "A new beginning awaits you if you'll speak your heart's desire."

Concentrating on the words, Tory closed her eyes, lowered her chin to her chest, then scratched her beard. "And I said my heart's desire was for us to start the new year with a better understanding of each other." She opened her eyes to a chest lightly sprinkled with hair—her chest, at least for the time being. Unnerved, she glanced up quickly.

Dillon placed the strip of paper on the bed. "So . . . what do you think?"

"Maybe this is our chance to do just that. I mean, to get a better understanding of each other. What better way for you to get a grasp of my life than to actually live it?"

Again, Dillon pressed a hand to the small of his back. "Hey, no offense, Babe, but I've had about as much of a grasp of your life as I can stand. Let's just call in sick at work for as long as it takes for whatever they put in our food to wear off."

"We can't do that. We don't know how long it might take."

She stood and started pacing. "Michael's short-handed. One of the secretaries asked for some time off. And I'll be taking maternity leave soon. I can't ask for time off before then. You can easily handle my work at the office. It's a no-brainer. Besides, I'm sure you're needed at the restaurant, too."

Dread streaked across Dillon's face. "What exactly are you saying?"

"I'm saying that I have to go in to work for you today and every day until we switch back. And you have to do the same for me. For as long as it takes, I live your life and you live mine."

He groaned. "Isn't your baby shower tonight?"

She stopped pacing and faced him. "I forgot about that. I really hate to miss my shower, but I guess it can't be helped."

Dillon stretched out on his back across the foot of the bed and stared up at the ceiling. "Lisa will want to know what we decided about her offer to let us buy in to the new restaurant," he finally said. "What will you tell her?"

With all that had happened in the last several hours, Tory had forgotten about the restaurant, as well as her acceptance to law school. It seemed the urgency of their new problem had obscured the old ones. Dillon's question made her realize the old problems still lurked in the shadows, waiting to be resolved.

"What do you want me to tell Lisa?" she asked quietly.

"Tell her. . . ." He hesitated, kept his gaze focused on the ceiling. "Tell her we need some more time. Tell her I'll give her an answer at the restaurant's New Year's Eve party. Surely this will all be over by then."

Apprehension fluttered in Tory's heart. It wasn't the answer she'd hoped for, but it was fair enough. "Okay," she said. "I'll tell her."

Huffing and puffing, Dillon pushed himself up from the bed. "It's still a couple of hours until I have to get up. I'm gonna lie down on the couch and try to get some sleep."

Tory tossed him a pillow. "You only have a little over an hour."

"It's just five-fifteen," he said, starting for the door.

"You forget . . . you have to put on makeup and fix your hair."

Halfway across the room, Dillon stopped walking and faced her. "You're joking! No way am I wearing makeup. I don't care—"

"Maybe not, but I do. I'm not letting you show up at the law firm looking like you just climbed out of bed. I mean, *we* may know you're not me, but nobody else will."

"Jeez," Dillon said, shaking his head as he resumed his pregnant waddle toward the door.

"Dillon?" Tory tossed him another pillow when he turned. "Put one under your knees and one just above your hips at the small of your back. You'll be more comfortable."

Chapter Three

Dillon placed a stack of papers into the copier and pushed the button. Leaning against the machine, he freed a foot from one shoe and wiggled his toes. He'd always liked the way high-heels accentuated a woman's legs, but after almost three hours of wearing them, he'd decided, sexy or not, they should be banned from the face of the earth. His feet were killing him. And while he was banning things. . . .

Grimacing, Dillon pinched at the waistline of his dress until he caught hold of the elastic band on his pantyhose. He tugged it out an inch with one hand and scratched his belly with the other.

With a sigh of relief, he closed his eyes. "Oh, man, that feels good."

"Tory?" A woman giggled. "Are you okay?"

Dillon jumped and looked up. The pantyhose elastic popped against his skin when he released it. Nan Jones, one of Tory's co-workers, a woman in her late fifties, stood off to one side of the copy machine with an armload of documents and an amused expression on her face. "Hi, Nan." Despite the heat that crept into his cheeks, Dillon managed a grin. "I, uh—"

"Hey," Nan said, raising one hand while peering over the top of her reading glasses. "You don't have to explain anything to me. I've felt like doing that a time or two myself. Especially when I was in your condition. Why are you so dressed up today, anyway?"

Dillon slipped his shoe back on and shrugged. "I don't know," he answered, suddenly suspicious about Tory's motives this morning when she'd insisted he wear these clothes. "That's a very good question."

When Nan pursed her lips and frowned, Dillon looked away. He hadn't done anything right since arriving at the legal office where Tory worked as a part-time runner. Before leaving the house this morning, Tory had filled him in on the basics of what would be expected of him at her job, and he'd filled her in on his restaurant duties the best he could. But he was at a disadvantage.

Tory had spent the first two years of college working as a waitress. He, on the other hand, had never worked in an office.

When the copier finished, he gathered his papers together. "It's all yours," he told Nan, then took the originals and copies to Tory's boss, Michael, before returning to her work station. His next assignment sat in a file at the corner of the desk with a note attached. Dillon hoped it was a delivery or a deposit. Surely he couldn't screw up a simple trip to another office or to the bank.

He read the note with apprehension, then, after glancing around to make sure he was alone, picked up the phone and punched in a number.

"Wishful Thinking," the person at the other end answered.

Dillon instantly recognized the voice of his friend, Joe Buckles, assistant manager at the restaurant. "Hi, Joe. Could I speak to Tory?"

"Tory Todd? She's not here." Joe paused, then in a suspicious tone asked, "Tory? Is that you?"

Realizing his blunder, Dillon clenched his fists. Tory's long, tapered fingernails dug into his palms. "Uh, yeah, it's me. I said you're speaking to Tory, didn't I?" He winced. "Is Dillon around?"

"Sure," Joe answered, sounding puzzled. "I'll see if I can track him down. It may take a minute. Thanks to your husband, I'm still limping around from my hockey injury, ya know."

Smirking, Dillon rapped his knuckles impatiently against the desk. "Give it up, Bucko, you big mama's boy. You've milked that sprained ankle for all it's worth. It wasn't that bad a fall."

"How do you know? You weren't even there."

"Uh . . . Dillon told me."

"Did he also tell you he's the one who knocked me down?"

Dillon laughed. "You were in the way. That's, uh, what Dillon said, anyway."

"You disappoint me, Tory," Joe said, his voice teasing. "I thought if anybody would give me sympathy, it'd be you."

"Sorry, Bucko. You're outta luck this time."

"Bucko? Not only are you starting to act like Dillon, you're starting to talk like him, too."

Dillon gritted his teeth. He'd have to remember not to use Joe's nickname until he was himself again. "Just go get Dillon, okay?"

"Okay, already. I'm going."

After several seconds, a deep voice reverberated across the line. "Hello?"

"Tory," Dillon whispered. "I need help here. You know that secretary who took some time off? Well, she called in and quit and they've got me doing some of her work."

"You're kidding. Jana quit? Just like that? After all these years?"

"Never mind that. I'm supposed to prepare this legal document." Dillon read the note aloud. "I'm a hunt-and-peck typist. What am I going to do?"

"Relax," Tory said. "I'll walk you through it. It's already set up as a file on the computer. All you'll have to do is pull it up and make a few changes."

As she explained how to log on to her computer, Dillon grabbed a pen and started taking notes. He tensed when he glanced up and saw Nan round the corner and start toward him. "How's it going at the restaurant?" he quickly asked Tory when she finished with her instructions.

"Hectic. But I've fudged my way through so far."

"Good. I guess I'll see you tonight then. I'll need your help getting ready for the baby shower, so try to get home on time."

He sensed an underlying tension in the silence that followed his statement. "When I say I'll be home at six, I'm home at six," Tory finally said.

Dillon didn't miss the subtle insinuation that he was always late. It was seldom easy getting away from the restaurant. Something or someone always seemed to need his immediate attention. But Tory could never understand that.

When Nan stopped alongside the desk, Dillon turned his back to her and muttered into the phone. "Did Lisa ask about my . . . your decision on her offer?"

"Yes . . . she did."

"And you told her—?"

"Exactly what you told me to tell her," Tory

snapped. "She seemed okay with getting an answer by New Year's Eve."

"Good." Despite his wife's curt response, Dillon relaxed. "Bye, Babe. Oh, and thanks." Turning, Dillon hung up the phone and shifted his attention to the opposite side of the desk where Nan stood watching him.

"How's Dillon?" she asked.

"A little out of sorts. He's cranky. He has a headache, his feet hurt, and he's hungry."

Nan lifted a brow. "Sounds like he's the pregnant one. How do *you* feel?"

"I'm cranky. I have a headache, my feet hurt and I'm hungry. But aside from all that, I feel great," he said, not bothering to cover his sarcasm. "I think I've spent more time in the bathroom this morning than at my desk. I must have the smallest bladder in the world."

Nan laughed. "It's been a long time, but I remember those days. When I was pregnant, I became pretty well acquainted with the potty myself." She motioned toward the door with a nod of her head. "Come on. We're cutting out of here early. I'm taking you to lunch. The boss won't mind. He knows your shower is tonight, and I can finish up that document for you this afternoon."

"I can't afford to eat lunch out. Besides, I've gotta get Kayla from the sitter's at one."

"That's over an hour from now, and I'm buying."

"Well, in that case, sure."

"What are you hungry for?"

Dillon licked his lips. "A big plate of greasy enchiladas and an ice cold beer."

Nan made a choking sound. "That must be one heck of a craving."

Dillon's stomach rumbled. He'd messed up again. Tory was a health nut. She wouldn't touch an enchilada, much less a beer, even if she wasn't pregnant. And, at the moment, the thought of all that grease and foam made him a little queasy, too. "Just kidding," he said.

An idea struck him. He could spy on the competition as well as get a free lunch. "There's a new place close by here. Wanna check it out? It's kind of off the beaten path, but I've heard it's good."

"Sounds great to me. You drive, okay? My car's been acting up."

A few minutes later he struggled to settle himself behind the wheel of Tory's old Volkswagen. No wonder she was always worn out. Climbing in and out of the tiny car with a bowling ball in your lap was no easy feat. When Nan closed her door, he started the car and took off, trying to recall Joe's directions to the new cafe.

"Brrr." Nan rubbed her palms briskly up and down her arms. "I forgot this thing doesn't have a working heater."

Shivering, Dillon shifted gears, changed lanes. "I forgot, too." When Nan shot him a funny look, he added, "Guess I'm just used to it."

He decided he might as well pick Nan's brain while he drove. Dillon didn't know her well, but he'd been acquainted with her a long time. And from what he'd gathered from Tory, she was a wise woman. Practical. Nan had her head on straight.

"When your kids were babies," he said, "did you work?"

"Nope. I was the traditional, old-fashioned, cookie-baking mom."

Dillon allowed himself a moment to feel smug. So, he'd been right about Nan. He sensed he'd found himself an ally. "Do you regret staying home?"

Nan's eyes were suspicious as she squinted at him over the top of her glasses. "Not for a second. Why do you ask?"

"I just—"

"Did you hear from the law school?" she interrupted, a note of excitement perking in her tone.

It occurred to Dillon that while he'd forgotten all about Tory applying, Nan obviously hadn't. As he slowed to a stop at a red light, he felt like the world's biggest heel. "Yeah, I did hear. I've been accepted for the fall semester."

"Oh, that's wonderful!" Maneuvering around the gear shift, Nan leaned across the space between the seats and hugged him. "Why didn't you tell me the minute you got to work?"

Startled by her embrace, Dillon scooted closer to his own door when the hug ended. Now he felt like the biggest heel in the universe instead of just the world. He hadn't hugged Tory when she'd told him her news. He hadn't kissed her or laughed with her or said any of the things he knew he should have said. "I don't know why I didn't tell you, I—"

"Uh, oh. Don't tell me you're having second thoughts? Is Dillon giving you trouble?"

Guilt tiptoed up his back and tapped him on the shoulder. He shrugged. "Sort of."

Nan shook her head and sighed. "Honey, that doesn't surprise me. I don't care if he's the most free-thinking man in the world, he's still a man. And men tend to feel threatened when their women strike off to do something on their own. Especially if that something could eventually make them financially independent."

"It's not that." Dillon glanced from Nan to the stop light. When it blinked to green, he took off again. "It's just that I feel—*Dillon* feels now's not the right time. The kids—"

"Just because you pursue a career, it doesn't mean you're a bad mother or that you don't love your kids."

"Then why did you stay home?"

"Because it was right for me. Now my sister,

on the other hand, would've gone nuts at home and would've driven the children nuts, too. She just wasn't geared for it. We had our kids at about the same time. I'm convinced Sis was a better mother when she went back to work and gave up trying to be something she wasn't: me, to be exact."

"What about her kids? Didn't they suffer?"

"Hmmm. Suffer? I just saw them both at Christmas. They seemed perfectly happy and well-adjusted. But I guess I could've been imagining things." Nan grinned. "Curtis graduated with honors last spring from OU. He's working on his master's in marketing now. Sarah's married and expecting her second baby. She's a dental hygienist . . . just like her mom."

Dillon wished he'd never initiated this conversation. He'd done so hoping Nan would back up his opinion that Tory should forget about law school for the time being. That she should support his restaurant plans and quit wearing herself out by taking on so much responsibility. That his kids needed a mother, not an attorney.

"Ever since I've known you, Tory, this is what you've been working toward, what you wanted," Nan said. "It'll be tough to accomplish, but don't give up on it unless you're absolutely certain it's *your* decision, not Dillon's. I know so many women my age who are looking back at their lives and realizing that, so far, they've lived someone else's dream, not their own. Don't be one of those women thirty years from now. You won't be doing anyone a favor. Not you *or* Dillon."

"But what about *his* dreams?" Dillon asked, though it wasn't only his future he was worried about—it was Tory's. For the past two and a half years, he'd watched her push herself to the point of exhaustion. He was afraid of what juggling law school and a new baby might do to her.

Nan scowled. "You've been accepted into law school. What will that take? Three years? He can have his turn then." She reached across and patted his hand. "Dillon will come around. He's just a little scared right now, afraid of losing you. Show him that's not going to happen, and he'll become your biggest supporter."

Dillon wanted to tell Nan she was wrong. He wasn't afraid, he just wanted what was right for his family. He didn't want to pass up any opportunity to take care of them in the best way he knew how. If he could make a success of this restaurant, in a year, maybe two, things would smooth out. Tory wouldn't have to work at all. The kids would be older. She could pursue whatever she wanted without so much stress. But he could see it was no use arguing with Nan. She was a woman, after all. And she was obviously on Tory's side in this issue. Besides, a part of him was afraid there was a grain of truth in what she said—but only a grain. Maybe it *was* selfishness on his part to want to be enough for his wife—just him and the kids. Maybe.

"Honey," Nan said, shifting to look out the window. "Where are we?"

Dillon frowned. "I thought Palmer Street was right along here. Joe said—"

"Why don't we pull into that service station up ahead and ask directions?"

"We don't need to do that. I'm sure we're close." He passed the station by. "It's one of these next side streets."

They crossed three more streets, none of which were Palmer. Dillon circled back, retraced his prior path.

"We're going to spend the entire lunch hour wandering aimlessly," Nan mumbled, staring out her window.

"Don't worry about it. I know what I'm doing."

"Look, Tory." She pointed. "Ask that lady at the stop sign if she knows where it is."

Dillon was beginning to get more than a little peeved by Nan's criticism. Did she think he was too incompetent to find his own way? "Joe told me how to get there." He paused at the stop sign, but refused to even glance at the lady standing on the curb.

"Sheesh!" Nan shook her head, her eyes rolling skyward. "You're as bad as my husband."

* * *

Tory made herself a sandwich and joined Joe at the counter. Wishful Thinking always closed for a few hours after the lunch rush for cleanup and preparations for the dinner crowd.

"Hey, Dillon, my man," Joe said around a mouthful of corned beef and sauerkraut. His scraggly red beard bobbed with each chew, reminding Tory of a billy goat.

"I'm glad that's over." She climbed onto the stool beside him. In truth, she'd rather enjoyed the hectic pace of the lunch rush. Without the added bulk of her pregnancy, she had energy to spare. Setting her plate on the counter, Tory lifted her arms overhead and stretched, bending slowly from left to right at the waist. "Mmmm. That feels like heaven."

When she lowered her arms, she noticed Joe staring at her, his sandwich poised halfway to his gaping mouth.

"What's the matter?" she asked.

"I . . . uh, never saw you do *that* before."

"Do what?"

"Stretch and, well, *purr* like you just did. You looked . . . you sounded—" He shuddered, glanced away, bit into his corned beef. "Never mind," he said between chews. "Just don't do it again."

Lifting her own sandwich, Tory shrugged.

Joe belched, then glanced back at her. "Are you sick or something?"

"No. Why?"

He slathered a french fry in ketchup, then popped it into his mouth. "What's that you're eating?"

"A cucumber sandwich."

"That's what I thought." Joe's lip curled with disgust.

Tory took another bite. Joe had a point. Normally, she loved cucumber sandwiches, but this one wasn't doing a thing for her appetite. She had the strongest craving for beef . . . smothered in cheese . . . with onions. "Maybe I'll make myself something else when I finish this." She dabbed the corners of her mouth with a napkin. "How's your ankle. Joe? I noticed you're limping."

"Yeah, but you won't hear me complain," he answered sarcastically. "You told your wife I've been acting like a wuss about it. You should've heard Tory on the phone this morning. She even called me a mama's boy."

Tory narrowed her eyes. She'd better have a talk with Dillon. He was making her look bad. Besides, Dillon should be more sympathetic and apologetic. After all, he was the one who'd knocked the poor guy down during a hockey game. Accident or not, Joe's sprained ankle was Dillon's fault. Well, she was in a unique position to do something about her husband's rudeness, and she wasn't about to pass up the opportunity.

"I'm sure Tory was just teasing you, Joe. I really feel bad about your ankle, and so does she. I'm sorry."

Joe barked out a laugh. "Yeah, right."

"No, really." Tory leaned in, placed a hand on his forearm. "I'll try to be more careful next time. I won't be so rough."

The stool screeched against the floor as Joe jerked his arm from beneath her hand and scooted away from the bar. "You think I can't handle you at the rink? I can take you any day of the week. Meet me there tonight and I'll prove it. Just you and me. I'll show you rough."

Stunned, Tory sucked in a breath of sauerkraut-scented air and leaned back. Was Joe just strutting his stuff, or was he truly offended? "I don't think . . . I was just trying to apologize. Besides, I can't meet you at the rink. My—Tory's shower is tonight. I have to stay home with Kayla."

"Lucky for you." Eyeing her warily, Joe eased his stool back up to the bar, putting some added distance between them.

"I'm sorry." Tory lifted a hand, reached out to him.

Dodging her, Joe leaned to one side. "Hey! Don't touch me again, Dillon. You're givin' me the creeps."

When a dark-haired waitress paused on the other side of the counter, Joe blushed profusely.

The young woman didn't seem to notice. In fact, she didn't seem to see Joe at all. "Hi, Dillon," the waitress said, then winked so quickly Tory almost thought she'd imagined it.

Lowering her hand, Tory searched her mind and came up with a name. She smiled. "Hello, Melissa. How are you?"

Melissa's eyes lit up. Cocking her head, she grinned . . . and winked again. "I'm fine. Wonderful, actually. Thanks for asking." She started off toward the kitchen, her hips swinging like a pendulum.

"What's with the wink?" Tory wondered aloud, watching the girl walk away.

With an uneasy expression, Joe glanced around the restaurant at the other members of the staff who were busily cleaning up. "You know Melissa. Especially when *you're* around."

Tory turned to him. His face was still splotched red from embarrassment. She wanted to ask him about his last statement, but the guy seemed edgy as a razor. "Joe. . . ." She frowned. "I'm really sorry. I mean it."

"Quit saying you're sorry." Joe shook his head. "Criminy!"

"Sor—" She bit her lip. No wonder men had so much trouble talking intimately with women. If Joe was any indication, they obviously had no experience with it. Tory couldn't imagine not being able to be honest and express her feelings with a best friend. "Maybe we should just . . . change the subject."

"Sounds good to me."

"So . . . what would you like to talk about?"

Joe's bushy brows drew together. "You're starting to sound like my girlfriend. Speaking of women . . . what did Tory think about your new restaurant?"

The cucumbers in Tory's stomach soured. "*My* new restaurant?"

"Yeah. Lisa's offer to buy in."

"He—I'm not sure I'm going to do it."

"*What*? Get outta here, man! You were so pumped about it. What happened?"

She shrugged, stared down at her plate, toyed with a sprig of watercress. "Nothing, really. I just got to thinking—"

"Is Tory nagging you about it?"

Tory looked up quickly, her body temperature rising ten degrees in a second's time. "Have I ever said Tory nags me?" She squinted at Joe, almost daring him to lie. Dillon Todd had better hope his buddy gave the right answer, or there'd be big trouble tonight.

"Not in so many words, no."

"What does that mean?" She shoved her plate to the far side of the counter and crossed her arms, her mind spinning. "So, I—Tory's—a nag, is she? I guess that's the impression I've given you. What else have I told you about her? I guess

I gripe about her all the time, don't I? Admit it, Joe. Do I or do I not complain about my nagging wife all the time?"

Wide-eyed, Joe shifted his gaze to the ceiling, then back again. "*What* is freakin' going on here?"

Tory felt her lower lip begin to quiver. Covering her mouth with one hand, she turned away from Joe. Prickles of hair tickled the tips of her fingertips. Out of habit, she'd almost shaved her legs—*Dillon's* legs—in the shower this morning. But she hadn't thought to shave her cheeks or chin. "Excuse me," she said, her deep voice teary. Shoving back her stool, she stood and started for the restroom.

This time, she made sure she went into the men's instead of the ladies'. At the sink, she splashed her face with water, then headed for the toilets. Three urinals lined one wall. No seats, no privacy. Beyond them stood a single stall. Tory started for it, but before she could enter, the restroom door burst open and Joe limped through.

"Okay, man," he said, his eyes shifty, anxious. "I've heard of things like this happening. After years of hanging out together like two regular guys, some dude pops up and tells his friend he's—" Joe glanced to the side, pinched his goatee. "Are you . . . ? Hey, if you are, just . . . don't tell me . . . okay? I don't wanna know."

"What are you talking about?"

"You. The way you're acting. Eating cucumbers and talking funny. Putting your freakin' hand on my arm. And the way you walked *in* here. Your hips . . . they. . . ." He lifted both hands in front of him, moved them right to left, then lowered them. "Never mind. I don't wanna talk about it."

Tory glanced away from him. "What happened to the door on this stall, Joe?"

"There is no door."

"Why not?"

Joe shrugged. "Never has been. You know that."

When she faced him again, Joe was approaching the urinals while releasing the top button on his baggy pants.

"Joe . . . don't!"

His zipper zipped down. So did Tory's eyes. To brace herself, she grabbed hold of the edge of the stall and froze. "Oh . . . my . . . God . . . !"

Joe's zipper went up again. Quickly. "Don't look at me like that!" he shrieked. "Criminy! I was right about you, wasn't I?" He stumbled backward. "You of all people. I can't freakin' believe it. You are, aren't you?" He raised both palms. "Don't answer that. I don't wanna know." Pushing through the door, he disappeared.

Tory stared at the swinging door, her heart pounding, her knees like watery gelatin. If she lived to be a hundred, she feared she'd never get over the sudden restroom phobia she'd developed in the past two days.

Thinking of Dillon, she let go of the stall and exhaled slowly. She could clearly imagine his reaction if he found out about this . . . about what Joe suspected. It wasn't a pleasant picture.

Chapter Four

Bone weary, Tory unlocked the apartment with Dillon's key, then opened the door and stepped inside.

"You're late."

Tory looked up. Dillon stood in the middle of the toy-cluttered den with Kayla on one hip and a stressed expression on his feminine face. He wore a stretched-out pair of his old sweats and a slouchy pair of wool socks.

Stuffing the keys into her pants pocket as she came into the room, Tory spared a glance at the Christmas tree they had yet to take down. All the ornaments within Kayla's reach had been removed and tossed on the floor beneath the branches. "I was ready to leave on time, but your replacement didn't show. Then a little boy got away from his parents and dropped a salt shaker down the toilet in the men's room. We had water everywhere." She reached for Kayla. "Hi, sweetie pie. Come to Mommy."

"You're *Daddy*!" Kayla squealed, giggling and squirming as Dillon passed her over.

Daddy. Tory's breath caught. How strange it seemed to hear Kayla call her that. She held her daughter close, stroked her soft, dark hair. She'd missed Kayla this afternoon. Glancing across at Dillon's stomach, she realized she'd missed the baby, too; missed feeling it move around inside of her throughout the day.

"You can finish getting ready for the shower now," she told Dillon. "I'll take over with Kayla."

"I'm as ready as I'm getting," he said curtly, lifting his chin. "Just look at this place! It's a mess. Kayla's a mess. *I'm* a mess."

Hoping to avoid, or at least postpone, a confrontation, Tory turned away from him and headed for the bedroom to change Kayla's soggy diaper. After the day she'd had today, the last thing she wanted to do was listen to him gripe.

"You don't even care," Dillon continued, following behind her. "You're not even listening to me."

"I *am* listening. You said the apartment's a mess."

"Couldn't someone else have handled the overflowing toilet? Where was Joe?"

"Joe had already gone for the day. I couldn't just leave the staff in a lurch."

"What about me? Was it okay to leave me in a lurch? Don't I count?"

Tory lowered Kayla to the bed and glared over at Dillon's agitated face. "Are you saying my being late was on purpose?"

"*Stop it*!" Kayla said in a stern voice. "Be nice."

Tory glanced down to see her tiny daughter pointing a finger at them, her brows drawn together, her lips pursed. She recognized the scolding expression and warning voice—they were a perfect imitation of her own. Feeling guilty and ashamed, she fastened the clean diaper in place.

Dillon sat on the edge of the bed, his shoulders slumped. "I can't please Kayla. She wants things done a certain way . . . the way you do them. I couldn't even get her down for a nap. I can't do anything right."

"That's ridiculous. You shouldn't feel that way."

The instant the words slipped free of her mouth, Tory regretted them. She sat beside Dillon. Pulling Kayla onto her lap, she stared down at her daughter's pudgy bare toes. "I'm sorry. I know exactly what you're going through right now. I always hate it when you tell me I shouldn't feel a certain way. It seems like you're saying my feelings aren't justified. But that's what I just did to you. . . ."

From the corner of her eye she saw him studying his fingers where they rested against his stomach. "And I always hate it when you lay a guilt trip on me the minute I walk in the door," he said. "But that's what I just did to you. . . ."

The corner of Tory's mouth twitched as the irony of the situation kicked in. "Maybe this is one of the lessons we're supposed to learn from all this. I mean, seeing the other side and all that." She peeked across at Dillon.

He grinned, though his heart didn't seem to be in it. "Yeah, I guess."

They turned at the same time, their eyes meeting. "Please tell me I don't ever sound as pathetic as you did when I came home," Tory said.

"Tell *me* I don't come home acting like a heartless jerk."

During the silence that ensued, Dillon lowered his gaze, as if afraid for either one of them to read the truth in the other's eyes.

After a minute, Tory stood, lifting Kayla onto her hip. "I'll get your dress," she said.

Dillon stood, too, and sidestepped toward the door. "No way. I refuse to put on another pair of panty hose and high heels. Why did you make me dress up for work today, anyway? Nan asked me about it."

Tory wasn't sure if the sudden pain in her side

was from a jab of Kayla's knee or a stab of guilt. Turning her back to him, she started for the closet. "Occasionally I have to dress up for work. If we have clients coming in for depositions or whatever."

"Yeah, but today wasn't one of those days."

She nibbled her lip. He'd caught her. "You'll probably only be me for a short time. I wanted you to get the full impact. You know what I mean?" She looked over her shoulder at him and winced. "Sorry. I guess my mean streak's showing."

Kayla squirmed in her arms. "Down, Daddy," she said.

Tory lowered her daughter to the floor, then reached for the dress she'd purchased to wear to the shower.

"You have to put this on, Dillon. If you show up in sweats people will think I'm letting myself go."

As Kayla attempted a somersault, Tory laughed out loud.

Dillon chuckled, too. "While you're occupying my body, would you try not to laugh?"

"Why?"

"Because you snort when you laugh."

"I do not!"

"You do. Trust me."

Tory put her hands on her hips. "Why haven't you ever told me before?"

"I didn't want to embarrass you."

"Then why are you telling me now?"

"Because I don't want *you* to embarrass *me*."

Recalling Joe in the men's room at Wishful Thinking, Tory raised a brow. "My snorting is the least of your worries."

"What do you mean by that?"

"It's just . . . I guess I could use some coaching on how to act like a man."

He scratched his cheek, searching for sideburns again, Tory guessed. "Okay," he said, drawing out the word. "Such as?"

"Are you and Joe on the outs or something?"

"Not that I know of. Why do you ask?"

"I never noticed before how mean he talks to you."

Dillon huffed a laugh. "Mean? That's just the way we communicate. Insult him every now and then. And don't forget to give him a sucker punch or two if he's within arm's reach."

"Don't you ever . . . *talk*?"

"Sure we talk. We talk about sports and—"

"No, I mean, don't you ever talk about things like"—she lifted a shoulder—"I don't know, your feelings, your goals?"

Dillon's face paled. He closed his eyes. "Jeez, Tory. Please don't tell me you talked to Joe about feelings when he thought you were me."

Tory handed him the dress and grimaced. "Don't ask."

"You're scaring me."

"Forget it. Let's get back to the subject of the shower."

Dillon opened his eyes and scowled down at the maternity dress. "The shower scares me, too."

Wondering what could possibly be scary about a baby shower, Tory gave Kayla a gentle push on the rump to help her roll over. She applauded the somersault and laughed when Kayla looked up at her.

"Kayla and I will take you and pick you up afterward so I can help load the presents into the Jeep," she told Dillon. "I'll show up a little early and say I had the time wrong so I can catch the tail-end of things."

Dillon slipped the dress off the hanger. "Do I really have to wear this?"

"It would mean a lot to me if you would."

He made a face. "Okay. I guess I'll be a good sport since you had to deal with the men's room problem at the restaurant. Even if you did con me into over-dressing for work."

Tory decided she'd be wise not to fill him in on the other problems she'd dealt with in the men's room today.

"This shower . . ." Laying the dress on the bed, Dillon stood, tugged his sweatshirt off over his head, then shoved down his pants and stepped out of them. "What should I expect? I keep imagining all these secret women's rituals."

She cut her laugh short when she realized he

was right about the snort. "Rituals? Like what?"

"I don't know," he said, slipping into the dress. "A flock of clucking old women holding me down and painting my toenails purple or something."

"It's a pretty safe bet that's not going to happen. You'll basically eat cake, drink punch and open presents. Make sure to oooh and ahhh over everything, even if you don't have a clue what it is."

Dillon turned so she could zip his zipper. "The cake and punch I can handle. The oohs and ahhs are pushing it."

He faced her, then surprised her by settling his arms around her masculine waist. Tory looked down at him, wishing his male image gazed back at her instead of her feminine one. She loved his face—his slanted black eyes, his dark coloring. She loved *him*, period. She loved the family they'd created together. Was that what she was supposed to learn from this crazy episode in their lives? That nothing was worth breaking the bond that held the four of them together; she and Dillon, Kayla and the baby? Why did marriage have to make things so complicated? Why couldn't she and Dillon be like they'd been with one another before life got so chaotic?

"I never thought I'd say this," Dillon drawled. "And I still think the timing's wrong, but I guess I'm beginning to understand why law school might look appealing to you. This woman stuff is exhausting."

"Are you saying law school is a man's thing?"

"Uh-oh. Your nostrils are flaring. That's not what I meant."

Pleased that he'd confessed to a little understanding of the law school matter, even if he had followed it with a male-chauvinist comment, Tory narrowed her eyes and smiled. "Hmmm." An urge to keep the mood light came over her as she tucked a long, spiraling curl behind his ear. She was tired of being tired. Tired of worrying about being a woman in a man's body with a husband in a woman's body. Tired of agonizing over what would become of them . . . of their marriage . . . when they finally changed back. "Since you're looking so pretty tonight," she teased, "I guess I'll give you the benefit of the doubt. Just promise you'll make me look good at the shower."

He blushed and made a face. "Watch out who you're calling pretty."

Pushing worries about their future to the back of her mind, Tory slipped away from Dillon, pulled a pair of panty hose from a dresser drawer and tossed them to him, then crossed to the closet to get him some shoes. "It looks like my feet are swollen," she said. "You can wear flats instead of heels."

She looked back to see Dillon holding the hose

at arm's length, clasped between his thumb and index finger. "Gee, thanks," he said.

"If you hurry," she told him, drawing the corner of her lower lip between her teeth to keep from grinning, "I'll have time to touch up the polish on your nails."

Propping his feet on the footstool the hostesses had provided, Dillon gulped down his fourth cup of Miss Piggy's punch. All that oohing and ahhing worked up one heck of a thirst. The punch was sweet, pink and fizzy, but drinkable. He just wished they'd give him a glass instead of these wimpy little cups so he wouldn't need to keep getting refills. The cake wasn't so bad, though the icing tasted like pure shortening with a five-pound bag of sugar mixed in.

He scanned the room of women with nervous eyes. He'd fantasized a time or two in the past about being the only man in a room full of attentive women. But in his fantasies, not one of those women had had blue hair, and the gifts they'd given him hadn't come wrapped in pastel paper.

And as for secret women's rituals . . . he hadn't been too far off the mark. At the beginning of the shower, one of the hostesses had passed around a spool of ribbon and scissors. Each woman cut the length of ribbon she guessed would reach around the circumference of his stomach. After he opened a present, the woman who'd brought it came up and tied her ribbon around him. The guest who came closest to guessing the correct length won some sort of door prize. All he got out of the deal was humiliation and fifteen or so ribbons wrapped around his gut. He felt like he'd been hog-tied.

Women. He might as well give up ever trying to understand them. He just didn't get it. What was the big attraction in getting all dressed up to gather together in someone's living room to eat mints and cake with waxy icing? To sip fancy Kool-Aid? He didn't get what all the oohing and ahhing was about, either . . . *or* the ribbon thing . . . *or* all the giggling and hugging . . . *or* why everyone seemed to think the color-coordinated food table was so darned adorable. Most of all, he didn't get the passing around of gifts for everyone to see. It didn't matter what the item was—be it an elaborate hand-knit blanket or a practical box of disposable diapers—the gift made the circle and was exclaimed over as if it were free tickets to the Super Bowl.

Give him a few guys, a slap or two on the back, a football game on the tube, beer and pizza. He'd choose all *that* any day of the week over this. *That* he could understand.

"How old is your baby now, Sara?" Dillon heard his boss, Lisa O'Conner, ask when he picked up on the thread of conversation he'd been trying to ignore.

Sara, who'd been Tory's roommate before Dillon came along, snapped to life across from him. "She's a month old today. She keeps me so busy, I don't know how I spent my time before she was born."

Dillon forked into his second slice of cake.

"I heard you had a rough time of it in labor," Lisa continued. Her voice had dropped an octave, as if she and Sara were speaking in confidence, though the whole room was listening.

Sara nodded, her eyes going wide. *"Twelve hours*. I thought the doctor was never going to let me start pushing. Near the end, I thought I'd split in two if I didn't die first."

The cake went dry in Dillon's mouth. He glanced around the room. Everywhere he looked, women young and old were nodding their agreement, talking amongst themselves in low tones. Sharing war stories, he guessed.

"My sister was in labor for almost eighteen hours," he heard another guest say. "Near the end, she was cussing out the nurses and assuring my poor brother-in-law he'd never touch her again. She had to sit on a doughnut for a solid month afterward."

"Ouch," Lisa muttered, grimacing. Then she snickered. "Maybe someone should've given you a case of hemorrhoid cream, Tory."

Dillon tried to smile at her, but couldn't quite manage it. He shifted uncomfortably in his chair and tried to concentrate on choking down the cake.

"It's well worth all the trouble, though," Nan added, peering at him over her glasses. "I doubt any of you mothers will argue with that. When my kids were born, I hardly remembered any of the pain by the very next day. I was too focused on my precious little reward."

"Oh, definitely," said Sara. "Even sore, cracked nipples are worth it, as far as I'm concerned."

Everyone giggled. Everyone but Dillon. He lowered his chin, glanced down at the breasts he'd always been crazy about, and for the first time, saw them from an entirely different perspective.

"Oh, no." Nan looked sympathetically at Sara. "Don't tell me you're having that problem?"

"Unfortunately," Sara said. "I've tried everything. Creams, ointments. Nothing seems to work. When the baby latches on to nurse, I almost go through the ceiling."

Dillon felt sick to his stomach. This wasn't the first time he'd heard about labor and pushing. He'd stayed by Tory's side through Kayla's birth, after all. He even vaguely remembered a cracked nipple phase sometime in the weeks afterward. But, somehow, seeing and hearing about it all when he was sure he'd never go through it was entirely different than seeing and hearing about it now. Now that a baby was kicking him in the ribs from the inside out and he had breasts the size of blue-ribbon melons.

"Air dry after you nurse," Nan told Sara.

Lisa nodded her agreement. "I used to walk around the house with my shirt unbuttoned and my bra flaps hanging down. I mean, who was around to care? It was just me and the kids all day long every day." She giggled. "Just make sure you remember to cover up if someone shows up at your door. My mailman got quite a view once."

Sara shrieked, her eyes wider than ever. "I'll try that," she said between bursts of laughter. "At this point, I'll try anything, believe me. A couple of days ago my left one got so bad it bled."

Dillon lowered his fork and touched his stomach with a shaky hand. What if he didn't change back before the baby came? What if he went into labor and had to push this kid out? What if cracked, bleeding nipples and hemorrhoid cream were his destiny?

Forgetting he had a plate in his lap, Dillon kicked the foot stool aside and stood, toppling cake to the floor. "Excuse me," he blurted, "I—" He stepped forward, the faces around him blurring into each other like one of Kayla's watercolor paintings. "I think I'm gonna be sick."

Lisa's arms went around him just as his knees gave out. Above the high chatter of concerned voices, he heard one deep one. Dillon recognized it as his own and knew Tory had arrived.

* * *

An hour later, Tory hung up the phone and turned to Dillon. He was rocking Kayla, who had fallen asleep in his lap. She was relieved to see that some color had returned to his cheeks. "Dr. Piaro wants to see you first thing in the morning," she told him. "I'll call Lisa and Michael to let them know we'll both be late for work."

Dillon stopped rocking, his face going instantly white again. "He won't examine me, will he? I won't have to take off my clothes and put my feet in those. . . ." He swallowed. "Those. . . ."

"Stirrups?"

"Yeah, those," he said, sounding frantic.

"I don't know. Don't worry about it. I mean, he may just want to check your blood pressure and the baby's heart beat."

Tory studied her husband and tried not to smile. Poor Dillon. She recalled a time or two when her feet had been hiked up in that cold, metal contraption, her knees spread wide, when she'd wished he and *every* man could experience that particular event. It seemed only fair. But now, looking at Dillon's nauseated expression, she couldn't wish that on him. He'd been through enough.

"Are you ready to talk about the baby shower yet?" she asked as she crossed the room to his chair.

He visibly tensed. "I'd rather not."

"What's wrong?" she whispered, lifting Kayla from his arms, settling the child's damp head against her chest. "Did they compare episiotomy stories or something?"

He looked up at her. "Don't tell me there's more? Epis . . . what's that?"

"Well, in the delivery room, the doctor cuts—"

"Never mind," he said, lifting a hand to halt her words.

She started for the hallway to the bedrooms but stopped and turned just short of leaving the room. "Dillon?"

He reached for the newspaper on the floor. "Hmmm?"

"Do I nag you?"

His head came up. "I've never said that."

"Not to me you haven't. You know better. But to Joe, maybe? Do you ever tell Joe that I nag you?"

"What's this all about, Tory?"

She sighed. What was this all about? Joe hadn't exactly *said* Dillon said she nagged him. It was just the way Joe worded things. She'd jumped to conclusions. But now she was afraid she *did* nag Dillon. Nagged him about coming home late and working too many hours, then complained that there was never enough money. The guy couldn't win. "Nothing," Tory said, turning her back on him. "Forget I asked."

She took another couple of steps down the

hallway, then backed up. "Dillon? What's with that waitress Melissa and the wink?"

Dillon's chin lifted. The newspaper spread across his lap rustled. "The wink?"

"Joe said—"

"You and Joe sure seem to be doing a lot of talking," Dillon grumbled.

Frowning, Tory gave up on the conversation and carried Kayla to bed.

Chapter Five

The next morning, after an examination that widened Dillon's eyes to the size of ping-pong balls, the obstetrician assured them all was well. The fainting spell at the baby shower had probably been nothing more than the result of standing up too fast—that combined with stress. Tory's eyes had locked with Dillon's and both of them grinned when the doctor said that. Stress was too mild a word to describe their current state of existence. But, of course, the good doctor had no idea. Still, despite his reassurances about the pregnancy, he'd said stress at this stage of the game was nothing to take lightly. It was time to quit work . . . and no more sex, not that they'd had any lately.

Dr. Piaro was from the old school. Current studies might suggest that, unless there was a problem with the pregnancy, a couple could engage in sex right up until the day of delivery. But Piaro advised against it. Tory suspected that, after years of dealing with pregnant women, the wise old doctor was simply tuned in and sympathetic to what a mother-to-be needed . . . and didn't need. He'd gone on to say that total bed rest wasn't necessary, but it was time to take things a little easier from this point on.

So Dillon had called the law office to give Michael the news, then spent his first full day at home.

Tory came home late again, exhausted. One waitress and two bus boys had called in sick at the last minute and she'd had trouble finding replacements. The only thing that had made staying at work seem worthwhile was the time-and-a-half pay she knew would be on Dillon's next check. For the first time, she had an inkling of the struggle he must go through each time he had to choose between extra pay and a smoothly run job, or time at home and a financially poor, but smoothly run family life.

At eight o'clock, after putting Kayla to bed, Tory went to bed herself. When muffled noises in the living room awakened her three and a half hours later, she almost had to pry her eyelids apart. Stirring, Tory sat up and climbed out of bed. She wrapped Dillon's bathrobe around her and went to check things out.

Except for the glow of the television and the twinkling, colored lights on the Christmas tree, the living room was dark. Soft, melancholy music drifted from the set. Dillon sat on the couch, his swollen feet propped up on the coffee table. On the end table beside him sat a half-eaten carton of chocolate chip cookies and a glass of milk. Dillon didn't see her; he seemed captivated by the romantic drama unfolding on the screen. Tory recognized the old Susan Hayward movie. As she crept further into the room, she realized with surprise that Dillon was weeping. With a tissue clutched tight in his hand, he dabbed at his eyes.

"Dillon?"

He jumped, sniffed loudly, then hurriedly wiped his face. "Oh, uh, hi. I couldn't sleep."

"Take the bed," she said, studying him, stunned by his obvious emotional condition. "I'll sleep on the couch so I don't bother you."

"I'd rather have the couch." He grabbed the remote control from the cushion beside him and quickly changed the channel. A snarling wrestler appeared in Susan Hayward's place. "The television. . . ." He swallowed, his eyes shifting restlessly. "I might need it in the middle of the night."

"Need it?" Tory blinked more fully awake and took an even closer look at him. Strung-out, exhausted, miserable: Those were the words that popped into her mind. His red-rimmed eyes were puffy, and the T-shirt he still insisted on wearing to sleep in had rolled up, exposing the lower half of his belly, as well as the tops of his overstretched boxers.

"Yeah, I might need the television for company." He nibbled his lower lip, as if to keep it from quivering. "It's miserable being so tired but not being able to sleep. And you're in there—"

"I know," she interrupted, crossing the room to stand beside him. "And I'm in there snoring like crazy, right?"

He nodded and looked away.

Tory reached down and picked up the pillows beside him. She fluffed and rearranged, then grasped hold of Dillon's shoulders and settled him back against them. After tucking a blanket around him, she knelt on the floor at his side.

"Thanks," Dillon said. "That feels better. I'm sorry to be such a baby about all this."

She grinned. Some things hadn't changed. When Dillon didn't feel well he always needed to be pampered. They could both have the flu, and his would be worse—in his mind anyway. "That's okay. Believe me, I know what you're going through."

"How do you do it? Those humiliating doctor

visits . . . constant backaches . . . sleepless nights. Before we switched, why didn't you tell me how hard it is to be pregnant? Why didn't you ever wake me up when you couldn't sleep?"

She *had* told him about being pregnant. More times than she could count. Apparently, hearing about it didn't have the same impact as experiencing it first hand. "I'd been pregnant before," Tory said, choosing not to get into a discussion about his lack of listening skills.

"Yeah, but you didn't wake me up the first time, either."

"Maybe it's because it's more natural for me. I mean, I was a pregnant *woman*. Not a man in a pregnant woman's body."

He shrugged. "Maybe. But nobody, woman or man, should suffer through this alone. I'm sorry, Babe. You should've woken me whenever you were sitting up at night feeling horrible. When we change back, I want you to." His mouth curled up at one corner. "If you do, I'll rub your feet."

"Is that a hint?"

"Yeah." He lifted a hand to her cheek, then hesitated and lowered it. "I guess it is." When she started to stand, he clasped her wrist and drew her back down. "I want to kiss you," he said, easing his grip, tracing circles into her palm with his fingertip. "But you need a shave. It would be like kissing myself." He shuddered. "Too weird."

She laughed. "Close your eyes. They're the same two pairs of lips they've always been."

He stared at her a moment, then complied. Tory closed her eyes, too, then leaned forward until only their mouths touched. "I want to do more than kiss you," she whispered against his lips, "but I guess Dr. Piaro wouldn't approve."

When Dillon quickly broke their connection, Tory blinked.

A look of disgust crossed his face. He let go of her hand. "I can't believe I'm saying this, but if you try anything, I'm going to have to have a headache." He shuddered again. "Talk about too weird."

Tory stood and smiled down at him. "You're safe with me. But, one thing this body switch has accomplished is to make me more sympathetic to the male sex drive." She glanced down at the lower half of her anatomy. "This thing seems to have a mind of its own."

"You're right about that." Dillon looked hopeful. "So . . . will you remember that when we change back?"

Making a face at him, she moved to the end of the couch. She slid beneath Dillon's feet, then settled them into her lap. "That's not exactly the better understanding of one another I had in mind when I opened that fortune cookie and stated my heart's desire." They sat silently for a few minutes as Tory rubbed his foot.

"I think I'll keep Kayla home with me the rest of the week," he finally said. "I was bored all alone here today. I slept a lot in the morning. Then after I picked up Kayla, she took a nap and I napped with her. For some reason it's easier to sleep during the day than at night. Now I'm wide awake." He yawned. "Did you know Kayla can sing every word to that song from *Dumbo*?"

Tory nodded. " 'Baby Mine' has always been her good-night song."

"She kept asking me to sing it to her but I didn't know all the words. So I said for her to sing it to me, and she did. She sang every word of it. Sang me right to sleep." He glanced down at the edge of the blanket, stroked his fingers along the silky binding. "I should've known the words. I should've known *she* knew the words. I should've known that was her song."

Tory was surprised at how angry he sounded; angry at himself . . . and ashamed. She was torn between wanting to make him feel better and wanting to hear him say that when this was all over, he'd find a way to be home more. But, after living his life for only two days, she didn't know how he could possibly make that promise. They had bills to pay, a child to feed, a new one on the way.

Opting for compassion, she lifted her shoulders slightly, then lowered them. "You can't be here at nap time. You can't always be here in the evenings when she goes to bed, either. I realize that now. I wish it could be different." When he didn't respond, just continued to stare down at his fingers, she added, "You get Kayla up in the mornings. You take her to the sitter. That's something."

Lifting a hand from the blanket to reach over his shoulder, Dillon grabbed a cookie. "It's not enough." He released a long, discouraged breath before taking a bite.

Disheartened that they weren't any closer to a solution to their family and career conflicts, Tory looked down at the puffy feet in her lap. On top of everything else, she badly needed a pedicure. And now Dillon was polluting her body with processed sugar. "Dr. Piaro said you need to take things easy. You won't be able to get much rest if Kayla's home with you all day. She's used to playing with the kids at the sitter's every morning."

"We'll take it easy," Dillon insisted. "What could be so exhausting about spending the day in the company of one little girl?"

Tory started to tell him, then decided it would probably be best to let him find out for himself. One day should do it. She finished massaging his left foot and started on the right one. "When I was rocking her to sleep earlier, she called me mommy."

Dillon stopped chewing, his brows lifting.

"You're kidding. How could Kayla know it's really you? She must've just made a mistake."

"I don't think so. I mean, think about it. Kayla knows us by more than just our appearance. She knows us by our touch and the tone of our voices, the things we say to her and the things we do."

"Amazing," Dillon said, fumbling beneath the blanket until he came up with the remote control. He changed the television channel. "I realized today that I've never spent an entire day alone with Kayla, just the two of us. Not that I don't like having you with us, but I'm looking forward to some one-on-one with her. This will be a good time to potty train her," he said, flicking from channel to channel. "She's too old to be wearing diapers. Besides, it'll be expensive buying them for two after the baby comes along."

Tory pursed her lips. So . . . he planned to completely potty train their daughter in the next few days. How relaxing. Funny, she'd been working on that for weeks now and still hadn't totally accomplished the feat.

Dillon stopped changing channels when he came to a late-night talk show. Lifting her gaze to the screen, Tory continued massaging his feet and listened to the comedian's joke. Just before the punch line, Dillon switched the channel. Frowning, she glanced across at him. "Some lady called the restaurant today for you. A Mrs. Winston. She wanted to know if you'd twisted Lisa's arm yet. I didn't have a clue what she was talking about."

"Oh, yeah, the catering," Dillon said absently, his eyes focused on the television, his finger pushing the remote button in a steady rhythm. "I think that lady sits on the board of every woman's organization in the city. She keeps trying to convince Lisa to get into catering. Says she could keep us booked single-handedly."

Tory glanced at him, then back at the television. "Lisa isn't interested?"

"She doesn't have the time to get it started, much less run it. Not with the new restaurant plans. And that's another thing. Mrs. Winston owns several office buildings downtown. For the last year or so, she's been after Lisa to put a smaller version of Wishful Thinking into one of them and just keep it open for breakfast and lunch. If the Norman restaurant does well, Lisa's considering it."

Though she knew time was running short and they'd be forced to discuss Lisa's offer soon, talk of the Norman restaurant made Tory nervous. "Oh, look," she said, glancing back at the television. "A *Little House on the Prairie* rerun. I love that program."

Dillon flipped on past it, paused for a moment to watch a documentary on gorillas in the wild, grabbed another cookie, then flipped again. He might look like a woman, Tory thought, but he was still one hundred percent male when it came to his TV habits.

When he paused to watch the *Three Stooges*, Tory lifted his feet and slid from beneath them. "I'd better get to bed."

"Don't leave yet," Dillon said, his eyes as pleading as his voice. "I'm lonely."

She leaned back and crossed her arms. "I'll make you a deal. I get the remote. You stop eating cookies. We watch Little House. I stay."

He lowered his gaze to the half-eaten cookie in his hand and frowned. "You know I hate sappy tear-jerkers."

Tory raised a brow. "When I walked in here earlier, seemed to me the tears were flowing pretty freely."

Dillon looked like he'd been caught watching porno instead of an old romantic movie. He handed her the remote, hesitated, then gave up the cookie, too.

Thirty minutes later, Tory sniffed back tears as she watched the Ingalls family celebrate a sparse Christmas around an even sparser tree. She heard a soft sniffling beside her and glanced over at Dillon.

"Man, how embarrassing." He reached for the tissue he'd discarded earlier. "What's the matter with me?"

"Pregnancy hormones are pretty powerful."

Smiling through her tears, Tory bit into a cookie. "And so is a man's appetite."

The next day, Tory joined Joe at the counter when they took their usual break after the lunch rush. "When this shift ends, could you follow me to the auto shop, then give me a ride home?" she asked him. "The Jeep keeps stalling on me. I don't think they fixed it right the last time."

"Sorry," Joe said around a mouth full of corn chips. "No can do. You said I could cut out early, remember?" He swallowed, grabbed a toothpick off the counter, then began working on the space between his upper front teeth. "I have an early dinner date."

"Then why are you eating a late lunch now?"

Joe exchanged the toothpick for a meatball sandwich. "This is just a snack."

Carrying a tray of napkin-wrapped cutlery, Melissa paused on the opposite side of the counter. "I'd be happy to follow you to the shop, Dillon." She winked, her full, berry-colored lips spreading wide to expose a mouth full of bright, white teeth.

"Sure, okay," Tory answered. "Thanks. The shop closes at six so we'll need to leave here around five-thirty."

"Whenever you say." Melissa winked again.

Tory narrowed her eyes. What was the deal with that wink? It almost seemed more of a reflex than anything deliberate. She didn't know Melissa Ellenburg well. The young woman had worked at the restaurant less than two months, and prior to this week, they'd only met twice, three times at the most. Melissa had always been friendly enough. But, despite the fact Tory was only a couple of years older, she recalled feeling middle-aged and frumpy with her ungainly pregnant body those times she'd been around the high-breasted, firm-bottomed, flat-bellied Melissa.

"Well . . . better get back to work," Melissa said.

Tory waited for the wink, but this time it didn't come. Instead, their eyes met and held, and Tory instantly felt uncomfortable. She tried to reason why but couldn't. All she knew was that she felt immense relief when Melissa finally smiled and walked away.

Crossing her arms, Tory watched the waitress leave. So what if Melissa's hair was straight and sleek instead of chaotic and curly? So what if a runway model might easily envy her figure? That couldn't be what caused the anxious prickle at the back of her neck, could it? Tory didn't like to think of herself as being *that* shallow.

"Hey, my man," Joe murmured, diverting Tory's attention away from Melissa. "You sure you know what you're doin'?"

"I'm getting a ride home from the auto shop. Why?"

Joe pinched his chin, his eyebrows wiggling like nervous caterpillars. "It's *your* butt, I guess. Just be careful. You're treading into risky territory."

Understanding seeped slowly into Tory's brain. It was the *way* Melissa had looked at her that had made her uneasy. The woman's eyes had offered more than a mere ride home. And, understandably, Melissa thought she was making that offer to Dillon, not Tory.

"Joe . . . ," Tory said, feeling jealous now instead of wary. "What do you mean by risky?"

"You know what I mean." Joe smirked, then mimicked the wink. "Sweet Melissa has that catch-me-do-me gleam in her eye whenever she's around you."

"Catch-me-do . . . ?" A flash fire burned a path up Tory's neck and across her face. "Why would she . . . ? I'm not chasing Melissa. Have I ever given her any reason to believe I'm chasing her? Have I ever made *you* think I'm chasing her, Joe?"

Tory didn't give him a chance to answer; she was half afraid to hear what he might say. "It's just a ride," she blurted, her gaze darting across the room where Melissa stood talking to another waitress. "Isn't it? Have I ever . . . ? Do I ever . . . ?" She swallowed.

"The way you watched her just now when she walked away . . . ," Joe said quietly. "Well, just take some advice from a friend. You might wanna rethink accepting that ride. I know women, and you'll be deep in you-know-what if Tory ever finds out about it."

As she sized Melissa up, jealousy nipped at Tory like a taunting dog. "Her body," she said, more to herself than to Joe. "I could have a body like that. I mean, after the baby's born, of course."

"The baby?" Joe sounded baffled. "What does the baby have to do with it? You could have her body right now if you want it. I'm telling you, she's willing if you are."

"No," Tory said, her eyes still on Melissa, her mind eaten up with suspicion. "I mean my body could *look* like hers if I wanted. So could my hair." She lifted a hand to her head. "The right stylist could—" Realizing her goof, Tory lowered her hand and glanced sideways at Joe. She'd never seen a more startled expression on anyone.

"Criminy . . . ," he said. "Don't tell me we're back to that again."

"Forget it, Joe. I was just thinking out loud."

"It's what you're thinking that worries me. I'm serious, Dillon." He scooted a few inches off to the side and settled his forearms against the counter. "I'm really startin' to worry about you."

"Well, that makes two of us." Tory lifted her

water glass. "I'm starting to worry about me, too."

"I hate to say this since I like Tory and everything. But, at least if you and Melissa—well, you know—at least then maybe I wouldn't be so worried about the other thing."

"*What* other thing?" Tory snapped, more alarmed than she could believe. Dillon had never given her any reason not to trust him, and she felt ashamed doubting him now. But she had to admit, things had been strained between them, even before the unthinkable happened and this body switch occurred. They hadn't had much time for one another. She'd been preoccupied with school, her pregnancy and Kayla. He'd been preoccupied with his work. At least she'd *thought* it was work on his mind.

Joe puffed out his cheeks, shook his head. "I just hope you know what you're doing."

Oh, she knew what she was doing, all right. She was going to find out once and for all if anything was going on between Dillon and that walking, talking, winking Barbie doll. That's what.

Chapter Six

The afternoon was sunny. The air, though crisp and cool, lacked the usual bite of late December. Bundled up in a jacket, Kayla bounced on the playground horse, singing loudly. Nearby, at one of the fast-food restaurant's outdoor tables, Dillon sat watching her as he sipped hot chocolate. Across from him, Joe gulped a milk shake between bites of his second chicken sandwich.

"You surprised the socks off of me when you called and asked me to meet you, Tory," Joe said. "What's up?"

"I haven't seen you in a while. How's work?"

"Busy," he answered, deserting his sandwich

momentarily to tackle a pile of french fries. "And my guess is it's only gonna get busier. We hardly see Lisa anymore. Her time's tied up making plans for the new restaurant. And if Mrs. Winston has her way, Lisa will be working on the plans for a third sometime around next Christmas. She came in again today."

"Mrs. Winston did?"

Joe nodded as he finished off his milkshake, slurping noisily.

"What did she say?"

"Dillon can tell you more than I can. She spent most of the time talking to him. But apparently, the lease will be up on a place in one of her downtown buildings toward the end of the new year. She thinks it's the perfect spot for a Wishful Thinking to go in."

Joe picked up a napkin and wiped his mouth, "Surely you didn't ask me here to talk about this? You can get all this information from Dillon."

Dillon set down his steaming styrofoam cup and reached up to stroke a non-existent sideburn. He hadn't had much of an appetite today. The hot chocolate didn't even taste good. He felt on edge, antsy. Tory's recent vague comments concerning conversations with Joe, not to mention her request for lessons on acting like a man, made him fear his reputation might be on the line.

"I was wondering," Dillon said, watching Joe

carefully for anything suspicious in his reaction. "Is Dillon dealing with some kind of problem at the restaurant? He's acting sort of odd lately. To tell you the truth, I'm worried about him."

"You, too? He's flat out givin' me the creeps."

Joe propped an elbow on the table, scratched his goatee and squinted. It seemed as if he wanted to say more but was uncertain as to whether he should. It occurred to Dillon that he'd placed the guy in an awkward predicament. As far as Joe knew, he was being questioned by his best friend's wife. He wouldn't want to betray their friendship by revealing anything Dillon might want kept quiet.

"This is weird," Joe said, his words delivered cautiously. "All this time, I've been thinking Dillon must be having problems at home, while *you're* thinking he's having problems at work." He paused. "It's none of my business, but you two are getting along okay, aren't you?"

Dillon shrugged. "We're fine. Why? What has Dillon said to you?"

"It's not so much what he's said. It's more the way he's acting. Like he's going through some kind of personality change or something."

Dillon felt queasy. He glanced at Kayla, watched her slide safely off the horse's back then start toward the table. "What do you mean?" he asked Joe.

Joe shifted in his chair. "I'm not real comfortable talking to you about this."

When Kayla tugged at the hem of his maternity blouse, Dillon spared her a quick glance. "Just a minute, sprite." He looked up at Joe again. "If something's going on with Dillon and you know about it, I want you to tell me. How can I help him if somebody doesn't tell me what's going on?"

Scratching his beard with one hand while nervously tapping the table top with the other, Joe turned to watch a boy go down the slide. "This isn't easy for me, Tory."

Kayla jumped up and down as she jerked on Dillon's arm. He patted her hand. "Hold on, sweetie." Returning his attention to Joe, he said, "Nothing you tell me is gonna turn me against Dillon."

"Well . . . there's this girl at work." Joe lifted a hand and quickly added, "Now, don't get me wrong. Dillon doesn't give a damn about her. He's crazy about you. He'd be crazy *not* to be crazy about you. But this girl . . . she comes on to him."

Melissa. The hot chocolate Dillon had consumed started to curdle. "And?"

"And normally, Dillon brushes this girl off—you know, doesn't give her a second look. But today was different. Today he looked twice. And, well . . . she's giving him a ride after work since his Jeep's acting up."

"Are you saying he's interested in this woman?" Dillon knew the question was crazy; he could answer it himself. He wasn't interested in Melissa. But Tory must think he was or she wouldn't be paying attention to Melissa in a way that would make Joe suspicious.

Joe raised a shaggy brow. "This might sound nuts, but I don't think Dillon's *sexually* interested in this girl. I think he's more interested in finding out where she gets her hair and nails done."

"*What*?"

Kayla yanked Dillon's sleeve and squealed, but he was so startled by Joe's statement, he ignored her. "No way, Joe. Are you implying what I think you're implying?"

Joe shook his head, his face turning as red as the Christmas lights that still hung around the exterior of the fast-food restaurant. "I don't know what to think. Yesterday, I overheard Dillon giving one of the waitresses advice about PMS. I swear, he sounded like he knew what he was talking about. Then today. . . ." Joe's voice rose an octave. "*Today* I caught him checking out his butt in the restroom mirror. He asked me if I thought he looked too thin when he wore black."

"Joe—"

"I shouldn't be talking to you about this, Tory," Joe interrupted. "But, damn it, I can't help it. The way Dillon's acting is spookin' me big time. You might wanna check your underwear drawer. I wouldn't be surprised if he's wearing your panties on the sly."

"I don't wear women's underwear," Dillon blurted, mortified by Joe's embarrassing speculations.

Joe blinked. "You *don't*?"

"No, I don't! And I don't like men, either, if that's what you're thinking!"

Joe's mouth fell open. A french fry dropped from between his fingers and landed on the ground. "Not you, too?" His adam's apple quivered. "Just what kinda marriage do you and Dillon have? I thought—"

"*Daddy*!" Kayla shrieked.

Joe gasped. "She called you *daddy*. Criminy! You've even got the poor kid confused!"

Dillon's mind spun as he looked into Kayla's distraught, upturned face. He lifted her onto his lap and discovered her pants were soaking wet. He should've listened to Tory and changed Kayla out of her training pants and into a diaper before taking her out of the house.

And Melissa. He should've told Tory a long time ago about how the woman came on to him. If Melissa played out her usual routine, what would Tory think?

Giving his watch a quick glance, Dillon slid Kayla off of him, took her hand, and struggled to stand. He'd swear his stomach was growing larger by the second. "Come on, kid. Let's get you cleaned up." He spared Joe a glance and saw that the guy still looked shell-shocked. "Sorry to run off," Dillon told him. "I just remembered something I've gotta do."

He had to get to Tory . . . before Melissa did.

After finishing her business with the auto shop mechanic, Tory climbed into Melissa's shiny blue Mustang and closed the door. "I appreciate the ride. Better take me back to the restaurant. I have some things to wrap up before I call it a day."

"Want me to wait for you?" Melissa asked in a silky voice. "I could take you home." She tilted her head to one side, her eyelids dropping to half-mast.

"That's okay," Tory said, fighting back a snarl. "I'll get a ride from someone. You've done enough."

"I don't mind waiting. Really." She smiled and shot Tory the wink. "I'd love to give *you* a ride anywhere."

Tory clenched her hands into fists. *Guess what I'd love to give you*. She leaned slightly in toward Melissa. "I think. . . ." She squinted. "Yes, you do . . . you have lipstick smeared on your teeth."

Melissa's smile fell faster than a cake when the

oven door slams. Bowing her head, she lifted a hand to her mouth.

"On the right eye-tooth," Tory said, feeling justifiably wicked. "The really pointy one."

After a few seconds of frantic rubbing, Melissa looked up again, her face flushed scarlet, her eyes narrowed. "Damn you, Dillon Todd!" she said, as embarrassment shifted to coyness. "You're teasing me! Look at you—you're trying not to laugh." She dipped her chin, her lips pouty, her eyes flirtatious. "Well, I'm glad you're finally relaxing around me. It's about time."

Scooting across the seat, Melissa slowly loosened the knot in the tie around Tory's neck. "You're always so tense when you're with me. So serious," she said quietly, inching closer. "It's almost like you're holding your breath or something."

"I am holding my breath. I'm sorry to say this, but that perfume you're wearing. . . ." Tory wrinkled her nose. "It really stinks."

Melissa's hand went still against the necktie. Her face paled and one corner of her mouth twitched spasmodically. "What's the matter, Dillon?" she asked after a moment. "Are you chickening out?" She lifted her brows, her eyes lighting up with that "catch me" look Joe had warned about. "That's it, isn't it? Accepting this ride was a big step for you. Now you're afraid of what you want, so you're trying to put me off by hurling insults."

She traced a fingertip down the edge of the tie. "Don't be afraid. We're making such progress. I was beginning to think I'd have to strip naked and camp out in your car to get you to notice me. That's okay. I knew you'd be a challenge. The other girls . . . they said I should forget about you; that you only had eyes for your wife. They said you're one of the few who believes a ring on your finger actually means something. You know what I told them?"

"No, what?" Tory asked, feeling relieved, silently scolding herself for ever doubting Dillon's faithfulness.

"I told them"—Melissa whispered, her hand encircling the tie—"that if anyone could make you forget that ring"—she tugged gently—"it would be me."

"You think so, do you?"

"I know so." Melissa lifted a finger and touched a sideburn, then slowly traced it down Tory's cheek to her lips.

Tory sucked in a startled breath. She reminded herself that Melissa was unaware the lips she stroked weren't Dillon's any longer. The woman had no idea that his body was currently out on loan. Summoning her wits, she opened her mouth to give the woman a piece of her mind, but Melissa slipped her finger inside.

"*Ouch*!" Jerking back her finger and wincing, Melissa scrambled back behind the wheel of the car. "Son of a—you bit me!"

Savoring the moment, Tory leaned against the door and crossed her arms.

"You *bastard*," Melissa snarled, her voice low and threatening, reminding Tory of a hissing cat. "Get out of my car." She held her injured finger against her chest. "Get out!" This time, the words were shrill, hysterical. Uneven red splotches appeared on her face. "Find another way home to your precious job and your boring little wife. I thought she was a lucky woman, but I was wrong. You're a spineless, passionless weenie, that's what you are. I doubt you know the first thing about satisfying a woman—especially a woman like me."

Tory opened the door and stepped outside. A *weenie*? She choked down a giggle. Obviously, Melissa wasn't accustomed to being spurned.

As she slammed the door, love for Dillon puffed up inside of her until she thought she might lift off the ground like a helium balloon. She ducked her head inside the car window for a few final words. "Nice try, Melissa, but you didn't have a chance. I can't really blame you for your efforts, though." She gave Melissa the wink, then smiled and pointed at her own chin. "What woman could possibly resist this face? I know I can't."

"You pathetic, conceited jerk. Listen to yourself." Melissa huffed a sound of disgust. "Find another waitress. I'd rather starve than work for you."

Tory stepped back and watched Melissa drive out of the parking lot. She laughed out loud. *Mission accomplished.*

Straightening her tie, she started toward the auto shop. She'd use their phone to call the restaurant. Maybe one of the bus boys would come pick her up.

Just as she reached the door, car tires screeched behind her. She looked over her shoulder and saw her own red Volkswagen. The driver's door opened and Dillon, wearing her coat, struggled out from behind the steering wheel. He left the engine idling as he hurriedly waddled across the parking lot toward her, one arm cradled under his belly.

Tory met him halfway. "What are you doing here? Is something wrong?"

"They told me at the restaurant where to find you." He paused to catch his breath. "Is everything okay?"

She nodded. "Everything's fine. Where's Kayla?"

He jerked his head in the direction of the Volkswagen. "Inside. Asleep in her car seat."

His brows squeezed together as they walked side-by-side toward the clattering old vehicle.

Leaning against it, Dillon met her gaze. "I passed Melissa Ellenburg down the road. Why aren't you with her?"

"She emasculated me, then kicked me out of her car. Oh, and she quit her job, too." When Dillon's eyes widened, Tory added, "I bit her finger."

He barked out a laugh. "Seriously?"

"She deserved it."

"I don't doubt that." He chuckled a moment, then sobered. "About Melissa. I hope you know I never—"

"I know." Tory's heart raced as she stepped nearer to him, so near the swell of their baby brushed against her shirt. "Back when we were ourselves," she said, looking down at him. "Sometimes, when we'd kiss, you'd hold me so close I couldn't tell where I stopped and you started. Maybe if we shut our eyes and do that now, it could be like old times. Maybe we could forget for a minute that things aren't right."

"Tory—"

"I know," she interrupted, sweeping a hand down the length of her body then lifting her arm toward him. "I know you think this is all too weird. I think so, too. But—"

Dillon cut off her words by pulling her against him. She closed her eyes and felt two arms wrap around her shoulders. Her arms encircled his waist. Their bodies pressed together. Their lips brushed once, then met again and held. And suddenly, it was as it had always been. The same familiar desire, the same stirring warmth, the same wonderful feeling of completeness. She was finally whole again, connected, and so vitally alive.

When the kiss ended, they continued holding each other. Dillon pressed his face into her shoulder; Tory closed her eyes so tight they hurt. She didn't want the moment to stop. But reality came rushing back, bringing with it all the problems and confusion. "What are we going to do?" she asked softly.

"We'll change back somehow. This can't go on forever."

"But after that . . . I mean, what are we going to do then? About law school? About your restaurant plans?"

"I don't know. We've been avoiding the subject." He paused, and Tory felt his warm breath through the fabric of her shirt. "I'll ask Lisa for more time," he finally said. "We can't make a rushed decision on this. It's too important."

"I've been thinking," Tory said. "When I applied to law school, I think deep down I knew the timing was wrong. But I'd been working so long toward that goal that I just didn't want to face the facts. I think that's really why I didn't tell you I'd applied."

The Volkswagen's engine died, and an almost unbearable silence replaced the sound of the surging motor. "God, I miss being a mother and a wife," Tory said. "I miss it so much. I hope you know how much I love you. You and our family are my happiness. I need and want you more than anything else."

"But you need and want other things, too." Lowering his arms, Dillon stepped away from her. He smoothed a palm across his stomach and glanced down. "I understand that now." Suddenly, his hand stilled, his eyes went wide.

"What's wrong?" Tory asked, alarmed by his expression.

"The baby . . . it's moving. He's been extra active today."

Amused, Tory tilted her head. "He?"

"Or she." Dillon shrugged. "Either way, it doesn't matter which to me." He met her gaze again. "Before this happened . . . before we switched, I had no idea. . . ." He shook his head. "I never guessed it would feel like this. It's amazing."

"It is, isn't it?" Tory smiled.

A wistful look of peace settled over his face. "This may sound crazy, but I feel a really strong sense of connection to this baby now, and to you and Kayla, too. I've always loved all of you. But this is more powerful than anything I've ever felt before. It's different. More intense."

Emotion welled up inside Tory, tightening her throat. "That doesn't sound crazy at all."

Dillon pressed his fingers against the tight swell of his stomach. "I think I can tell where the head is," he said, speaking quietly, his voice hardly more than a whisper. "And here's a knee, or maybe an elbow."

Tory reached out a hand and felt, too.

"Is it always like this?" he asked. "Being pregnant? Like, with Kayla . . . did you feel . . . ?" He paused, as if he couldn't explain what he was feeling.

Tory didn't need an explanation. "Yes," she answered, smiling a watery smile. "There's nothing else like it."

She toyed with a button on the coat he wore, then slipped her hands into the pockets to pull him against her again. The fingers of her right hand brushed against paper. She lifted a narrow, white strip from the pocket. "What's this?"

Dillon frowned as he studied it. "Oh, yeah. The other fortune. I forgot about it. I read it the other night at Confucius Says while you were in the restroom." He shook his head. "I was so out of it I can't even remember what it said."

Straightening the curling slip of paper, Lisa recited the printed words aloud. "When the old year fades into the new, your lover's kiss will transport you." Filled with sudden hope, she waved the fortune in the air. "Maybe this is the answer!"

"What?"

"The traditional kiss at midnight on New Year's Eve. Maybe it will send us back to our own bodies!"

"I can't believe it could be that simple."

"We have to believe it. What else do we have?"

Slowly, Dillon grinned. "It won't hurt to try." Leaning forward, he pecked her on the lips. "I do love kissing you."

Chapter Seven

Streamers streamed. Music blared. A space had been cleared for a dance floor, and some of the more adventuresome guests made use of it by jiving to the beat of a 1940s big band tune. Tables of food and drink lined one wall, and just to the side of the entrance, Lisa had posted a sign stating that the cost of a cab ride home was on the house.

Dillon stared into the crowd and wished they'd stayed home with Kayla and the sitter. Mrs. Merriweather, their elderly neighbor, had been making hot chocolate when they'd left; she'd rented some movies, too. Right now, that calm, warm, atmosphere seemed far preferable to the noisy, cheerful chaos going on around him. He could sorely use some of Mrs. Merriweather's motherly pampering.

Beyond pretending to himself, Dillon silently admitted he was afraid. Tonight could be the night. Tonight might hold the key to his future. Would he become a man again, or stay forever trapped in the body of a woman—his wife? The thought of that possibility brought with it a tremor of pure panic. Dillon could remember times in his past, times alone with Tory, when he'd wanted nothing more than to crawl right inside of her. But this was taking that desire to the extreme. This was ridiculous, unbelievable, terrifying.

All day long he'd recited the second fortune again and again in his mind, praying that Tory was right about the message.

When the old year fades into the new, your lover's kiss will transport you.

Tory took hold of his manicured hand. "Ready?" she asked.

Dillon swallowed, his eyes scanning the celebrating mob. Most of the faces were familiar. Among them, Lisa and Michael, Lisa's friend Val Potter, and Michael's law partner Jarrod Wilder. In the center of the crowd, Dillon spotted Tory's co-worker, Nan, with her husband. They were talking to Joe and his date.

Because he couldn't seem to squeak out a response to Tory's question, Dillon nodded once while trying to psych himself out of turning and bolting through the door. When Tory squeezed his hand gently, he looked over at her.

"I've set your watch alarm for a minute before midnight," she said, glancing down at her wrist. "Let's try not to lose sight of each other. No matter what, we've got to be kissing when the clock strikes twelve."

Dillon nodded again, and Tory let go of his hand.

"Don't forget to talk to Lisa about what we discussed," Dillon told her. "We need more time."

Sending him a reassuring smile, Tory said, "I won't forget."

As they wove their way through the throng of people, Lisa caught sight of them and waved.

"There you are," she called out. "I was about to give up on you two." Tucking a straight strand of light brown hair behind one ear, she moved toward them, giving Dillon a hug when they came face-to-face. "How are you feeling, Tory?"

"Fine," Dillon lied. The noisy atmosphere had the same shredding effect upon his nerves as fingernails scraping down a blackboard.

"I heard the doctor has you staying at home now since you fainted at the shower."

He nodded while scanning the room for a place to sit down. He felt Tory's hand take hold of his again and guessed she'd sensed his edginess.

"We're only three weeks away from the due date," Tory said.

"Only three weeks?" Lisa's grin stretched ear to ear. "I can't wait! I miss having a baby around. Kayla grew up into a little girl too fast for my liking. You haven't told me what she thinks about having a new brother or sister."

"I'm not sure she understands," Tory continued. "We talk to her about it, but I don't think she knows what she's in for."

Lisa laughed. "Can you believe all that's happening in your lives?" She linked her arm with her husband's when he came up beside her.

"Speaking of happenings," Michael O'Conner said. "Did I tell you Tory was accepted into law school, honey?"

Lisa's eyes widened. "No, you didn't tell me! That's fantastic! Congratulations!"

"Thanks," Tory said. "I, uh, mean Tory thanks you, don't you, sweetie?"

"Yeah, thanks," Dillon murmured distractedly, his eye on a nearby empty chair he desperately wanted to claim. His back ached worse than usual tonight. And his feet were so swollen it felt as if the toes might pop off one by one, like ten champagne corks from ten spewing bottles.

"Good grief," Lisa said, her voice conveying a note of concern Dillon picked up on. In the years they'd worked together, he'd learned to read her well. "Law school, another baby, possibly a new restaurant. You two have a busy year ahead of you."

"Which brings up a subject I really need to talk to you about." Tory nibbled her lower lip. "I know this isn't the time to discuss business, but—"

"No, that's okay," Lisa interrupted. "I've been anxious to hear what you've decided. Let's get it out of the way."

"Tory," Michael said, slipping his arm free of Lisa's, "I had a pregnant wife once—twice actually. I bet you'd like to get off your feet." He nodded at a table a few steps away. "While these two talk shop, why don't we sit and I'll tell you all about the joys of law school?"

Once seated, Dillon kept his eyes focused on Michael but his ears tuned in to the conversation transpiring behind him between Tory and Lisa. Pretending to be enthralled by Michael's words, he linked his hands across his stomach. It felt hard as concrete tonight . . . and tight. Nerves, he decided. He had to settle down. The over-anxious state he was in couldn't possibly be good for the baby.

"I sympathize with your dilemma," he heard Lisa say. "But I really need to know something soon. I want you as a partner, Dillon. You have the experience and the business sense to make the restaurant a success, and besides that, we work well together. But if you bow out, I'm going to offer it to Val. She's fed up with her job and I think she'd jump at the chance for something new. She'd be good at it. Val's good at anything she tackles."

And Val Potter was Lisa's best friend, Dillon thought, experiencing a sudden jab of fear. The opportunity of a lifetime might be slipping away from him. But the jab subsided as quickly as it had come. Only a week ago, he'd known without a doubt that buying into the restaurant was something he wanted to do. Now he wasn't sure *what* he wanted anymore in that regard. In fact, about the only thing he *was* sure of was that he wanted his own body back.

"Another week," Tory said. "That's all I'm asking for."

"A week. . . ." Lisa's voice trailed off. "I feel like I'm starting to sink here, Dillon. I need to make some decisions, and I need the input of whoever's walking into this with me. It seems like every time I turn around another problem pops up. If not with the new restaurant, with this one. Melissa, for instance. She'd talked to me about transferring over to the Norman store when it opened, so I know she was planning on working long-term. I can't figure out why she quit."

"I think she expected fringe benefits she didn't get," Tory muttered.

Turning his back on Michael mid-sentence, Dillon looked over his shoulder. Tory's eyes glinted with humor when they met his. He grinned at her. She mimicked Melissa's wink. Their gazes held. And in that instant Dillon sensed that everything would be okay. He and Tory had each other and their children. They were the only things he was sure of. And when he looked at his life, stripped away all the vanity and pride, his own manufactured expectations and those of others . . . when all that was left was the naked truth of it, sharing a future with Tory and raising their family was all that really mattered.

Sending him another smile, Tory returned her attention to Lisa, and Dillon faced Michael again. "Did you know we're potty-training Kayla?"

Michael tugged his earlobe and shrugged. "I . . . uh . . . no, Tory, I didn't know that."

"She went all day long today without an accident. First time she's done it. That's a big deal."

Michael's jaw twitched. He smiled. "Sure it is. It's been a long time since my kids were that age, but I remember."

Dillon settled his forearms on the table and leaned in. "No, I mean it's a really, really big deal. Oh, I know what you're thinking. I used to think it, too. I'd say all the right things when I heard details about Kayla's day. You know . . . *that's great. Awesome. Way to go*." He lifted his brows.

"Buzz words. That's all they were. I didn't have a clue how important those little accomplishments in my kid's life really are. Important to *me*."

Michael crossed his arms, his gaze darting toward his wife then back again. He looked baffled and intensely uncomfortable with the conversation, but Dillon couldn't seem to stop himself from going on.

"She likes green beans better than peas, Kayla does. I never used to know that. Did you know those kind of things about your kids?"

"Umm—"

"She has this afternoon routine. The same thing everyday. Lunch, play time, then there's this program she watches. After that, a nap. If you foul up her schedule, you pay the price." He laughed. "Know what I mean?"

Michael's answering chuckle was nervous. Tugging his earlobe, he shifted to look at Lisa and cleared his throat . . . twice.

Lisa glanced toward the table then back at Tory, ignoring her husband's subtle call for help. "Okay, Dillon," she said slowly. "Think it over another week. But after that, you've got to let me know something one way or the other."

She and Tory exchanged a few more words before joining Michael and Dillon at the table. Dillon pulled back the chair beside him so Tory could sit down.

When Lisa came up beside Michael, he quickly

stood. "We haven't talked to all of the guests yet, honey. There's quite a crowd here." He grabbed her hand and started away from the table. "Better get started. Midnight will be here before you know it."

"Enjoy yourselves," Lisa called out over her shoulder. "Remember, Dillon, only one more week. We'd make a great team."

Dillon watched them leave. They stopped a moment to speak with Joe and his girlfriend, Leah. Then Joe and Leah made their way to the table.

"Hey, Dillon, my man."

"Have a seat," Tory said, nodding at the chair beside her.

Shaking his head, Joe lead Leah to the opposite side of the table. "No offense, Dillon, but I think we'll sit over here. This new touchy-feely thing you've got goin' just isn't my thing, if you know what I mean."

Joe pulled out a chair for his girlfriend. "How are you feeling, Tory?" Leah asked as she sat.

"Okay," Dillon said, deciding she'd probably rather not hear the truth. He cradled an arm beneath his stomach and all but sprawled out in his chair.

Joe sat beside Leah, his eyes narrowed to teasing slits as he peered across the table and pinched his goatee. "Let me tell you about these two, sweetheart. They may look like the all-

American couple, but don't let 'em fool you." He lifted a hand, cupped it around his mouth; tilted his head toward Leah, and whispered, "Tory told me she doesn't wear ladies' underwear. But I'm not so sure about Dillon."

"*Joe*!" Leah swatted his arm. "What a thing to say."

Rubbing his stomach, Dillon made a face. "Ha, ha. You're such a smart ass, Joe. I—" The words died on his tongue. Though it didn't seem possible, his stomach pulled even tighter than before, like a leg cramp after running too many sprints . . . only worse. Sucking in a quick gasp of air, he grasped hold of the chair's arms and squeezed.

Joe didn't seem to notice. "Smart ass?" He scowled and turned to Tory. "Your wife just called me a smart ass."

Dillon felt Tory's hand on his shoulder. "Are you okay?"

"I—" The cramp had him catching his breath and holding it. He stared down at his fingers where they gripped the chair and watched his knuckles turn white. Only they weren't his knuckles at all, they were Tory's, and he was suddenly so confused and so afraid. He lifted his gaze to her face, but saw his own face instead. It blurred and swam, then slowly came into focus as the cramp began to ease.

"What's wrong?" Tory asked, her eyes wild with worry.

Dillon blew out the air he'd held trapped in his lungs. "I don't feel so good. I . . . I need to get out of here."

"Let's take her outside," he heard Joe say from across the table.

The next thing he knew, Joe held one of his arms and Tory held the other. With Leah leading the way, they guided him through the revelers and out the front door.

Outside, they stopped on the sidewalk beneath one of the street lights. Dillon drew chilled air into his lungs and, to his relief, his head began to clear.

"Feeling better?" Tory asked after a few moments of tense silence.

"Better," he answered . . . and then another spasm began. Dillon closed his eyes, dug his fingertips into Joe's and Tory's arms. "Oh . . . jeez! It's happening again."

"Get the car, Leah," Joe ordered. "She must be havin' the kid."

Dillon's eyes popped open. "*I what*?"

"The baby," Joe said with forced cheer, though he looked a little peaked. "Maybe you're havin' it. What do you think, Dillon?"

"It's too early," Tory said, her deep voice trembling. "But I guess it could be possible."

Feeling as if he'd drifted deeper into a nightmare, Dillon watched Leah dash into the parking lot, heard her high heels clicking against the pavement.

"No!" he shrieked, his breath sending puffs of white steam into the frigid darkness. "I'm not having this baby!" He let go of Joe's arm to grab hold of Tory's other shoulder. "Do you understand? I refuse to have this baby! I won't! I don't know how!"

Something warm and wet trickled down the inside of Dillon's right thigh.

"She's hysterical," he heard Joe say in a perplexed voice.

Lowering his head, Dillon stared down at his feet. The trickle became a stream that pooled on the sidewalk below. He glanced up just in time to catch sight of the burst of fear in Tory's eyes. She pressed her lips together and winced, her brow wrinkling. "Oh, no," she whispered.

"What is it? *What is it?*"

"I . . . I think our water just broke."

Chapter Eight

Tears dampened Tory's face as she entered the restroom just off the maternity ward delivery room. She'd cried all the way to the hospital. And, this time, if Joe had thought Dillon less than macho because of it, he didn't let on. In fact, she'd glimpsed Joe's reflection in the rear-view mirror a time or two as he broke every posted speed limit trying to make it to the hospital in time, and he'd looked as if he might be more than a little emotional himself.

It wasn't just her fear for Dillon that had Tory so upset. The simple truth was she felt short-changed. She'd carried this baby for eight months. Regardless of the pain, *she* wanted to be the one to bring their child into the world. Giving birth was the most exhausting work that existed. It was also the most rewarding. And, as a woman, it was *her* right, not Dillon's.

Not that Dillon would argue the fact. He'd declared loud and clear on the ride over that he wholeheartedly agreed. The last thing he wanted to do was cheat her by delivering the baby in her place. When this was all over, she didn't know how they'd ever explain to Joe and Leah some of the things she and Dillon had said.

A young nurse poked her head into the room. Tory glanced up.

"Better get a move on, Mr. Todd," the woman said with excitement. "It won't be long now." She helped Tory into a gown, cap and mask, then led her into the delivery room.

Flat on his back on a table, Dillon's feet were propped up in stirrups, his legs draped with sheets. Dr. Piaro hadn't arrived yet, but a stout gray-haired nurse stood between his spread knees preparing for the birth.

Tory went to her husband's side. "Oh, sweetie," she said, touching his shoulder. "I'm so sorry. I never meant for something like this to happen when I made that wish. God, why couldn't we have just stayed home with Kayla that night instead of going out to dinner? You wouldn't be going through this right now."

The nurse stopped whatever she was doing between Dillon's legs, looked up, and cocked a silver brow. Tory ignored her. Who cared what the woman thought? Who cared what anyone thought? She and Dillon were stuck in a terrifying dream, yet his pain and her fear were all too real.

"No, Babe," Dillon said, his voice groggy. "I'm the one who's sorry. You went through hell to give me Kayla. I know that now." He drew a sharp breath and flinched.

Tory stroked his face. It might look like her face, but Dillon lived behind it, and right now she didn't care how strange that seemed. "You gave me Kayla, too."

"Yeah, but I only had to do the fun part. I guess it's only fair that with this second baby, I get the rough part, too."

"No, it's not fair." She sobbed. "I mean, it's not supposed to be this way. I can't stand seeing you in such pain. I feel so helpless. When I was having Kayla, I never realized how helpless you must've felt." Tory remembered shouting curse words at him when things got rough. She nibbled her lip, wishing she hadn't done that. When she heard the two nurses whispering, Tory looked up and saw their bewildered expressions.

"It's okay," Dillon said. "It's. . . ." His face went rigid. His eyes widened. "I need to push. Ohhhhh, ohhh, ohhhh, I need to push!"

"Not just yet," the older nurse said in a calm,

encouraging voice. "Just a little longer. Hold on."

Turning to Tory, Dillon lifted his head off the table. "Tell them to give me a shot or something!"

"But we're doing Lamaze—"

"Forget Lamaze! I want a shot, damn it! Make them give me drugs! Now!"

Alarmed by Dillon's outburst, Tory looked up at the nurses and saw Dr. Piaro enter the room.

"Ready to have this baby?" he asked.

With a mouth too dry to speak, Tory gave a nervous nod.

Dillon cursed.

The watch on Tory's wrist beeped. She jumped. "It's a minute before midnight!"

Dr. Piaro chuckled. "Determined to have the first baby of the New Year, are you?" He took the nurse's place at the foot of the table. "Okay, Tory. Give me a good strong push."

Leaning over Dillon, Tory peered into his red, strained face. He looked up at her, gritted his teeth, and bore down.

"Kiss me," she whispered.

Dillon groaned, but she muffled it by covering his mouth with her own.

"Mr. Todd," Tory heard the gray-haired nurse say, "this is hardly the place or the time."

When the younger nurse grabbed hold of her arm, Tory tried to shake the woman off while keeping her lips firmly planted on Dillon's.

The nurse yanked. "Mr. Todd, *please!*"

Dillon moaned.

"*Push!*" Dr. Piaro ordered.

With everything she had in her, Tory kept kissing.

Dillon was spinning . . . twirling on an out-of-control carousel stuck at warp speed. The pain spun with him, clung with piercing, tugging tentacles, sucked at his body like a leech. And there were sounds . . . confusing, warbled words that roared, faded to murmurs, then roared again. Somehow, through it all, he heard Tory moaning . . . moaning, but the haunting wail seemed to come from within himself. And all at once he was aware of Tory's mouth on his, drawing the agony from his body, taking it into her own. The relief was sudden and overwhelming, stopping the carousel with an abrupt jerk and a sharp grinding of gears.

"*Push,*" he heard Dr. Piaro say. "That's it."

"Mr. Todd! I'm going to have to ask you to leave." Dillon felt a hard tug on his arm and staggered back. Opening his eyes, he gasped for breath.

The last thing he remembered seeing was his own face, his own slanted eyes gazing down at him with fear. Now, he was the one looking down, and Tory's beautiful face stared up at him from the table, her green eyes hazy with exhaustion, her pale skin splotched red and damp with perspiration.

Ignoring the nurse's protests, Dillon stepped toward the table. "I'm here, Babe," he said. "I'm right here beside you."

"One last push now, Tory," Dr. Piaro said.

And then Dillon heard a cry. Their baby's first.

Five hours later, Tory looked up from her newborn daughter's face as Dillon slipped quietly into her hospital room. "What are you doing here? It's five o'clock in the morning." She sent him a smile. "You're supposed to be home with Kayla getting some rest."

"You think I can sleep? Mrs. Merriweather's with Kayla. She offered to stay the night so I could get here early."

He sat at the edge of the bed and, with a fingertip, stroked the downy-soft head nestled at Tory's breast. "Look at her," he whispered. "Such a miracle."

He glanced up, looked deep into Tory's eyes. His own eyes were moist with tears and so filled with love the sight left her breathless.

"You and I," he said, "we do make the most beautiful daughters."

Tory kissed him gently. "Happy New Year."

"The happiest," he murmured as he lifted a hand to her cheek. "I'm so glad everything's back as it should be, if you know what I mean."

"That makes two of us." She reached up, covered his hand with her own. "I love you. You know that, don't you?"

"I know that."

They sat quietly for several minutes, both of them content to just be together, studying their new baby girl in the pre-dawn silence and the soft glow of lamplight.

"Tory," Dillon finally said. "Lisa and Michael took me home last night from the hospital. We had a long talk. I turned down the Norman restaurant deal."

"You *what*? But she gave us a week to think it over."

"I don't need to think it over. I—"

"I couldn't stand it if you come to resent me some day in the future because of this. If you feel like I forced you into giving up this chance—"

Dillon lifted his fingers to her lips. "You didn't force me into anything. It's my own decision. I don't want to do it. Not now, anyway."

"Why, Dillon?"

He bowed his head, touched the baby's cheek. "Being at home with Kayla this past week . . . it made me realize how much I've missed by working such long hours. I want to be more a part of both of our daughters' childhoods."

"But if you keep your current job, your hours will be the same as they've always been."

"Lisa and I . . . we're making some changes. Remember Mrs. Winston?"

"The woman who wants Lisa to open a restaurant in one of her downtown buildings?"

"Yeah. And she wants us to get into catering, too. Lisa agreed to let me get that going. The catering, I mean. I'll still be a manager at the restaurant, but she's promoting Joe to manager, too, so I can cut back on my hours. I can schedule the catering and handle a lot of the business from the apartment. There are still a lot of details to work out."

"Are you sure this is what you want?"

He nodded. "In a year or so, maybe we'll open a new restaurant downtown. If so, Lisa's willing to let me in on that deal instead." He stopped for a breath. "Anyway, what I'm trying to tell you is that you don't have to worry about law school. Even if I buy in next year, we'd only be open for lunch, so I'd be home more. It still won't be easy . . . we'll have to pinch pennies more than ever since you're quitting your job, but, well, you have my blessing where law school is concerned. Not that you ever needed it."

Tory laughed softly. "I'm not going."

"You're *what*?"

"I said I'm not going to law school. Not this year anyway."

"Tory . . . I told you . . . the door's open. Everything's taken care of. You can go. I *want* you to go."

"I don't *want* to go." She lifted a hand. "Don't misunderstand. I mean, I still want to be a lawyer. I'm just not in any big hurry. I guess being away from Kayla so much this past week made me re-think things, too. So . . . I called the dean of the law school yesterday. He said I could defer for a year."

"You mean you can start school a *year* from this fall?"

She nodded. "This will give all of us time to get adjusted to having a new baby in the house. Time to get to know her. I can keep working part-time at the law firm and save some money. I bet Michael would even be willing to let me take over some of Jana's work—you know, she's the secretary who quit. If so, I'd get a raise. Best of all, I'll have extra time with my babies. That's what I want most of all."

"You're sure?"

She nodded. "I can have it all, just maybe not all at once."

Smiling, Dillon released a long breath that sounded like pure relief.

"In only a week, we've both had the same change of heart," Tory said, laughing. "How do you explain that?"

Dillon brushed a kiss across his daughter's

head. "You told me once that pregnancy hormones are powerful things." He shrugged, then shifted the kiss to Tory's lips. "Blame it on the baby," he whispered.

A Little Bit of Magic

Kimberly Raye

For Natasha,
the best agent in the business.

Chapter One

She was *not* going to look.

Samantha Skye kept her gaze riveted on the stack of mail in her hands and tried to ignore the man who'd just walked through the front double doors of the brownstone where she lived.

He stopped just a few feet away, in front of his own mailbox. The creak of hinges, followed by the slow slide of paper echoed through her ears. Her fingers trembled around a letter.

Keep the faith, girl.

If she didn't look, she wouldn't want to touch, and touching Jake Morelli would be a big, *big* mistake.

She knew that firsthand.

One touch would turn to a kiss. One kiss to a really hot kiss. One really hot kiss to a bunch of really hot kisses and then—

"Sam." His deep, rumbling acknowledgement disrupted her thoughts and sent a trembling down her spine.

You know the drill. Politely nod and get up to your apartment. Pronto.

"Hi." So much for Pronto. She smiled. Her eyes, the traitorous things, shifted to him and her heart pounded.

Tall, dark and handsome. That described Jake Morelli to a T. With short dark hair, the faintest hint of stubble darkening his jaw and deep chocolate-brown eyes so rich they put a pint of her favorite Double Fudge Ecstasy to shame, Jake had the kind of classic good looks usually reserved for the pages of *GQ*. Not to mention, a lean muscular body that would have done any Calvin Klein ad proud.

Said body hid beneath a charcoal suit and pinstriped tie, however, because Jake Morelli made his living as a corporate lawyer. A *single* lawyer, Great-Granny Gigi had made a point of mentioning when he'd moved into the Lake Shore Drive brownstone where she and Sam lived. Single, with no bad habits his past landlord would divulge, a sizeable bank account, *and* great dimples. Great-Granny Gigi had a thing for dimples.

But getting hooked on Jake Morelli, dimples

or no dimples, was completely out of the question. He wanted only one thing from a woman.

Unfortunately, that one thing wasn't sex.

Even so, the truth didn't keep an image from sliding into Sam's head. The two of them, bodies touching, mouths tasting, the summer heat pressing into them from the outside, and a completely different heat burning them up from the inside.

". . . all right?" His deep voice startled her from the memory and her mail took a nosedive toward the carpet.

"Darn it." She bent down, and so did he. Their hands collided and heat shot through her at the contact.

"Is everything okay?" Deep brown eyes warm with concern peered at her as he collected her scattered mail. "You look flushed. You're not coming down with something?"

"Uh, I'm fine. Just a little tired." She took the stack he handed her, careful not to touch him again. "Christmas was three days ago and I'm still trying to get back on track."

"I don't even try. I just cruise through until New Year's, then jump back on the wagon."

"So sayeth the man who just landed a senior partnership in his law firm." Great. Not only was she flushing, she was talking to him. So much for a quick getaway.

"If I didn't know better, I'd say you were keeping tabs on me."

"Don't go getting a swelled head." A gleam lit his eyes and her heart kick-started. *Great choice of words, Sam.* "Um, Granny Gigi just happened to mention your promotion in passing. She's the one keeping tabs."

"So how are things in the toy business?"

She shrugged. "Same old, same old." *Same old, same old*? Was there a lack of oxygen in the room or had she just caught a major case of stupid? In the past six months since she and Jake had . . . well, anyway . . . *since*, she'd been handed the biggest account of her career. A project guaranteed to land her a vice presidency, along with an office overlooking Lake Michigan, her very own key to the executive unisex bathroom and full creative control for Three Kisses, Inc., one of the biggest toy manufacturers in the country. Her career was on an upswing, yet the only thing she could think about with Jake Morelli staring so intently at her was how badly she wanted a kiss.

His kiss.

Her gaze hooked on his mouth—so firm and sexy and close. Now if he would only move a fraction forward, dip his head a little more. . . .

"You've been working late." His lips moved around the words so seductively, that for a few heart-pounding moments, her throat went dry.

"H . . . how do you know?"

"One of the perks of living on the first floor. Right beneath you." His gaze darkened. "I can hear you moving around at night. The living room, the kitchen, the bedroom."

The last word slid into her ears, teased her senses and reminded her of a hot summer night when she'd found the mutt from hell going through the trash on the front stoop. She'd spent an entire evening going door to door in search of his rightful home. Jake hadn't been the lackadaisical owner, but he'd helped her lug the dog around and check with the rest of the tenants. After a fruitless and exhausting search, they'd wound up back at his apartment. And then he'd touched her. And then he'd kissed her. And then. . . .

She wiped at a sudden trickle of sweat near her temple.

Stop it. That was over and done with, a weak moment better forgotten. She'd been frazzled and frustrated, and he'd been so sweaty and handsome and half-dressed, wearing only a pair of worn jeans. The sight of all that tanned flesh, dark hair and those wicked eyes had caused temporary amnesia. She'd forgotten all about Three Kisses, about her briefcase full of work, about the overgrown dog licking at her toes.

She'd forgotten everything except Jake.

Never again.

She took a deep breath, desperate to revive the

thousand or so brain cells that had collapsed at his nearness. Remember the Double Fudge Ecstasy, she told herself. After one teeny, tiny taste at the campus ice cream shop, she'd spent half a semester in graduate school being a slave to her craving. By her final year, she'd managed, after an extra ten pounds, to lick that obsession, and she could, *would* lick this one.

Ugh, *licking* was not the verb to be thinking of with Jake so close and looking so, mmm . . . *lickable*.

She leaned in, he leaned in. Despite the twenty-something degree weather, the Christmas lights draping the lobby, and her determination *not* to kiss Jake Morelli, their breaths mingled and it was that hot summer night all over again.

"Does somebody know where I can find Gigi Stevens?"

Sam's head snapped back and her gaze darted past Jake to see a teenaged kid wearing a purple and orange tie-dyed T-shirt, baggy jeans and a dozen multi-colored love beads around his neck.

He held up a white paper sack with a half moon logo imprinted in blue and gold. "Mystic Muffin at your service."

"What?" Jake asked.

"Mystic Muffin," the boy repeated. "Where we feed your body and your spirit."

"A New Age shop," Sam explained.

"And totally organic bakery," the kid added.

"I've got a package of blessing seeds and two jumbo muffins that are losing their freshness, so if you guys'll point me in the right direction, I'll be gone and you can carry on with your love fest."

Love. The word stuck in Sam's head and a wave of anger swept through her, effectively killing the desire which had momentarily fogged her common sense.

Desire, of all the lowdown, dirty, manipulative . . .

"I don't believe this," she muttered. *Granny Gigi*. "I'll take the delivery to her." She reached for the bag.

"No can do." The white bag dangled out of her reach. "See my button? It says 'delivery guy'. That means me. I'm the guy. Besides, no delivery, no tip, and this guy's gotta eat."

"Here." She fished in her purse and handed him a five. The bag landed in her hands as the boy took the money.

"It's all yours, lady. Skeet's the name if you need anything else."

But the only thing Sam needed was distance. She'd nearly kissed Jake Morelli. Worse, she'd *wanted* to kiss him.

She still did.

"I, uh, it was nice seeing you. Gotta go." She plopped her briefcase and the Mystic Muffin bag on top of the large box she'd hauled home from work, and hefted it into her arms.

"Let me give you a hand—" Jake started.

"No. I'm fine." Or she would be the minute she put about thirty feet and a few floors between herself and the sexy Italian currently sending her hormones into overdrive.

"Wow, dude," Skeet said as Sam headed for the elevator as fast as she could. "She's got really great karma."

"Tell me about it." Jake's deep voice floated into the elevator after her.

Sam melted against the wall and closed her eyes. *Willpower*, she told herself, summoning her control and resisting the urge to march back out and lay one on his sinfully handsome mouth. *It's all about willpower*.

Which Sam obviously didn't have, because by the time she reached the third floor and Gigi's attic apartment, she still felt *this* close to stripping naked and worshipping at Jake Morelli's feet. She was flustered, her nerves buzzing, her lips still tingling.

"Granny Gigi," she called out when she opened the door to the old woman's attic apartment. She plopped the box inside the doorway and peered through the huge potted plants growing here and there, making the room look more like a *Wild Kindgom* episode than an attic loft. "Front and center. Right now!"

A shock of white hair appeared from behind a large potted fern. "Why, hello, dear."

Sam glared at her ninety-two-year-old great-grandmother, a small slip of a woman in round wire-rimmed glasses, a pink mumu and white orthopedic shoes. She resembled a New Age version of Granny from *The Beverly Hillbillies*.

"You did it, didn't you?" Sam demanded.

"Did what?" Gigi pulled off her gardening gloves. Her dozen or so silver bracelets tinkled like chimes as she reached for a watering pitcher.

"I almost kissed Jake Morelli and it's all your fault. You put a love spell on me."

"I did not. Why, I haven't done a love spell since . . ." Her words trailed off as she seemed to think. "Why, since I tried to hook Rose up with that exotic male dancer we hired for her sixty-fifth birthday party, which, I might add, was over ten years ago." Her forehead crinkled. "Or was that eleven years ago?"

"Rose? Rose Spellman? Isn't she married to a plumber?"

"That's Rose Spellman-Harper now, and I'm afraid the plumber was my fault. You see, when I recited the part about Rose needing a professional to keep her equipment working properly, my own toilet had backed up and I think I got a little confused."

"From a G-string to a pair of overalls and a tool

belt. Yeah, I'd say some wires got crossed on that one."

"Not wires, dear. Energy. Anyhow, it all worked out for the best because Harvey turned out to be quite the expert when it comes to pipes, especially his own." Gigi's face crinkled with another smile, her blue eyes twinkling. "So what's this about nearly kissing that darling Jake Morelli?"

Sam's eyes narrowed. "You swear you haven't been combing my hairbrush when I'm not looking?"

"If I were going to cast a love spell, I'd go for nail clippings, dear." A frown furrowed her forehead. "Or maybe it's hair *and* fingernails." She shook her head. "No, I think those are ingredients for a voodoo doll. I'll have to ask cousin Merline. Voodoo's her specialty. . . ."

So much for blaming Granny Gigi for her near fall from grace. Her weakness for Jake was completely her own. Darn it.

"Besides," Granny Gigi added, "the only thing I have of Jake Morelli's is this lovely business card." Her eyes twinkled as she pulled the card from her pocket.

"Give me that." Sam snatched the card and shoved it into her skirt pocket. Just in case Gigi decided to make a few calls to cousin Merline. "Here." Sam handed over the bakery bag.

"For me?" Gigi's face lit with excitement as she

peeked inside. "How ever did you know I was in need of blessing seeds?"

"You ordered them."

"I did?" She seemed to search her memory for a minute. "Why, yes. Yes, I think I did. I called the Mystic Meatloaf just this morning, in fact. Or was that yesterday?"

"That's Muffin, Granny Gigi. Mystic *Muffin*."

"Why, whenever did they start serving muffins?"

"They've always served muffins."

Gigi looked doubtful. "But I could have sworn that was meatloaf they delivered with my eye-of-newt order last week. Or was that my essence of eucalyptus? Oh, well. Whatever it was, it was very good." She put the bag off to the side and sat down on an overstuffed pink couch. Granny Gigi had a thing for pink and plants. "So you really kissed him?"

"*Almost* kissed him."

"The intent was still there. The desire. The passion." Gigi sighed. "I miss your Great-Grandpa Hal."

"He's been gone for twenty-eight years."

"The twenty-eight most lonely years of my life." Gigi gave another deep sigh. "Now it's just me all by my lonesome."

"You and a few hamsters and a cat and about two dozen fish, and me," Sam added. "You've always got me."

"That's nice, dear. But I'm talking about great-great-grandchildren. Babies. Lots of babies. Mona has twelve daughters and nineteen grandchildren, and Esther has seven boys and fourteen grandchildren and Rose. . . ."

Mona, Esther and Rose. The infamous Spellman sisters and Gigi's weekly poker buddies.

"Rose has fourteen children," Gigi went on, "and double that number in grandchildren, including a brand-new great-grandbaby born just two months ago."

"I'm getting hives just thinking about it."

"Children are a blessing."

"Messy blessings that cry and poop and kick. Especially kick, and I've got the bruised shins to prove it."

"Did Patrick kick you again?"

Patrick was one of the toddlers in research and development, and a walking poster boy for birth control, as far as Sam was concerned. "He not only kicked, he bit me yesterday."

"He's probably just starved for attention."

"He took a big enough bite out of me to rule starving out of the equation. Face it, Granny Gigi, I'm just not a kid person."

"Not now, but once you have a few of your own—"

"I'm not having any of my own. I don't have time for kids. Or Jake Morelli."

"He wants twelve."

"Who?"

"Jake Morelli."

"So?"

"*Sooo*," she drew the word out, "I'd love to have twelve great-great-grandchildren."

"You'll have to settle for the Chia pet I got you for Christmas, and this." Sam opened the box she'd lugged in and pulled out her surefire ticket to the vice presidency of marketing for Three Kisses, Inc.

"What is that?"

"A doll." *The* doll. "She looks like a three-month old. Feels like a three-month old. And—" Sam planted a kiss on the baby's satiny cheek. The infant cooed. "She responds like a three-month old," Sam declared with all the pride of a new mother.

Mother? Wait a second. No way was she a *mother*. Creator. She'd been in on the project at every level from inception, until now, the verge of Miss Kiss's debut the day after tomorrow on New Year's Eve.

"Her skin is heat-sensitive," she told Gigi. "You kiss her or stroke her and she coos, and she doesn't feel like plastic. Josie down in research and development is an Einstein with synthetics. Miss Kiss feels real."

"But she isn't real."

"Thank God. And look, she comes with this neat carrier that's the same size as a real infant carrier. The whole concept is to introduce a life-size, life-like replica—"

A loud bark cut into her spiel. She glanced down to see her monstrous-sized mutt—a cross between a Great Dane, a German Shepherd and a St. Bernard—crawl from between two huge flower pots. A dollop of white cream topped his nose and yellow cake crumbs trembled on his whiskers.

"Granny Gigi, how many times do I have to tell you? Keep Prince out of the Twinkies." She shifted Miss Kiss, carrier and all, to Granny Gigi's sofa as she knelt by the dog. A large tongue lapped at her cheek. "The vet says too much sugar is bad for him."

"Oh, pooh. A little sugar never hurt anyone. I'm telling you," Granny Gigi went on, "you don't know what you're missing. Babies are warm and cuddly and loving."

"I don't want kids in my life right now. I've got enough to worry about with Prince. Speaking of which, I'll pick up the doll later after I get him settled downstairs." She grabbed the dog's collar and tugged him toward the door. As if Prince knew a nice, nutritious—tasteless—bowl of dry dog food waited for him, he dug in his paws and tried not to budge. "I'm happy just the way I am. Single and busy."

"We'll see." The soft voice followed her, but when she turned around to give Granny Gigi a warning look, the woman was little more than a pink blur behind an overgrown ficus.

"We will not see," she called out. "Do you hear me? No funny business."

"Why, I wouldn't dream of it," the ficus replied.

"It's not the dreaming I'm worried about," Sam grumbled as she grabbed her briefcase and tugged Prince out into the hallway. "It's the doing."

Sam's muffled good-bye echoed over the air-conditioning vent and Jake stifled a pang of guilt. Okay, so he'd been eavesdropping, but it wasn't as if he had a choice. With the cold weather, he had to turn the air conditioner off, and without the hum of the unit, there was nothing to keep him from hearing the goings on in Gigi's apartment—if he really listened.

I like my life the way it is.

Sam's words replayed in his head and made him frown. Why, he wasn't so sure. After all, Samantha had never claimed to be anything other than the career-driven woman she appeared. She was busy, focused, and not the least bit interested in anything long-term, and Jake should know. For the past fifteen years, he'd been the king of the busy, focused, living for the here-and-now bachelors, and he'd known dozens of women like Sam.

Known, as in past tense.

At thirty-six, Jake Morelli had made senior partner in one of the most prestigious corporate law firms in the country. He'd achieved every career goal he'd set for himself, and now it was time for the next step in his life. Settling down.

But then Samantha Skye threw a wrench in the works when she showed up on his doorstep with a giant, half-starved dog overflowing her arms. It wasn't so much that she'd been drop-dead gorgeous with her long, jet-black hair, creamy white skin and the brightest, most mesmerizing green eyes he'd ever had the pleasure of gazing into. What had snagged his interest more than anything had been the desperate look in those eyes, the compassion, and all because of a homeless dog. Jake had been a goner, and totally convinced he'd found *the* woman. The one he intended to have a happily-ever-after with, complete with a house in the suburbs and a dozen kids to add to the massive Morelli clan—his nine brothers and sisters, all of whom had settled down and started families.

All except Jake.

He'd only meant to kiss her, to get a taste of the sweet, compassionate woman destined to be the next Morelli, but at that first meeting of mouths, something had happened. Heat. Sizzle. *Bam*.

She'd been soft, warm, giving, and so out of control in his arms; he'd been hooked. Then he'd received a wake-up call. He'd opened his eyes early the next morning to find the bed empty, a note with the single word, "Thanks", and his happily-ever-after had taken a nosedive straight into a one-night stand.

Later that day he'd seen her headed to work: cool, sexy, and detached in a crisp black business suit. It didn't take a genius to realize that Samantha Skye was a sleek, polished, well-put-together career type only interested in a night of pleasure.

The very type of woman he'd left behind when he'd traded in his black two-seater Porsche for a fully equipped Suburban with family extras, walked away from his high-rise apartment with a jaccuzi and mirrored ceilings, and given up everything else he'd come to love and cherish as a single, successful bachelor.

His gaze hooked on the big screen TV taking up half the opposite wall. Well, almost everything. As long as he watched at least a half hour of family television in addition to ESPN, he figured the TV didn't count as a last grasp at his bachelorhood.

But he'd made the real commitment to finding the future mother of his Morelli dozen three days ago. On Christmas day he'd agreed, after a home-cooked turkey dinner, home videos and enough laughter to make any man homesick, to let his youngest sister find him a woman.

"We'll call it Project Jake," Gina had said eagerly. "With my contacts, we'll have you fixed up in no time. But first things first, we need a list. The three things you absolutely must have in a woman. First off, she has to cook."

Jake liked to eat as much as the next guy. "Sounds good."

"And she should be able to sew. After all, kids are forever ripping hems and tearing sleeves, and she'll surely want to make curtains for the nursery."

Jake wouldn't mind having someone to sew on his buttons. "Sounds good."

"And last but not least—"

"Great in bed?" Instant chemistry? *Bam*?

"Bridge, silly. Mom, Maureen and I need a fourth, and not one of our brothers has managed to marry anybody halfway decent with a deck of cards."

Though Jake hadn't been in wholehearted agreement with all three qualifications, he wasn't having much luck on his own.

What did he have to lose?

Time. Energy. In three days, Jake had been on two lunch dates and two dinner dates, for a total of four prospective candidates, not one of whom Jake had felt more than a passing interest in, much less *bam*.

A last grasp at his bachelorhood.

That explained his overwhelming attraction to

Samantha. She was just another bad habit left over from his sex-crazed single days, and Jake was an expert at overcoming bad habits. It was all about strength, about taking charge and resisting his baser urges.

The big-screen TV stared back at him as if to say, "Yeah, right."

Hey, even Superman had his kryptonite.

"Your destiny lies right beneath your nose." Samantha read the fortune cookie that had arrived with a carton of sweet-and-sour chicken and some fried rice from Le Duck, her favorite takeout restaurant around the corner.

Right beneath your nose. . . . Her gaze strayed to the carpeted floor where she sat Indian-style near her coffee table, Prince sprawled a few feet away. In her mind's eye, she saw beyond, to the apartment below. Jake's apartment. *Jake.*

Before she could dwell on the thought, her phone rang.

"Are you ready for tomorrow?" Josie Farrington demanded when Sam said hello.

"I'm going over the presentation right now."

"So am I."

"I thought you had a date tonight." Josie had had a date almost every night since she'd hit the big 3-4 and decided it was time to find Mr. Right.

"*Had* being the operative word. You know, Sue over in statistics was right. You can tell everything about a man by his E-mail address."

"And here I thought it was his shoe size."

"I'm talking character. Take tonight's date for instance. Bob Cantrell from sales and marketing. I should have known when I saw *S&MBob* on the company roster that something was up, but I figured the first part referred to his department. Big mistake."

"How big?"

"We go back to his place after dinner and the next thing I know, he's standing in front of me wearing a spiked collar and nothing else, and asking—no, *begging* me to tie him up." She sighed. "You're so lucky, Sam. You never reel in the wierdos."

"That's because I'm not fishing."

"Me either. At least not anymore tonight. Now about tomorrow's presentation. . . ." Josie launched into a recap of all the important points of the Miss Kiss project while Sam fingered the business card she'd confiscated from Granny Gigi.

". . . original Miss Kiss is blond-haired, blue-eyed, but we'll do the full range of hair colors, from brunette to redhead, silvery blond to strawberry—"

"What if they just use their first name?" Sam cut in.

"I don't think it matters. They'll all be Miss Kiss dolls."

"Not the dolls. The men. What if they use their first name for an E-mail address?"

"Well, it usually says they're relaxed, friendly, nice."

And handsome. And sexy. With the most incredible eyes and a wicked smile and . . .

Earth to Sam. Jake isn't the man for you, remember? No man is the man for you because you're not looking for a man. You're looking for a vice-presidency.

Men were too distracting, and if there was one thing Sam didn't need right now, it was a distraction. Even one as good-looking as Jake Morelli.

Especially one as good-looking as Jake Morelli.

She knew from watching her own father that it took complete focus and concentration to reach the top. While growing up, she'd rarely seen him, even though they'd lived under the same roof. Quality time had consisted of a monthly dinner, a tradition still carried on today. Of course, her father often brought along business contacts when they met on the first Monday of each month, and so quality time felt more like corporate hour, but Sam didn't really mind. She was proud of him. He now owned one of the largest investment firms in Chicago, an accomplishment he owed solely to his dedication and drive.

And Sam was no less driven.

Her gaze strayed to the fortune, her attention lingering on the word *destiny*.

Crazy, because Sam didn't believe in such a thing, not for herself, anyhow, not since she'd been five years old and had realized that she would never do any of the things her late mother had been capable of: no levitating inanimate objects, knowing when someone was at the door before he knocked, or changing her eye color with just a few whispered words. Her mother, who'd died in a car accident when Sam was only four, had been a natural witch. It had been her calling. Her destiny.

Unfortunately, said destiny skipped a generation and Samantha had turned out to be plain, old Sam with boring green eyes. Her only natural talent had been her creativity, which she'd geared toward a career in advertising. The hours were long, the work tough, but she thrived on the competition.

A chip off the old block.

Grabbing a spreadsheet off the coffee table, she placed it in her lap. There. Her so-called destiny lay right beneath her nose, all right—in a pile of work on the new Miss Kiss project.

A surefire ticket to the top of the corporate food chain as long as the next few days played out according to plan. Tomorrow was the presentation to the shareholders. The day after, the preview of the first advertising pilot, and then the grand finale, the New Year's Eve gala and the official introduction of Miss Kiss to the local media.

"Sam?" Josie's voice finally penetrated her thoughts.

"Right here." She crumpled the slip of paper and tossed it into an already overflowing waste basket. There. No more fortunes.

And most of all, no more Jake.

Chapter Two

"Maybe she has some sort of disease that makes her allergic to the little buggers." The suggestion came from Rose Spellman-Harper, one of the three blue-haired ladies gathered around Gigi's dining room table.

"My Sam does not have any sort of disease."

"It's nothing to be ashamed of." Rose's gaze dropped to the small infant in her arms, a three-month-old little girl with porcelain skin, jet-black hair and cornflower blue eyes. "Elizabeth's father is allergic to her. At least that's his excuse for not making his monthly visits. But that's all right," she said to the baby, "Great-Grandma Rose loves you."

Gigi fought down a wave of envy as she watched Rose fawn over Elizabeth. "Sam does not have any allergies, much less a disease. She's the picture of good health."

"It could be psychological. Maybe she was traumatized as a child." Mona Spellman-Fisher, the oldest of the three sisters, handed Rose a formula bottle before picking up the cards Gigi dealt her. "That would explain her hesitation when it comes to having her own family."

"She did take her mother's passing pretty hard, but she seemed to adjust well enough after that. She was only four and children that age are very resilient."

"Of course, dear." Esther Spellman-Smythe studied her cards. "All right, I'll see your eye-of-newt and raise you three packages of blessing seeds." She added the bet to the center of the table. "Perhaps she just doesn't *like* babies."

The possibility hung in the air around the table as three speculative gazes examined Gigi as if to say, "Well?"

"Nonsense," Gigi declared. "How could she not like babies?"

"Well, I don't like dogs," Mona said.

"And I don't like goldfish," Esther chimed in. "And Rose can't stand snakes."

"A baby is not a snake. No, I think Sam's problem is that she's never really been around babies. Why, I hated olives until I ate them at my cousin

Sonya's wedding. One taste and you couldn't tear me away from the buffet. Samantha just needs a great big taste of what she's missing."

Agreement floated around the group and the conversation turned to some serious poker for the next forty-five minutes, until the last hand had been dealt and Rose walked away with the winnings—the makings for a pot full of Lovin' From the Oven, a love potion for Elizabeth's mother.

"I do envy you getting to take care of that angel," Gigi said as Rose gathered up baby Elizabeth's diaper bag.

"You'll have one of your own to fuss over one day."

"Chin up." Esther patted Gigi's shoulder. "Miracles happen every day."

But Gigi was afraid it would take more than a miracle to bring Samantha around. This situation called for some major intervention. A life-changing event. A little bit of magic.

The clock struck midnight as Gigi closed the door behind the last sister.

"You already know what I'm thinking, don't you, girl?" she asked Diva. The black cat purred an enthusiastic response as Gigi eyed the Miss Kiss doll Sam had left sitting on her couch earlier that evening. Bright blue eyes stared back at her from a perfectly shaped face dotted with rosy cheeks. "You may look real, sweetie, but you're not." A smile curved her lips. "Not yet, that is."

"You're beautiful, Sam." Jake hovered over her, moonlight sculpting his muscles, making him look so big and fierce and oh, so sexy, and Sam couldn't help herself.

She was weak. Hungry. Starved.

She slid her arms around his neck and pulled him down. His lips met hers, tongues tangled and heat sizzled through her body. Her nipples throbbed, her thighs ached. His hard body pressed into hers, pushing her deeper into the mattress.

His mouth worked a blazing trail down her neck, and then the slope of her breasts where he paused to draw one aching tip into his mouth. He suckled her and she clasped at him, body arching, hips rotating, begging for more. For . . .

The thought trailed off as his mouth moved lower. And lower. And . . .

"Oh, yes," she gasped. "Do that." She caught her bottom lip. "And that." Mmmmm . . . "And *that*—"

Caboommmmmm!

Wow. She'd heard of fireworks going off. She'd even felt some heavy duty roman candles with Jake that first time. But this was a bonafide explosion.

Her eyes popped open.

No Jake. Just a big throw pillow resting on top of her heaving chest and one strategically wedged between her . . .

A dream. A very vivid, very erotic dream. But a dream, nonetheless. Not real. No kissing and panting and—

The thought shattered as another muffled boom shook the ceiling, followed by a loud cry that completely returned her to the here and now and the fact that something very strange was happening.

Her gaze was riveted overhead as the ceiling seemed to tremble.

Granny Gigi.

Sam tore out of the apartment, stabbed at the elevator, only to give it up and rush up the back staircase. A few frantic moments later, she shoved open Gigi's apartment door.

"Granny Gigi!" Her frantic voice bounced off the walls. "Are you all right? Are you hurt? Oh, my God, where are—" The words suddenly stuck in her throat as her gaze fastened on the doll carrier sitting on Granny Gigi's couch.

Only it wasn't the carrier that caught her attention, it was the doll kicking and cooing inside. Or rather, the baby kicking and cooing and—

"Surprise!" Granny Gigi burst through two palm fronds and Sam's heart stopped beating altogether.

"This can't be happening." Sam shook her head. "It *isn't* happening."

"Of course it's happening." Gigi clapped her hands. "Isn't it wonderful?"

Sam turned a horrified gaze on Gigi. "This definitely is not happening." A hysterical bubble of laughter burst from her lips. "It's a dream. You're a dream. That's a dream." She pointed to the cooing bundle. "Just like Jake."

Granny Gigi's eyes lit up. "You've been dreaming about Jake?"

"Yes. I mean, no. I mean, yes I have been and I can say that because you're not real and—ouch!" Cat claws burned up her leg courtesy of Diva, sending a very real bolt of pain through her body and completely shooting her dream theory to hell and back.

"Diva gets a little nervous when you raise your voice. Isn't that right, baby?" Granny Gigi scooped up the cat and deposited her near a neon pink scratching post. "Now, dear. Back to the dream." Her eyes twinkled. "To Jake."

Shock beat at Sam's senses. "Granny Gigi, there's a baby sitting on your couch and you want to know about my Jake dream?"

"Every juicy detail. Were you working on the Morelli dozen?"

"Yes. No." She shook her head and tried to get a hold of herself. "Who cares? There's a *baby* sitting on your couch."

"It's your doll," Granny Gigi explained. "I mean, it isn't anymore because my spell worked, but it was."

"Your spell?" The room started to spin as the truth hit her. A spell. As in magic. As in . . . *baby*.

"The first two times, I got a little confused," Gigi rushed on as Sam leaned against a nearby wall and did her damndest not to hyperventilate.

"But the third time was a charm," Gigi was saying, her mouth moving but her words not quite keeping up, or maybe it was Sam's brain that couldn't keep up. "I said the incantation, and ta-da, instant change."

Sam's heart pounded, her blood rushed, her thoughts whirled. *Get a grip,* she told herself, gathering what little control she had. She let out a deep, shaky breath. "This is a real baby?"

"Yes, dear."

"A real *real* baby?"

"Yes, dear."

Her gaze collided with Gigi's. "But why would you do something like this?"

"So you could see how wonderful babies are, and realize how much you want one."

"The only thing I'm realizing at this moment is that I really should keep some valium on hand." At the rate her heart was beating, she'd have a cardiac arrest before she ever got a chance to see the inside of her new office courtesy of Miss Kiss and . . . "Oh, my God. My doll!"

"Yes, she is a doll, isn't she? So cute and cuddly looking. Why, she puts Rose's great-grandbaby Elizabeth to shame."

"This prototype is one of a kind. The star of the next three days. The center of my universe. The ticket to my promotion." Her gaze swiveled back to the cooing infant. "I think I'm going to be sick."

Gigi's eyes filled with concern. "Is it something you ate?"

"Change it back," Sam blurted. "Now. Change it back."

"But—"

"*Change it back*. I need it for tomorrow."

"Tomorrow? My goodness, that is a pickle. Why, it took me all evening to do this. And now I'm so plum tuckered out, I can't even begin to—"

"Now!" Sam's pleading gaze shifted to Gigi. "*Please.*"

"Okay." Gigi nodded vigorously. "Just calm down, honey. Let me see . . ." Gigi went silent for a long, coo-filled moment that made Sam's heart pound even more furiously.

"Well?"

"I'm thinking."

"About what? Just change it back."

"It's not that simple."

"Why not? You did the incantation, it worked. Just reverse the incantation."

"I know."

"So do it."

"Okay . . . abracadabra, three winks and a kiss . . . or was that five winks and a kiss? Or one wink and three kisses? Or three kisses and five winks?"

The baby started to cry. "Don't you have a book or something?" Sam demanded.

"Sure I do. Every good witch has a spell book. It's right there next to the baby . . ." Her words trailed off as her gaze fell on the spell book and the long trail of drool draped over the page.

"Oh, no," Gigi snatched up the book and slapped at the wetness, which smeared the writing even more. *"Oh, no."*

"Don't tell me you can't read it."

"Okay, I won't tell you."

"Granny Gigi! You have to do something." The cat started to meow. The birds started to caw. The baby cried louder. The noise level rose, and Sam barely resisted the urge to scream. "You have to!"

"I know."

"So think. *Remember!*"

"I'm trying." Granny Gigi touched her temples. "But it's just so noisy in here. I need quiet. Calm. Serenity. My energy's frazzled. My karma's got a kink. My thoughts are—"

"I'll take the baby while you regroup." What the hell was she saying? "Five minutes." Sam turned toward the baby and summoned her courage. "You've got five minutes."

* * *

Ten minutes later Sam stood downstairs in her apartment, the carrier on her dining room table, and stared at Miss Kiss. Tear-filled blue eyes stared back at her as the baby cried. And cried. And cried.

Calm. Cool. She told herself. Just stay calm and cool the way you did when the ad copy got lost for the Squishy-Squiggy-Glob Man. And then there'd been the total revamp of the Dancing Dottie doll that she'd done in less than twenty-four hours. . . .

"Come on, Gigi," she prayed, waiting for a miracle.

Instead, the infant continued to cry, Sam's temples started to throb and Prince started to bark.

She was going to have to do it—to pick it up. She took a deep breath, slid her hands beneath the wiggling bundle and lifted. She held the baby at arms length, as if she were holding a ticking bomb.

She wasn't. It was just a baby. A doll that just happened to be a baby. And not just any baby, but Miss Kiss, and she'd held Miss Kiss dozens of times. She'd dressed her. Undressed her. Even accidentally popped off a leg, an incident that had sent Josie straight into a box of Godiva chocolates until Sam had managed to shove the appendage back on without so much as a scratch.

She knew the blasted doll inside out, naked and clothed, one leg versus two. She could handle this.

She pulled the baby in closer. She jiggled, cuddled, and begged some more. "Please, baby."

Samantha barely heard the ringing phone over the high-pitched wailing and her own frantic voice.

She juggled the baby to one arm, snatched up the phone and cradled it with her chin. "Oh, hi, Mrs. Walker. Sure. I know it's half-past midnight. Yes, yes. I'll turn my TV down right away. I know hard-working tenants are trying to sleep—oops, my other line." *Click*. "Oh, hi Mr. Rigby. Yes, yes, I know you and the missus don't get too much time alone and I'm sorry I'm ruining your—got to catch my other line." *Click*. "Yes, Mrs. Walker, I heard that boom earlier. Mr. Rigby was probably playing with his son's chemistry set. And no, I'm not crying. Yes, yes, I know if you were single and living alone at my age, you'd be crying, but trust me, I'm fine. It's the radio—sorry, got another call." Five more calls, five more apologies and Sam finally managed to punch in Granny Gigi's number.

"Have you figured it out?"

"No, but my goldfish turned purple."

"What?"

"I think I confused the realism spell with color morphing."

"Just fix it. Please, Granny Gigi."

"Give me five more minutes."

Fifteen minutes later, Sam had a splitting headache, the baby was still crying and she'd finally figured out why. The baby's dress was soaked through, along with the front of Sam's best silk nightgown. Without a diaper in sight, she finally admitted that the situation required more than a simple fix. She needed help.

Grabbing the phone, she punched in the number and settled for the next best thing.

"Hello." Jake Morelli's deep, rumbling voice floated over the line and made the hairs on the back of her neck tingle.

"I need you," she blurted out.

"Samantha?"

"Now."

She needed him.

Jake's first impulse was to snatch the phone backup and tell her to find another boy toy. Okay, so it wasn't his first impulse. But it ran a close second, right behind the sudden need to race upstairs, rip off his clothes, and give her what she wanted.

Not that he would. They were totally wrong for each other. He was past those carefree days of mindless, thoughtless, gratuitious sex. He wanted meaning. Depth.

Or at least a little breakfast the morning after.

Even so, he found himself standing on her doorstep a full minute later, panting from the mad rush up the stairs. Fully clothed, of course. He hadn't completely lost his mind.

Just his control. Momentarily. But as soon as she opened up the door and threw herself into his arms, he would set the record straight. No boy toy, here.

"Thank God you're here," she declared as she opened the door. She looked so relieved, so flushed and so . . . wet?

His gaze riveted on her chest, on the taut outline of her nipples against the damp silk of her nightgown and he swallowed. Okay, so maybe one more night of lust couldn't hurt. He'd have a chance to work her out of his system. He'd be willing to eat Pop Tarts alone for another up-close-and-personal look at Miss Samantha Skye minus the wet top. . . .

The thought faded as he noticed the crying coming from inside her apartment. "What's that noise?"

"A baby."

"What baby?"

"My doll—" Her throat seemed to close around the words. Her frantic gaze darted behind her. "My, uh, *friend* Dollie, yeah that's her, is, um, having, um, surgery and she dropped her baby off here." She nodded. "Yeah, surgery. She can't very well take care of a baby if she's in the hospital, so I'm baby-sitting for her."

"So why did you call me?"

"I haven't exactly done much baby-sitting and it's a little more intense than I expected." Her desperate green gaze collided with his. "Can you help me?"

He stifled his disappointment, gave one last lingering glance at her perfectly taut nipples and walked inside. "Where is he?"

"It's over there."

"It?"

"She," she clarified. "I think. I mean. . . ." She nodded. "Yeah, it's a she. Miss Kiss."

"Miss what?"

"Kiss, uh, *Krissy*. Yeah, that's her name. Little Miss Krissy."

"Well, little Krissy," Jake said, eyeing the beautiful baby girl. "What seems to be the trouble?"

"She's wet," Sam said over his shoulder. "I'm wet. We're both wet."

"Then a diaper change might be a good idea."

"I don't have any."

He turned an incredulous gaze on her. "You don't have diapers?"

"No."

"What about formula?" She shook her head. "Your friend dropped her baby off without diapers and formula?"

"It was an emergency."

He watched her nibble on her lower lip, a sight that caught him completely off guard because Miss Samantha Skye, executive extraordinaire, never nibbled. She was the picture of calm, detached coolness. Usually. All except for that one night when she'd stood on his doorstep, so soft and compassionate and worried over that damned dog. And now.

"I'll go after some diapers," he said. "And formula."

"And leave me here?" Panicked eyes met his. "I mean, she's wet and she's crying and I don't have anything—"

"You go and I'll stay." *Sucker*. "Come on, darlin'." He hefted the baby into his arms. "Uncle Jake's here," he said as Samantha disappeared into the bedroom to change.

She emerged a few minutes later wearing a T-shirt and jeans and looking as sexy as ever even in a dry shirt. "Thanks, Jake," she said, pausing, her coat in hand. "If I can do anything to repay you, just let me know."

He could think of a few things. The press of her body against his. Her full luscious lips leaving a blazing trail across his skin. Her heat sucking him in, deeper, deeper—

"Water," he blurted out. "It's, um, a little hot in here."

She gave him a puzzled look before motioning

toward the kitchen. "Sure, help yourself."

If only.

The first thing Sam noticed when she returned home after hitting five convenience stores, was the unusual quiet.

"Jake?" she called out as she opened the door, set the bags inside and started unbuttoning her coat. "Is everything okay—" Her words stumbled into one another as she caught sight of him lying on her couch, the sleeping baby cuddled on his chest.

"She conked out right after I changed her."

Her gaze traveled to the baby's bottom. "Is that my scarf?"

"Saw it in the pile of laundry over in the corner. Soft, square-shaped. Worked like a charm."

"That's a two-hundred-dollar scarf."

"And worth every penny. I tried two different linen napkins and some cashmere thingie before I hit pay dirt."

"My napkins? My cashmere shawl?"

"Cashmere's soft, but itchy. Isn't that right, Krissy?"

The baby sighed and snuggled closer to Jake, and the anger died in Sam's throat. It wasn't as if she couldn't afford another scarf. After the Miss Kiss coming-out party, she could afford a dozen. *If* there was a party.

She forced the thought aside. Granny Gigi

would get the spell right, Miss Kiss would revert back to sensitized plastic, and Jake would be out of her apartment, and her life. Again.

Her gaze went to Jake's handiwork and she found herself smiling. "That's pretty ingenious."

He grinned, a wicked tilt to his sensuous lips that sent a spurt of heat through her. "I didn't get elected favorite uncle among thirty-eight nieces and nephews for nothing."

Her mouth dropped open. "Thirty-eight?"

"With twins on the way courtesy of my youngest sister, Gina. She's newly married. The twins will be her first. I've got three sisters and six brothers, all married and carrying on the Morelli name."

"Ten kids. Family get-togethers must be something."

"We rented the Sears Tower for Christmas dinner." Her gaze flew to his and she caught him smiling. "Just kidding. There aren't that many of us."

"But there will be once you add your dozen to the brood?"

"How do you. . . ." His words trailed off as his gaze lit on a nearby air-conditioning vent.

"Not me. It's Granny Gigi," she added. "The most I pick up is David Hall in 3D, part-time construction worker and full-time Casanova, at least according to the stories he tells his buddies about his latest babe conquests." She picked up the bags and walked the few feet into the adjoining kitchen.

"A dozen," she mused as she started unloading the first bag. "I can't imagine one, much less a dozen. The most I ever had was a Betsy Wetsy doll."

"No brothers and sisters?" Jake's voice carried from the living room.

"I'm an only child. My mom died when I was four."

"So your dad raised you?"

"No, three different housekeepers did that." Now why had she told him that? "My dad had a very demanding job," she rushed on. "He was just really busy. Granny Gigi was always there for me, but she didn't live with us. I saw her mostly on weekends. Other than my dad and a few distant cousins, she's all I have."

"What does your dad do?"

"Investment banking."

"Investment banking . . . as in Skye Investments?"

"That's him."

"I saw him at a corporate fund-raiser once. He was sitting in the corner, a laptop in front of him. My impression is he works nonstop."

"He's very driven." *A chip off the old block*. Sam wasn't sure why the thought didn't give her the usual rush of pride. Her fingers tightened around a tube of diaper rash ointment she pulled from the bag.

"My dad's a retired plumber. Him and my mom just celebrated their forty-fifth anniversary on Christmas Eve. I got them season tickets to the Bulls."

"That's thoughtful."

"My dad thought so. But my mom wasn't too thrilled."

"She's not into sports?"

"She's into daughters-in-law." At Sam's questioning glance, he added, "I'm the last single Morelli. But it's not as if I'm not trying to change that status. I've turned over a new leaf. I haven't had beer or Cheeze Doodles in over six months."

"You poor thing. I bet you haven't burped or scratched yourself in weeks, either."

"Now, I wouldn't go that far." His voice sounded right behind her and she turned to find him standing there, the baby cradled in his arms, a smile on his face.

Her heart pounded and she busied herself unloading the second bag. "You're young. What's the hurry to settle down?"

He leaned against a nearby counter, and crossed his long, jeans-clad legs. "I'm thirty-six. At my age, my dad already had half of us. If I want a large family, I have to act now, which is why I traded in the sports car, got rid of the mirrors on my ceiling—"

"Now that's a definite shame." Especially when she had a quick vision of tangled sheets and Jake, and Jake's reflection. A double whammy.

"So far, none of it has made much difference. I'm ready to take the plunge, but damned if I can find a woman to do it with. Most of the women I meet are lawyers, either happily married or happily single."

"And probably none of them are too thrilled about a Morelli dozen."

"I take it you don't want any kids?"

"Are you kidding? I barely have time to feed my dog."

Jake's gaze strayed to Prince, who overflowed a doggie bed near the kitchen table. "I can't believe you kept him."

"Me either." Prince yawned, his monstrous jowls trembled and she couldn't help but smile. "Worst mistake I ever made." Her gaze snagged Jake's again. "So why twelve?"

He shrugged. "I see my dad, how happy he is when he sees all of us together, how fulfilled he looks, and I envy him. You probably can't understand that."

But for an insane second, she could. Until she looked at the eight different brands of baby formula stacked on her counter. Next to the five different types of bottles. Some curved. Some small. Some large. Some with bags. *Crazy*.

"I wish you the best of luck. With twelve, you'll

need it." One, and she was desperate for divine intervention.

"And I wish you the best of luck." He glanced at the clock. "Because it's two in the morning, and I've got an eight A.M. meeting, so you have to take over."

"Oh." She eyed the sleeping baby. "*Oh*."

"She won't bite, Sam." He grinned. "Not for another few months anyway, until she starts teething."

His chuckle soothed her jangled nerves. She took a deep breath and held out her arms. "Okay. I'm ready."

"Glad to hear it, but first things first." He walked over and placed the baby on the dining room table where he'd double-folded her antique quilt and laid it out . . . oh, no, her antique quilt?

"It was the softest thing I could find," he said as if he'd noticed the stricken expression in her eyes. "Now, we need to put a real diaper on her. This thing is warm, but it's not going to absorb much of anything."

"No problem." She retrieved one of the various brands of diapers she'd purchased and handed it to him. "Here you go."

"Not me, Sam. You." He turned her until she faced the table. "You're responsible for her, so you need to know how to change her diaper."

"But I—"

"I'll help you." He stepped up behind her, his

hard-muscled body cradling hers as his arms came around her, his chest solid against her back. "First we'll undo the one she's wearing. Untie the edges."

Samantha worked at the knot, but with Jake so close and smelling so musky and hot and stirring, she went all thumbs.

"Like this." His hands covered hers, his flesh burning into hers, and an aching emptiness swelled inside her. "Now we ease the diaper off and put the other one under her." He guided her, his fingers strong and sure against her own trembling ones.

Trembling? Nerves, she told herself.

It certainly wasn't because of him. Because his body was so hard and warm and close and she wanted him closer.

"See?" his deep, husky voice rumbled in her ear when they'd finished the task. "That wasn't so bad." His lips nuzzled her ear.

She closed her eyes, arching back against him as he licked the sensitive shell of her ear and heat shimmied the length of her spine. Her heart pounded, drumming a wild, crazy beat that made her want to turn and touch him. Absorb him.

His hands moved, slid from hers upward, cupping her elbows, gliding along her upper arms before sliding down to her waist. He rubbed the soft cotton of her T-shirt, then higher, spanning her ribs until he cradled the weight of her breasts.

He massaged and kneaded and a low whimper burst from her lips. Then his hands curved and slid toward her aching nipples—

A soft *coo* bubbled in the air. Sam opened her eyes to see large, dark hands covering her breasts and Miss Kiss staring up at her.

"The baby's awake," she exhaled. What was she doing? This was wrong. Jake was wrong.

"Yeah." His voice was low, strained, as if he battled the same emotions pushing and pulling inside her. "I need to go."

"Yes." *Please*, she begged. Then her gaze swiveled to Miss Kiss. "I mean, no. The baby's awake." The realization suddenly hit her. Sleeping baby, quiet baby. Awake baby . . . she shuddered to think about the rest.

"You'll do fine. Keep her dry, feed her and rock her."

She turned toward him. "But—"

"Bye." He kissed her, a quick hungry kiss that made her head spin. Then he turned on his heel and left, the door slamming shut behind him as if he feared being near her another few moments, the way she feared being near him. He made her forget everything, from her No Jake policy, to the fact that her life, her career, was this close to falling apart.

A *baby*.

"I can do this."

Miss Kiss stared up at her as if to say, "Sure thing," before she opened her mouth and started to cry.

And Sam did the only thing a tired, overworked woman who'd been up half the night could do. She cried, too.

Chapter Three

"Where are you?"

"Josie?" Sam croaked as she grappled for the phone base which had taken a plunge the moment she'd reached blindly toward the nightstand.

"The board meeting is in a half hour, and they'll be calling me mud if you and Miss Kiss don't get your cabooses down here."

Sam forced her eyelids open against the blinding sunlight pouring through the bedroom window. *Sunlight*.

She'd overslept. On one of the most important days in her life, she'd *overslept*. When she, Samantha Skye, didn't dare oversleep on the unimportant days. And all because of. . . .

Images rushed through her mind. The crying. The chaos. The *baby*.

"I'll be right there." She slid the receiver into place and simply lay there. Listening. Dreading. But not a sound echoed through the apartment except the slow thud of her own heart.

A nightmare. Just a weird, distorted, hellish dream brought on by her near kiss with Jake in the lobby yesterday and all Granny Gigi's talk about babies.

Jake. Her body tingled as she remembered him behind her, his hands gliding up to cup her breasts. . . . Okay, that part had been more fantasy than nightmare.

She forced her eyes completely open, said a silent thank you that life as she knew it still existed, and rolled over.

Straight into a soft bundle of sleeping warmth.

"Oh, no."

Sam wasn't sure how she managed, but twenty minutes later, she was dressed and standing at Granny Gigi's door, her coat and briefcase in one arm, and a newly powdered, diapered and fed Miss Kiss in the other.

She knocked on the door with the toe of her pump. "Granny Gigi. Please open up."

Granny Gigi, clad in a pink housecoat, her white hair wrapped around matching pink rollers, opened the door. "Good morning, dear."

"That's a matter of opinion."

"Is something wrong?"

"Well, I've got a very important meeting that I'm late for, I overslept and I still haven't had my coffee." That, in itself, made her a walking terror. "And I'm still holding a baby, in case you haven't noticed."

"Well, my, yes you are."

"I take it you haven't had any luck?"

"Actually, I have. I managed to recreate, after a lot of trial and error, the first four lines."

"There must be an easier way. Can't you just call someone and ask to borrow their spell book?"

Gigi's face lit. "You know, you might be on to something. I mean, spell books are very individual. A witch spends her entire lifetime cultivating her own, but most witches have similar spells and while they won't be exactly like mine, they'll be close. Seeing something similar might help me to decipher my own." She smiled. "You're such a smart girl. I'll get on the phone right now and see what I can come up with."

For the first time, Sam noticed that Granny Gigi's usually rosy cheeks were pale, her eyes heavy lidded.

"How much sleep did you actually get last night?"

"About an hour." She looked puzzled. "Or was

that two hours? Once three A.M. hit, I did sit down to take a break, but a *Ricki Lake* re-run was on and they had transvestites who were sleeping with their boyfriend's father's plumbers, and I couldn't very well miss that. Once it was over, though, I took a nap."

"Granny Gigi, you need more than a nap." Even as desperate as Sam was, she wasn't desperate enough to sacrifice her great granny's health. Besides, Gigi couldn't very well think while exhausted. "Promise me you'll rest today, then you can work on the spell."

"But what will you do in the meantime? Take her to work?"

"Are you kidding? I can't do that."

Okay, so maybe she could, she decided after fruitless phone calls to half the day care centers in Greater Chicago. None of which would admit Miss Kiss without health records showing her latest immunizations. Sam had even broken down and called Jake on the off chance that maybe he was home and could babysit.

No luck. He was off at work, doing the manly thing, leaving the little woman to care for the rug rat all by her lonesome. Of all the chauvinistic, macho. . . .

Okay, so it wasn't *his* rug rat, but it was the principle of the thing. That and the fact that she still hadn't had her coffee.

A gurgle and soft *coo* drew her attention. She glanced down to see a trail of spittle leading from the corner of Miss Kiss's mouth, right across the lapel of her blue silk jacket.

And Jake Morelli really wanted a dozen of these?

Twenty minutes later, Josie met her as she stepped off the elevator on the top floor of Three Kisses, Inc.

"Thank God you're—what's that on your jacket?"

"Don't ask."

"Where's the doll?"

"Don't ask."

"We're in trouble, aren't we?"

She caught the scientist's gaze. "Don't ask. Let's just do this." Sam took a deep breath, mentally recited the story she'd cooked up in the five minutes it had taken her to drop off Miss Kiss in research and development with the other demon children. Despite the morning she'd had, Patrick had kicked her in the shin and started a major run in her pantyhose.

Could the day get any worse?

"Where are the cost-and-profit reports?" Josie asked.

On second thought. . . . She closed her eyes, seeing her hard work scattered across the floor near her coffee table, a leftover carton of sweet-

and-sour-chicken, and a pile of dirty diapers.

"You don't have the layouts, do you?"

She shook her head and Josie visibly paled. "That's not the answer a woman with a nonexistent love life and a broken coffeepot needs to hear this early in the morning."

Sam stared at the closed door and squared her shoulders. "I've been working for this opportunity for the past two years. Twenty-four hours, even twenty-four hellacious hours are not going to screw it up. I know the campaign inside and out. You know the doll. We can do this."

The door swung inward and Arthur Kiss, *the* Arthur Kiss, chief executive officer of Three Kisses, Inc, motioned them forward.

Arthur was all business, running the toy company the way her father ran Skye Investments, with no room for slacking, zero tolerance when it came to excuses, and a strict policy when it came to employees keeping their personal problems at home.

He glanced at his watch as Sam and Josie passed by, a stern expression on his face.

"I think I'm going to throw up," Josie murmured.

Sam took one look at the room full of directors, then another at Arthur, whose disapproving gaze was riveted on her drool-soiled jacket. "I'll race you to the ladies room."

* * *

"So how did it go?" Marge, Josie's research assistant and the woman in charge of the two dozen screaming toddlers, asked when Sam walked into research and development later that afternoon.

"On a scale of one to ten? I'd say a negative five."

"Josie said it was bad, but I thought I'd get your opinion." Marge knelt near a little girl playing with a Cryin' Crystal doll and noted the child's actions.

"Bad," Sam clarified, "but not irreparable. Not as long as I produce Miss Kiss in time for the New Year's Eve debut the day after tomorrow."

Marge moved on to another little boy absorbed in a Mighty Mack action figure. "I still can't believe you misplaced her."

Actually, Sam couldn't believe *misplaced* had been the best story she'd been able to come up with. Afterall, she made her living being creative.

Then again, she'd never had to think up a spectacular idea while changing a diaper in the backseat of a taxi during rush-hour traffic.

"I've been under a lot of pressure lately." Mainly since last night. "I'm sure I'll find her."

"I hope so," Josie said as she came around the corner. "Besides the fact that she's the only one of her kind and crucial to this campaign, she didn't come cheap."

Amen. Last night alone, Sam had spent a fortune on diapers, wipes and formula, and developed a new sense of admiration for mothers everywhere.

"For argument's sake," Sam hedged, "Let's say I can't find her." She hated to voice the fear that had been niggling at her all day. "How fast can you make another prototype?"

Josie retrieved a clipboard from her desk. "Let's see, I suppose if I worked round the clock . . ." She made a few small notations. "I'm certain I could have another one ready to go by the middle of next week."

The words sent a pool of dread swirling through Sam. This was it. Her life was over, her career down the toilet. Years of work, and now she'd have nothing to show for it.

"This baby is so sweet." Karen, another assistant, came around the corner with Miss Kiss cuddled in her arms and handed the baby to Sam. "So how long do you have her for?"

"I'm not sure." Sam hefted the baby to her other arm and picked up her makeshift diaper bag—an oversized purse she'd stuffed full of diapers and formula that morning. "Her mother's the spur-of-the-moment type. She might even be waiting for me at home."

"I still can't believe you got stuck baby-sitting," Josie said. "You don't like kids."

"That's right," Marge said. "I forgot, you don't like kids."

"Though it would be hard for anyone not to like this one." Josie studied the baby. "You know, with those blue eyes and that pale blond hair, she kind of reminds me of Miss Kiss."

"Really?" Sam spared a glance at the baby.

"Wow, she does," Marge said, coming around to study the baby. "A lot. Why, it's uncanny."

"Yeah," Karen agreed. "It's incredible."

"And kind of weird," Marge added. "Don't you think—"

"I need to get her home," Sam cut in. "I'm sure her mother's probably waiting. Worried. You know how mothers are."

"Yep, I don't let my three out of my sight for more than a few hours," Karen said.

Josie sighed. "I wouldn't know."

"You will." Karen patted Josie's shoulder. "You didn't tell me. How was your lunch date with the infamous Ira Montgomery-Arlington?" Ira was the consulting lawyer for Three Kisses, and the most eligible bachelor in the company.

"Fine," Josie replied, "when he wasn't entertaining me with stories about his past six girlfriends. I should have known *IMA.user* referred to more than his initials." Josie shrugged. "At least I had some good Italian. Of course, the object was to have *a* good Italian, so I can have a lot of little Italians. Or Germans or Englishmen, or whatever Mr. Right happens to be."

"I don't get it." Sam turned, Miss Kiss in hand,

diaper bag slung over her shoulder. Her conversation with Jake last night echoed through her head. "What's the big rush? It's not like you're going to spontaneously combust if you don't squeeze out a couple of kids before the age of forty. The world's already overpopulated as it is."

"She doesn't like kids," Josie told Karen.

"It's not about whether or not I like kids. I just think that the end all and be all of a woman shouldn't revolve around her ability to reproduce. Women are more than walking ovaries. We're lawyers and doctors and senators and astronauts."

"I could turn on the hot plate if you want to rip off your bra," Josie offered. "Geez, Sam, no wonder you lost the doll. You're much too tense."

Her career was flashing before her eyes, her future lay in the hands of a ninety-two-year-old woman who could recite every one of Rikki Lake's topics for the past month, but couldn't remember what she'd had for dinner the previous day. Of *course* she was tense. Not to mention Miss Kiss was cuddled in her arms just so and it felt sort of nice and, well . . . *nice*. Of all the ridiculous, crazy, rotten things.

"I . . . I have to go."

"Thata girl. Go home. Give Krissy back to her mommy, then treat yourself to a long, hot soak," Karen said.

"Right," Josie added. "Then maybe you can remember where you put Miss Kiss."

"Uh, yeah. Listen, thanks. You were a lifesaver—Ouch!" Pain bolted through her body and zapped her brain as her gaze swiveled to the cherub-faced boy staring up at her.

"I don't wike you," Patrick declared.

Sam smiled. "You don't, do you?" Okay, maybe her life wasn't totally screwed after all. Patrick still hated her and, she realized as her fingers tightened to keep from yanking him by the ear, she wasn't too fond of him, either, despite all the warm fuzzy feelings coursing through her.

Tonight, she promised herself, tonight everything would get back to normal and Miss Kiss would go back to being nothing more than heat-sensitive plastic.

And it wouldn't come a moment too soon. Already, her clothes were a mess, her apartment chaotic and her job this close to going down the drain. The sooner she got rid of Miss Kiss, the better.

No matter how much the thought suddenly bothered her.

Tonight.

She was on her own tonight.

Jake stared at his reflection, knotted his favorite Dior tie and did his damndest to ignore the crying coming from upstairs.

He couldn't rush to her rescue and risk another close encounter. No matter how much he wanted one.

He had a date tonight. Pamela Cohen, kindergarten teacher and his youngest sister's best friend. She made a great chocolate cake, sewed Halloween costumes for her class and played a mean game of bridge.

Perfect wife material and a far cry from a career-driven, workaholic marketing executive who shivered when he touched her and made this soft, little purring sound when he trailed his palms across her nipples.

He forced the thought away and shrugged on his jacket. The crying persisted, accompanied by the frantic click of footsteps overhead. *Frantic*, as in distressed—

No. He grabbed his cell phone and slid it into his pocket. He wasn't going up.

The noise persisted and he stiffened.

No. No matter how much crying. Or pacing. Or crashing. Or . . . *crashing*?

He hit the stairs at a desperate run. A few breathless moments later, he pushed open Sam's door, fully prepared for the worst.

His frantic gaze lit on her standing in the middle of the living room. "I—I thought something had happened. I heard a crash."

"I was headed into the kitchen and I bumped the coffee table and broke a vase."

Glass littered the carpet, but otherwise, she was okay. The knowledge sang through his head for a few moments, before his gaze zeroed in on her face and the tired circles beneath her eyes. The crying baby rested in her arms.

"I've fed her and burped her and changed her and I don't know what's wrong." Her eyes glistened, and the sight tightened a fist in his chest. "I mean, things were going so well when I left work. She was sleeping and we made it home in the taxi without an emergency diaper change and. . . ." The words faded into a sob.

"She probably has colic." Jake took the baby.

"What do I do?"

"Go in the bathroom, run a hot bath and soak."

Her brow furrowed and he barely resisted the urge to reach out and smooth the expression with his lips. "Isn't she young for a hot bath? Besides, I haven't had time to pick up one of those little bathtubs or any baby shampoo."

"The bath's for you, not her. You're tired and I've got a few extra minutes."

Earth to Jake. This is not a good idea.

No, but then neither was the thought of Sam passing out from exhaustion.

She cast a hesitant look from him to the baby and back. "She'll be all right, won't she? Colic isn't that bad, is it?"

"Everyone of my nieces and nephews survived. Now go." Before he did something even more stupid than rushing to her rescue. Like hauling her into his arms and kissing her. And nibbling the corner of her mouth until she opened those luscious lips and moaned his name. . . .

"A bath *does* sound wonderful."

A cold shower sounded even better. "Go."

Her gaze caught his before she disappeared into the bathroom. "Thanks, Jake."

Thanks. If she really wanted to show him her thanks, she could—

A fierce howl shattered the thought, thankfully, and drew his gaze to the bundle in his arms.

"Great timing, Krissy."

A chubby fist gripped his tie and before Jake could blink, his favorite pin-striped tie became a burp rag for her last feeding.

A dozen? Was he insane?

A dozen definitely bordered on crazy, Jake decided after a half hour with Krissy that had him feeling as if he'd just raced for the gold, and come in a sloppy second. He stared down at her closed eyes. At least she'd finally fallen asleep.

No thanks to Gina, who'd called on his cell phone twice wanting to know where he was—

The shrill ring of his phone interrupted the thought.

"I'm on my way," he growled before snapping the phone closed, placing the baby in her carrier and heading for Sam's bedroom.

"Sam?" Knuckles met wood as he rapped once, twice. "You done yet?"

No response. The only sound was the frantic thud of his heart as a visual image of what lay on the other side of the door rushed through his head. *Down, boy*.

With renewed firmness, he found his voice. "Sam, I really have to get going." No answer. "I'm opening the door. I'm walking in. I'm—" The words stumbled into one another as he caught sight of the figure curled up on the large bed.

She lay on her side, dark hair fanned out across the white pillowcase, and a white terry-cloth robe hiked up to mid-thigh, revealing endlessly long legs.

Gazing at her asleep, vulnerable and sexy-as-hell chipped away at his resolve and reminded him that no matter how much Samantha Skye appeared the calm, cool, detached executive in her power suits, she was just a woman beneath. The most beautiful one he'd ever seen, and Jake Morelli had seen plenty.

He'd blamed his lingering attraction to her on the fact that she wore tight skirts, sheer black stockings and appeared the sophisticated, put-together woman he'd always found so exciting.

But there was nothing put together about her now. No perfectly applied make-up, or tailored clothes to accent her curvy figure. She wore nothing but a homely robe that turned him on more than any black silk teddy ever had.

The neckline gaped, giving him an enticing view of the slope of one curvy breast. His memory quickly jumped in to paint a very vivid picture of all the robe covered. Pale breasts tipped with wine-colored nipples puckered and ripe from his mouth. . . .

Aw, man.

He swallowed and stepped forward—loudly—in a desperate play to wake her up before he reached the bed.

"Sam." He cleared his throat, coughed and stomped a few more times. "Time to wake up."

Okay, he'd have to touch her—but quickly. A tap on the shoulder. A jab with his finger. Then he was getting the hell out of here. Out of sight, out of mind, as the saying went, and Jake intended to put it to the test.

His first impulse was to nudge her awake, then quickly move out of touching distance. But he didn't nudge her, nor did he move away.

"Sam." His fingers slid around her shoulder and pulled her onto her back. The robe gaped even more, and he realized his imagination had nothing on the real thing. A soft, pink nipple peeked out at him and made him lick his lips.

"Jake?" Disoriented green eyes stared up at him. "What's wrong?"

Everything. "Nothing. You, um, fell asleep."

"Asleep?" Her brow furrowed as if she were recalling the past few moments. "I didn't mean to. I was just going to close my eyes for a few minutes. The baby had been crying and I had this terrible headache and— Ohmigod, the baby!" She struggled onto her elbows and the robe gaped even more.

Jake summoned help from every saint his mother had ever prayed to and kept his gaze fixed on Sam's face. "She's fine. I changed her, fed her and put her to sleep."

Relief swept her features and she relaxed back into the mattress, the movement pulling the robe back into place enough for him to breathe again.

"I'm no good at this baby stuff," she said, her expression so sad it twisted something in his chest.

"You just haven't had much practice," he heard himself say.

"Even with practice, I'd stink. But you. . . ." Her words trailed away as one hand smoothed his jacket lapel and she smiled. "You know just what to do, just how to touch her. You're good, Jake. Really good." She was talking about his way with kids, but the sudden flash of desire in her eyes told a different story altogether.

"I really have to go."

She nodded as if she'd just realized what she'd said. "Yeah. Maybe you should."

He licked his lips. "Before I do something I shouldn't do."

She licked her lips. "Something you *really* shouldn't do."

"Like kiss you." He wasn't going to, he promised himself with as much conviction as a guy could muster faced with such luscious lips glistening from the slow glide of her tongue.

But damned if he didn't go on and kiss her anyway.

She softened at the first contact, her lips parting, opening up to let him in. She tasted sweet. So damned sweet, he couldn't seem to get enough. He dipped his tongue inside, savored, explored before reality shook him and a voice prodded, *The future. Think about the future.*

Jake managed to grasp his last bit of control and pull away from her. "Can you cook?" he breathed, staring down at her, needing to hear the answers, to bolster his defenses and stop this now before. . . .

"What?" Her eyes fluttered open.

"Can you cook?"

"Peanut butter and jelly sandwiches." *Strike one.*

"Can you sew?"

"I'm hell with a stapler." *Strike two.*

"What about bridge? Do you play bridge?"

"No." *Strike three.* "But my granny plays poker."

"Close enough," he breathed, and then he kissed her again.

Her hands came up, curling around his neck, pulling him closer and Jake couldn't stop himself. She was an addiction that six months cold turkey hadn't been able to curb. He wanted her now even more than he had that hot summer night, despite her answers.

He touched her, his hands sliding down the smooth column of her neck, absorbing the heat and softness of all that sweet-smelling skin, feeling the frantic thud of her pulse against his thumb.

The robe fell completely open as he nibbled a path down her neck, inhaling her—the faint aroma of expensive perfume and soft, warm woman. . . .

She gasped as his tongue lapped at her nipple. Then he drew the tip deep, suckled her and relished the soft moan that filled the air around them.

Rrrrrrring!

He tried to ignore the shrill cry of his cell phone. It would go away. It had to go away because he couldn't stop—

"The phone," she murmured.

"Forget it."

They both did for a few more breathless, heart-pounding seconds until the damned thing started to ring again. He shut his eyes and focused on her, on suckling her other breast until the tip ripened and begged for more.

For him.

"Jake Morelli." Sam's breathless voice slid into his ears, and he glanced up to see that she'd retrieved his cell phone. "He's, uh, busy right now," she panted as he slid a hand beneath the edge of her robe and touched the inside of her thigh. "But I could . . ." Her words faded as his fingertips touched the drenched flesh between her legs. "Mmm . . . I, uh, could take a," she sucked in a sharp breath, "a . . . a message."

A moment of silence passed as the caller spoke, and then he felt her response even before he saw it. She stiffened. His gaze traveled to hers and the hard glitter of her stare froze him in place.

"It's for you," she told him. "It's your date."

Chapter Four

The next morning, Sam checked in with Granny Gigi to get an update on the spell reversal. The old woman was still two sentences shy, but had managed to get her hands on several of her friends' spell books and anticipated quick success. Sam grasped at that possibility as she headed for work with Miss Kiss tucked into her carrier.

The beginning of the day mimicked the previous one, starting with a frantic diaper change in the cab. Except today Sam had another worry besides the possible end of her career.

A *date*.

Jake was dating.

Good. At least that's what she told herself as she went about her normal routine, which involved media schedules, ad proofs, art boards, press contacts, not to mention, she'd undertaken the job of supervising everything for tomorrow's New Year's Eve party and media blitz at the fine arts museum. She oversaw everything from the invitations, one of which she'd even sent to her father, though she knew he'd be too busy to come, right down to choosing the menu.

While she had autonomy, she was out to please the higher ups, namely the person responsible for putting her in charge of the Miss Kiss account, especially after being late to yesterday's board meeting.

"We need elegant," she told Hank of Hank's House of Fine Swine, owner of one of the largest eateries in Chicago and Arthur Kiss' brother-in-law. "Absolutely no pigs in a blanket."

"They're Art's favorite."

"Okay, I'll take the pigs in a blanket. But make it an elegant blanket, with some dipping sauces or something to dress up the little porkers."

"I can do barbecue."

"This is white tie."

"Art loves barbecue."

"We'll need lots of napkins."

"I can do bibs," Hank told her.

Normally, Sam would have panicked. Perfection was key. Her future was riding on tomorrow night, on revealing Miss Kiss to an eager public amid flutes of champagne and platters of caviar.

"Bibs are fine."

Hey, Miss Kiss had pooped on her that morning. Pigs in a blanket hardly compared as an all-time low.

Discovering that Jake Morelli, the object of her most erotic fantasies was seeing another woman . . . well, there was the bottom of the barrel.

"A date," Sam moaned to Josie when she picked up Miss Kiss for the cab ride home. "Can you believe that?"

"Let's see. . . . A single, successful, handsome, healthy, heterosexual male being interested in the opposite sex? Yes, I believe it. In fact, hook me up."

"You're not funny." Sam loaded Miss Kiss into her carrier. "He told me she's a kindergarten teacher." Right after he'd told Miss Kindergarten Teacher that something had come up and he couldn't make it to dinner.

Not that his canceling had made any difference. Sam had been stunned and hurt, and she'd promptly told him to leave. Then she'd spent the rest of the night battling the urge to beg him to come back.

"A kindergarten teacher, of all things." She shook her head. "She might as well have a great big M for mommy stamped on her forehead."

"This is really bothering you, isn't it?"

"I bet she cooks," Sam rushed on. "Probably everything from soups to desserts."

"This *is* bothering you."

"And she probably makes her own pot holders, and mends socks and—"

"Why don't you just tell him?" Josie cut in.

Sam's gaze snapped up to collide with her friend's. "Tell him what? That I'm desperately in lust with him and I'd appreciate it if he didn't date anyone else, especially a domestic goddess who makes me look like chopped liver when it comes to the suburbia thing?" At Josie's knowing look, she added, "Not that I care if she makes me look like chopped liver. No way do I want to do the suburbia thing." Even if she *had* caught herself sniffing the travel-sized baby powder in her purse because she'd missed Miss Kiss and hadn't been able to get away from Arthur and the New Year's ad meeting to see the baby around lunchtime.

"This is my life." Sam glanced around her. "High-rise buildings, plenty of chrome and concrete, board meetings and ad budgets." The only life she'd ever known.

The only life she *wanted* to know, she reminded herself.

She liked her independence and the fact that she didn't have to rely on anyone else. She could make it on her own. She thought briefly of Jake, and the fact that he'd kept an eye on Miss Kiss while she'd soaked in the tub.

Okay, so usually she could make it on her own—when she didn't have a screaming baby on her hands. The exact reason why she didn't intend to have any screaming babies, and certainly not a Morelli dozen to interfere with her career.

"This is just lust," she told Josie. "No reason to go acting like a jealous girlfriend."

"True, but it's plenty of reason to act like an interested woman. Come on, Sam. I've never known you to back down when it comes to something you want."

And she wanted Jake Morelli.

Not in a forever kind of way, but there was this heat between them. Powerful. Potent. She couldn't breathe when he walked into the room, much less think. She'd thought she could deny the attraction and forget him the way she had every other man in her past. But six months away from him, and she still wanted more.

And he wanted more.

She'd seen the glitter of desire in his eyes, felt the tightness in his muscles when he'd pulled away from her last night, as if it had taken all of his control and then some. While he might be as intent on resisting her as she was him, he still felt the pull.

The chemistry.

Time and distance hadn't solved the problem, which meant she needed to try a different tactic.

Another night with Jake Morelli. That's what

she needed. A long, endless night with enough touching and tasting to fill her up and make her forget all about the way he licked that spot just below her ear sending shivers up and down her spine, and the way he held her just tight enough to make her feel safe and secure and—

One more night.

Then she could get on with her life—without Jake Morelli.

"I want you," she stated when he opened his door later that evening.

His head emerged from the white towel he'd been rubbing his damp hair with. "Come again?"

"I want you." She pushed past him into his apartment and set Miss Kiss—freshly diapered, fed and sound asleep in her carrier—on the sofa. She needed to lay out her plan before she lost her nerve. While she did go after what she wanted, she'd never wanted a man before, and she'd certainly never propositioned one. "And I think you want me, and this resisting one another obviously isn't working, so I've got an idea—"

The words died in her throat as she turned. He'd been partially hidden behind the door when he'd first answered her knock. He was completely visible now. Visible and nearly naked, with only a towel slung low on his lean hips.

He'd followed her into the apartment and stood barely an arm's length away. So close that she could feel the heat coming off him, smell the enticing aroma of clean soap and virile male. She took a deep breath as her eyes drank in the sight of him. The white cotton wrapped around him stood in stark contrast to his tanned muscle. Broad shoulders framed a hard, sinewy chest sprinkled with dark hair that tapered to a slim line and disappeared beneath the towel's edge. The same hair covered the length of his powerful thighs and calves.

He was every bit as gorgeous as she remembered.

Her gaze skidded up to his. Dark, ebony pools glittered back at her. A look she remembered, as well.

From that night six months ago.

From last night.

"I was in the shower," he explained. The muscles in his forearms and chest bunched as he balled up the towel he'd been using on his hair, chucked it into a nearby wicker basket and eyed her. "Now what were you saying?"

"That I . . ." She licked her lips. "That we . . ." She licked her lips again. "That I think we should try it again."

He folded his arms and eyed her. "Try what again, honey?"

She gathered her courage and blurted out, "Sex." She swallowed. "I . . . I think we should do it again. I mean, I still want you and I think you still want me, and ignoring it isn't making things easier. I say we just get together, do it again, get it over with, and out of our systems."

Jake had told himself the same thing over and over again during the past six months. But hearing her say the words didn't give him the expected rush of relief. Instead, anger washed through him because he knew that making love to Sam one more time wouldn't be nearly enough to sate his lust for her. He'd been with enough women to know that the heat burning him up from the inside out was different from anything he'd ever felt for a woman before. Hotter. More consuming.

He'd known it since day one, he just hadn't admitted it to himself until last night when his date had called, when he'd seen the flash of hurt in Sam's eyes.

Hurt, from a woman who'd climbed out of his bed six months ago and walked away as if they hadn't just loved each other within an inch of their lives. She shouldn't have cared whether he had a date.

She did.

It was a sweet revelation, because now Jake knew she felt more for him than just lust. And he felt more for her. He genuinely liked and respected her, and not because she was smart and independent and a fond reminder of his bachelor days.

The truth had hit him last night when he'd seen her straight out of the tub, as wet as a dishrag, and looking so damned appealing he'd nearly busted his jeans. But he'd felt more, as well. He'd experienced it in his chest, in the pause of his heartbeat and the nearly overwhelming urge to crawl into bed beside her and simply hold her, comfort her. Sam was more than every woman he'd ever wanted. She was *the* woman, the whole package rolled into one. Sexy as hell in sheer black stockings and a short skirt, and wholesome as apple pie in a T-shirt and jeans. Bossy and demanding one minute, and all trembling vulnerability the next. Smart, yet naive. Experienced, yet innocent. And he liked all of it. He liked her.

And she liked him.

She just wouldn't admit it. Yet.

"I haven't got my day planner, but if you give me a proposed time, maybe tomorrow or this weekend, early morning's out though, because—"

"Come here." But he didn't wait. He reached for her.

Her eyes widened and she managed a startled, "Now?" before he covered her lips with his own.

He held her face between his hands, thrust his tongue deep and made love to her with his mouth. Long and slow and thorough until she clung to him.

"But if now's a bad time . . ." He murmured after a few sweet moments when he pulled away.

"No." She clutched at his shoulders. "Now's good."

He pulled the blouse from her skirt, slid the buttons free and pushed the material off her shoulders. She wore a skimpy black bra, her nipples dark shadows beneath the lace. With a flick of his fingers, he opened the clasp.

"Just good?" Dipping his head, he caught one nipple between his teeth. He flicked the ripe tip with his tongue before opening his mouth wider. He drew her in and sucked until a moan curled from her throat. The sound fed the lust roaring through his veins.

"Great," she finally murmured when he paused his suckling to remove her skirt.

A flick of a button, a glide of a zipper and material pooled around her ankles. Her stockings followed, until she stood before him wearing nothing but her panties and open bra.

He discarded his towel, clasped her waist and backed her to the nearest wall. Pressing one hard thigh between her legs, he forced her wider until she rode him, her sweet heat pressed to his hard thigh.

She gave a small whimper of protest and he leaned back to see a rosy flush creep up her neck, as if she were shocked from the sudden intimate contact.

Shocked and thrilled. He could see her pulse

beating frantically at the base of her throat. He wanted to feel it against his lips, but he didn't move a muscle.

"Sam?" Her name was a question, because as much as he wanted her, he didn't want to frighten her.

She took a deep breath, the motion working her against his leg and a shiver went through her. But not from fear. Her eyelids fluttered and her luscious lips parted. "Better than great." Her voice was a breathless whisper. "Perfect."

A spurt of pure male satisfaction went through him and he touched her, stroked her, his thigh pressed intimately against her, working her until he felt the dampness through the thin material of her panties and he couldn't help himself.

He caught her lips in a fierce kiss as he dipped his hand into her silk panties. She was warm and wet and swollen. At the first touch of his fingers, a ragged moan curled from her lips and she came apart in his arms.

He scooped her up and carried her into his bedroom. He was about to slam the door shut, when sanity zapped him and he remembered the baby. He tamped down on his baser instincts long enough to check on Krissy and make sure she was sound asleep and secure before returning to the woman sprawled limp and sated on his bed.

But not for long.

He joined her on the bed, kissing her, stroking her, until she clutched at him, wanting more. He paused only to retrieve a condom from his nightstand.

Her eyes opened to watch him slide the sheath onto his throbbing length and a smile curved her lips.

That was his Sam. Blushing furiously one minute, staring hungrily at him the next. He liked both responses. Hell, he loved them. Couldn't get enough of them, of her.

He caught her legs and opened her wide, his gaze locked with hers. "You're so damned beautiful, Sam."

"So are you." She stared up at him with passion-glazed eyes before her gaze shifted past him to the ceiling. Her luscious lips hinted at a smile. "It's a definite shame you got rid of that mirror."

He grinned back. "I never thought I'd miss it. Until now." His expression faded as he grew serious. "Until you." And then he plunged deep, deep inside.

Sensation overwhelmed him for a long, breathless moment, the feel of her so hot and tight, pulsing around him, sucking at him, nearly making him spill himself then and there. But he'd waited too long to be back inside Samantha Skye to let go just yet.

He withdrew and watched the emotion play across her features, the sharp blush of arousal that colored her cheeks, her neck, her breasts. Then he pushed back, watching her lips part on a gasp, feeling her body instinctively tighten around his, milking him.

The motion grew as need blossomed, driving him, making him wild until he couldn't help himself. He pumped faster, deeper. When her body arched and she groaned with another climax, he followed, plunging one last time. His mind went blank as he exploded, emptying himself inside her, her muscles shivering around him.

Moments later, he gathered her close, feeling her heart pound against his, her breaths soft in his ear. No way was Jake letting her walk away from him. Not now.

Not ever again.

". . . don't do this to me!" Granny Gigi's voice penetrated the sleepy fog surrounding Sam.

Granny Gigi?

She had to be dreaming. She was naked in Jake's bed, his hard body pressed close to hers. Yes, just a dream. A warm, delicious, intoxicating dream.

". . . can't do this, I tell you!" The frantic sound of Gigi's voice yanked her completely awake. Her gaze snapped to attention and darted frantically around Jake's bedroom. Granny Gigi was *here*—

The thought stalled as her gaze lit on the air-conditioning vent.

"You can't do this to a poor old woman!" The voice filtered into the room and sent a burst of fear through Sam.

She bolted from the bed, her movements spurred by her Granny's shrieking, "No!"

Grabbing a T-shirt of Jake's off the back of a nearby chair, she yanked on the material. Visions of disaster rushed through her head as she tore out of the apartment and up the stairs.

She'd already reached Granny Gigi's door when her frenzied thoughts subsided long enough for sanity to push back. *Jake*. He could help her. She turned to bound back down the stairs.

"This is isn't happening to me!" Granny Gigi's high-pitched shriek sounded on the other side of the door, rising above the barking dog and blaring television, and fear jerked Sam back around.

Granny Gigi needed her. *Now*.

Frantic, she grabbed the ceramic flower pot sitting beside Gigi's doorstep, braced herself and shoved open the door. "Get your hands off my granny!"

"Sam?" Granny's Gigi's surprised stare swiveled toward the doorway where Sam paused, flower pot in hand.

"Hey, I don't do hands. Marlene at the Muffin, she's into hands. Can read a life line at twenty paces."

"Skeet?" Sam tried to calm the furious pounding of her heart as her gaze riveted on the teenaged boy.

"Are you all right, dear?" Granny Gigi asked.

"Me?" Her gaze darted from Skeet to Gigi and back, before sweeping the rest of the room. No masked men or disfigured serial killers. Just Skeet.

"Dear?"

"Uh, yes." She forced her gaze back to Gigi as relief swept through her. "Granny Gigi, what were you screaming about?"

"Screaming?" Granny Gigi looked puzzled. Then her gaze dropped to the white bakery bag in her hands and understanding lit her eyes. "Oh, yes. Yes, I was screaming."

"Why?"

"Skeet brought cream-cheese muffins when I specifically ordered blueberry."

"It was a mistake," Skeet said. "Marlene wrote it down wrong, but we're closing in five minutes and it takes me ten to go back. I'll bring blueberry tomorrow."

"But I need it now. I'm one sentence shy of the spell and I need a burst of energy."

"One sentence?" Excitement went through Sam. "Really?"

"And all I need is a quick burst of energy to fuel my my creative aura and figure out the rest. Blueberries do it for me every time."

"Sorry," Skeet said. "I'm off," he glanced at his

watch, "two minutes ago, so you'll have to wait."

"I'll give you a twenty-dollar tip if you go back and get blueberry," Sam told him.

"Deal." Skeet wiggled his eyebrows, his gaze going to her bare legs before he disappeared through the door. "Nice shirt."

Embarrassment flooded her as she realized she was standing in the doorway, wearing nothing but an oversized T-shirt. Jake's T-shirt. It occurred to her that if she could hear Granny Gigi, the old woman had probably heard Sam and Jake.

"Speaking of that shirt," Granny Gigi started. Sam braced herself for the coming speech about marriage, babies, and how delighted Gigi was that Sam and Jake had finally gotten together. "It reminds me of your mother."

"What?"

"She loved football. That's how she met your father, you know, at a Chicago Bears game."

"But my father hates sports."

"Now. But when they were first married, he loved everything from baseball to football. He and your mother went to every Bears game, wore matching shirts and even waved pennants. They also liked picnics." She smiled at the memory. "Why, your father would call in sick to work at least once a month. They'd pack a lunch and spend the entire day at the park."

"*My* father called in sick to work?" Sam tried

to digest the knowledge. "The same man who couldn't ever come to my piano recitals because it would mean leaving work a half-hour early?"

Gigi smiled. "He wasn't always like that. When your mother died, he stopped really living life and started just tolerating it. He loved her a lot, you know. He was always kissing and hugging her. Your father was a cuddler."

Sam thought about her childhood, about the monthly dinners and the cold man who barely glanced at her, much less touched her.

"Because you're so much like your mother," Granny Gigi said as if reading Sam's thoughts.

"But I can't do any of the things she could do."

"It's not about powers, dear. You have her eyes, so green and mesmerizing, and all that jet-black hair. I suspect every time your father looks at you, he sees her. When she died, it tore him up inside. He couldn't bring himself to smell her perfume or see a movie they'd laughed over, or hear a song they'd danced to. For him, it was easier to simply cut himself off from everything that reminded him of her."

"Including me."

"Yes." Granny Gigi patted her shoulder. "Not that he didn't love you. He did. He does. But when your mother died, he shut himself off emotionally. His problem. Not yours. And speaking of problems, where's Miss Priss?"

"That's Miss Kiss, and she's downstairs asleep."

"Ah, sleep. Such a wonderful concept." Granny Gigi settled on the couch and leaned her head back. "I hope he hurries with that muffin, otherwise I'm liable to drop off. I've almost got it, you know. A little more work, perhaps a bit of positive reinforcement . . ." Her words faded as Prince barked.

Prince? She'd left him curled up near his doggy bed before she'd gone over to Jake's—

The thought stalled as she caught sight of Diva. "Uh, Granny, your cat's *barking*."

"Yes, dear." Granny Gigi spared a glance at Diva who let out a loud *Rrrrruuuf*. "I've been trying so hard to reverse the Miss Kiss incantation, that I sort of cast a few little spells in the process. That's nothing compared to Diana."

"Diana?"

"That nice girl who lives down the hall in 3D."

"The only person who lives down the hall is David, the construction worker. . . ." Her words trailed off as understanding hit her. "Tell me you didn't."

"I'm afraid instead of building all those malls, he'll be shopping in them."

Sam had fully intended to climb back into bed with Jake when she returned downstairs a few minutes later. When she saw him sprawled on the sheets, so dark and sexy, his manhood nestled in a tangle of dark hair, images of their lovemaking rushed through her mind, stirring her senses, making her want him all over again. A feeling she'd prepared herself for. Afterall, the night was young, barely ten P.M., and she'd resigned herself to an entire night of hot, wicked sex with Jake Morelli. Anticipated it.

It was the sudden urge to snuggle into his arms, lay her head on his chest and hear his heart beating in her ear that caught her off guard.

And sent her scrambling for her clothes.

Snuggling?

No, no, *no*. This was lust. Passionate embraces, fierce kisses, wild lovemaking. *Chemistry*.

At least that's what she told herself as she yanked on her clothes. Chemistry.

"Come back to bed." His deep voice rumbled into her ears and rippled over her senses a heartbeat before large, tanned hands closed over hers. Her shoes thudded to the carpet.

"That wouldn't be a good idea." She caught her bottom lip against the heat flowering inside her as he nibbled her neck.

"Why not?"

"Because . . ." The thought trailed off as his hands slid underneath her T-shirt. "Because I . . ." He fingered her throbbing nipples, plucking and rolling until moisture flooded between her thighs. "I . . . I can't think when you do that."

And she needed to think, to plan, to. . . . The thought faded as his hands swept downward.

Thinking was definitely overrated.

"Just feel, Sam. Just *feel*."

And she did, as she turned into his arms and gave herself up to his kiss, and the rest of her long, anticipated night.

Tomorrow it would all be over and Samantha would get on with the rest of her life—without Jake Morelli to complicate things and distract her from her career.

If only the notion wasn't so utterly depressing.

Chapter Five

"Tonight's the night." Arthur Kiss paused in the doorway of Sam's office the next morning and eyed her. "I hope all the preparations have been made. A lot is riding on the success of this project."

"It'll be a night to remember," Sam assurred him. Either as the night Samantha Skye landed the vice-presidency for Three Kisses, Inc., or the night she blew a multi-million dollar ad campaign and lost the job of her dreams.

At this point, with the clock ticking away, Sam was placing her money on number two. While she hoped that Granny Gigi would come through, the chances of the spell being reversed by tonight were slim to none. As for the second prototype . . . Josie was close, but not quite there.

A fact that left one conclusion: Come tonight, Sam was going to have to tell Arthur that she'd lost the Miss Kiss prototype. And then he was most certainly going to tell her that she was fired.

Bye-bye vice-presidency. *Adios* executive washroom. *Caio* to her future at Three Kisses, Inc., and every other major company after the media caught tonight's fiasco on tape. Her only saving grace was that her father, who still hadn't RSVP'd to the invitation, would miss seeing his daughter's career spiral down the toilet.

She'd failed. Not just professionally, but personally, as well, because, despite her best efforts, she'd fallen for Jake Morelli.

Oh, she'd tried to convince herself that last night was over and done with. From the love-making, to the two of them sitting on his bed, eating cold pizza and talking, to the walking and rocking when Miss Kiss had awoke for her midnight feeding. When the baby had fallen back asleep, Sam had fallen right back into Jake's arms.

At the first rays of sunlight, however, she'd bolted, and this time he'd been too sound asleep to stop her. Thankfully. No way could she have left if he had asked her to stay. Distance, she'd told herself as she'd raced back to her own apartment. Only that hadn't worked either, because

Jake was under her skin, in her head, her heart.

He was handsome, successful and good-looking, but the appeal went even deeper. She liked the glimmer of pride in his eyes when he talked about his family and the gentle way he cuddled Miss Kiss. Most of all, she appreciated the way he smiled and winked and flirted and made her feel so wanted.

Crazy, because Jake Morelli was not the man for her. He wanted the little woman, not a corporate executive who's idea of nutrition meant eating a half-pint of ice cream before ten at night. She'd be as terrible a wife as she was a mother.

Three days with Miss Kiss and she was still all thumbs. Sure, she'd made some progress. The baby didn't cry as much as she had at first, and if she did, Sam knew just how to rock her so she would quiet. But she still couldn't get the baby's diaper on snug enough. She fed too much or too little. She forgot to do the burping thing. And figuring out those Onesie things with all the snaps was like trying to read a Chicago train map. Impossible.

She was not cut out for this baby stuff, which meant she wasn't cut out for Jake and his Morelli dozen.

It didn't matter that the idea set little butterflies loose in her stomach and made her think the most ludicrous thoughts about Jake, a preacher and a five-tier wedding cake. Only it wasn't some barefoot and pregnant Mother of the Earth helping Jake cut into the double-fudge layers complete with sugared strawberries on top. It was Sam herself.

Stress, she told herself. After all, it wasn't a new year that waited for Sam at the stroke of midnight. It was the end of her career. Her dreams. Her credit line at Saks.

If only the thought of losing all that bothered her half as much as the thought of losing Jake.

"How's that?"

"A little more to the left . . . there. That's it." Jake stared at the mirror hanging from his ceiling and grinned. "Thanks."

"No problem." Mick of Mick's Mirrors, Etc., climbed down the ladder, pulled off his gloves and winked. "Plan on entertaining a lot of guests?"

"Just one."

"And she's got a hankering for mirrors?"

"Something like that."

"My Wilma has a thing for handcuffs." He grabbed his clipboard and retrieved the invoice. "Damn near died of shock the first time she pulled them out, but the little lady was definitely on to something, and I've got forty-two years of wedded bliss to prove it."

"Forty-two years, huh?"

"Working on forty-three." He chuckled. "Not

one of our friends thought we'd make it past the first year. Me and Wilma are like night and day. She drinks herbal tea with lemon and I can't get my coffee black enough. But then love's a mystery, right?"

"The biggest in the universe," Jake said as he signed the invoice and saw Mick out. He was just walking back into the bedroom when the phone rang.

"I've talked to Pam and she's willing to give you another chance," Gina told him.

"I don't think the future Mrs. Jake Morelli would appreciate that."

"Ohmigod!" Gina shrieked. "You've found someone!"

Jake sprawled on the bed and stared up at the mirror. "You could say that."

"Does she cook?" Gina asked.

"No."

"Does she sew?"

"No."

"What about bridge?"

"No."

Jake wanted her anyway. She'd slipped away from him this morning, just the way she had six months ago, and so he hadn't had a chance to tell her how he felt. She wasn't anything he'd been looking for in a woman, yet everything. They were so wrong for each other, yet so right. He wanted her for his wife, for the mother of his children. He wanted her for keeps.

He was telling her today, and he wasn't taking no for an answer.

By the time evening rolled around and Sam left her office to rush home and change for the New Year's Eve party, she'd passed the scared-woman-awaiting-the-guillotine phase. She was on the chopping block, and it was panic time.

"My life is falling apart and you're playing poker?" she screeched when she walked into Granny Gigi's apartment, Miss Kiss in her arms, and found the Spellman sisters sitting around the card table.

"Of course not, dear." Mona passed by, a margarita in her hand. "Though we might take in a few hands later if all goes well."

"I told you all I needed was a little positive reinforcement." Gigi loaded more ice into her blender and salted the rim of a glass.

Positive reinforcement.

The phrase echoed in her head as Sam noted the long, flowing robes the women wore, identical to Granny's but in various jewel-toned shades. "You're all witches?"

"Born and bred," Rose told her as she walked from the kitchen, a tiny black-haired baby in her arms. "Not baby Elizabeth, of course. She belongs to my granddaughter."

"Where is Evelyn?" Gigi asked.

"Out with prospective husband number four since husband three turned out to be a lying, cheating scumbag just like one and two."

"I hope dear, sweet Evie taught him a lesson."

"She's stuck on the Do No Harm to Other Human Beings mantra. She hasn't realized that lying, cheating scumbags don't qualify, which is why, once this predicament's over, we'll have to give him our own present."

Mona clapped her hands. "I vote for a social disease."

"Blue balls," came Esther's enthusiastic suggestion.

"We could do both," Granny Gigi offered.

Sam was still trying to absorb the truth. "You're all witches." This time it was a statement rather than a question. "But I thought all you ladies did up here was play poker."

"Strip poker," Granny Gigi corrected, "and only during the full moon. Otherwise, we play gin rummy or practice our spells."

"Speaking of which, we figured that between our four spell books, each of which has its own version of the incantation Gigi used, we should be able to recreate the last line of Gigi's spell, which we've managed to do."

"All except for the last two words," Gigi added.

"You're kidding?" Okay, maybe the end wasn't in sight, after all. "You're just two words shy?"

A soft gurgle from Miss Kiss punctuated the question and all eyes dropped to the bundle in Sam's arms.

"My, my, what a cute little baby. Gigi, you did good work," Mona said as she reached for Miss Kiss. "Come now," she said when Sam hesitated to relinquish the little girl. "I won't hurt her." Mona scooped up the baby. "I've got a playmate for you, little one," she said, putting the baby into the playpen beside baby Elizabeth.

"But—" Sam started.

"You go on downstairs and get ready," Esther cut in, shooing her toward the door. "And let us get to work."

"Yes," Rose said from the dining room table where she was busy arranging various herbs. "I've almost got everything ready. In fifteen minutes or so, I'd say your troubles will be over. Don't you think, Gigi?"

"Yes, fifteen minutes should do it. Actually, the spell only takes about five minutes, but it takes a good ten minutes for us to get an adequate chant going because Mona's tone deaf."

"I most certainly am not tone deaf," Mona declared.

"Dear, you can't carry a tune in a bucket." Rose turned back to Sam. "Fifteen minutes. Twenty, tops."

Twenty minutes. Sam wasn't sure why she felt the sudden lump in her throat. Twenty minutes was perfect. It was still forty-five minutes until the start of the press party. She could change, pick up the newly fixed Miss Kiss and get to the museum in time to make a smashing debut with the doll and secure her promotion.

"Now run along," Rose told her.

"And take this with you." Granny Gigi shoved a margarita in her hand.

"What for?"

"Stress, dear."

"I don't need a drink to handle my stress."

"You never know," Gigi said.

Before Sam could protest, the door closed in her face. She found herself out in the hallway, a margarita in her hand.

"Hey, there, babe."

"Hey, David . . ." Her voice faded as she turned to the right and saw the stunning blonde with breasts out to there and legs up to here, standing near the elevator.

On second thought . . .

She downed the margarita in one long gulp.

The margarita did little to calm her nerves. Frantic with new hope, she rushed around her apartment preparing for the evening ahead. Between her shower, her hair and a few quick swipes of make-up, she made several last-minute phone calls to Josie, the caterer and even the valet in charge of tonight's parking. Samantha wasn't sunk yet. Everything might just work out.

Almost everything.

She loved Jake—which was why she'd avoided his phone calls all day and decided, first thing tomorrow, to look for another place to live. Talking to him, when she knew they could never have a future together hurt too much. To see him working on his own future, dating and looking for that perfect mommy for the Morelli dozen, would surely do her in.

"Tonight," she told Prince who sat on the couch and watched her. "I'm completely, totally focused on tonight." Prince purred his agreement as she snatched up her coat and purse. "The first night of the rest of my life."

Sam gave the dog a quick pat, opened her apartment door and ran straight into a warm, solid male. *Jake*.

He wore a T-shirt, faded jeans, and his jaw was covered with a day's growth of beard. The worry glimmering in his eyes stood out in direct contrast to the scowl darkening his expression. As if he couldn't decide which he wanted most—to wrap his hands around her throat and strangle the life out of her, or kiss her.

He did neither. Instead he glared, his eyes so bright with concern that she almost took the initiative and kissed him.

"Where the hell have you been?" he growled.

She attempted her most nonchalant voice. "I

had a lot of work to do, what with the Miss Kiss presentation party tonight."

"You could have picked up your phone just once."

She summoned her courage and faced him. "I could have, but I didn't. Last night is over."

"It doesn't have to be."

"It does."

"Why?"

"Because we're all wrong for each other." *Because the more time I spend with you, the more I want. Love, marriage, babies*.

He leaned in, his lips close to her ear, his body warm and solid blocking the doorway, "Last night felt pretty damned right."

Too right. "Please, Jake. I really need to go. The presentation's in twenty minutes."

"Not until we straighten out a few things. For starters, I don't care how wrong you think we are for each other, I think—" A loud boom interrupted him and his gaze flew to the ceiling. "What the hell—"

"They did it." Sam gazed at the ceiling as she remebered the tell-tale sound that had awakened her a few days ago when Granny Gigi had turned Miss Kiss into a real baby.

"Did what?"

"Changed Miss Kiss."

"Miss who?"

She tried to push past him. "Please, Jake, I have to get upstairs."

As if he felt her urgency, he stepped aside. "Lead on."

"What do you mean?"

"I'm going with you." His gaze held hers for a long, probing moment. "We're not done yet, Sam. Not by a long shot."

They were, but she didn't have time to argue with him. Without Jake, her career was all she had, and she would be damned if she'd lose that, too. "Whatever you say." She turned to leave, but he caught her hand.

A strange expression crossed his face as he stared at Prince. "I know this sounds crazy, but I think your dog is purring."

"Believe me," she said as she tugged him through the doorway. "You ain't seen nothin' yet."

Sam and Jake arrived seconds later to find Granny Gigi's apartment buzzing with voices.

"You did it, didn't you?" Sam asked Gigi.

"We did it, all right," Rose said.

"Only we're not quite finished," Gigi added.

"What do you mean?"

"Well, Gigi's aim was off," Esther said.

"It wasn't my aim. Mona distracted me."

"Now, Gigi, dear, don't you go placing the blame on me—"

"Blame for what?" Sam cut in.

"For this." Rose held up the most beautiful doll Sam had ever seen. Black silky hair framed an angelic face complete with rosy cheeks and wide blue eyes. Sapphire blue. "Oh, no." Sam's gaze shifted to Miss Kiss who kicked and cooed enthusiastically from the play pen.

"Look at the bright side, dear." Rose patted her arm. "We figured out the spell. Now all we need to do is the reversal."

"Which you're going to do right now," Sam told Gigi.

Her great granny shook her head. "In about an hour."

"An *hour*? What happened to fifteen minutes?"

"That was before we used all of our supplies. We're fresh out of blessing seeds."

"And braided wheat rope."

"And rosemary."

"But don't worry, we've already placed an order with Mystic Muffin. Skeet should be here as soon as he finishes a danish delivery to the Black Cat sisters out in Kennelworth."

"But that's over a half hour away."

"Actually, forty-five minutes if you count the time it takes him to swing back by the shop and pick up our order, which brings us back up to an hour."

Sam's heart thudded, as her career flashed before her eyes. "I don't have an hour. I have to have that doll *now*." Her gaze rested on baby Elizabeth, so soft and real-looking despite the fact that she was now plastic, and an idea hit.

"Everybody downstairs." Mind racing, Sam started issuing orders. "We'll stop off at Mystic Muffin on the way to the party and restock, then you guys have exactly a ten-minute cab ride to get the spell right."

"But the chanting—"

"Ten minutes."

"And if we can't?"

"Then we go to plan B."

Sam turned to head back down the stairs and walked into Jake. He'd been so quiet, standing in the doorway, drinking in the strange scene that she'd almost forgotten about him. Almost.

Her skin tingled at his nearness, every nerve in her body buzzing to full awareness as her gaze met his, so dark and unreadable. "I don't suppose I could call you tomorrow with an explanation for all of this."

"Not on your life."

Sam spent the entire cab ride explaining everything from her Great-Granny Gigi and the powers that ran in her family, to what had happened with Miss Kiss, to the Spellman sisters currently chanting away around them. Other than a few raised eyebrows, Jake drank in the information with a quiet intensity that made Sam very nervous.

"I know it sounds crazy and—"

"Actually, it explains a lot."

"—I wouldn't blame you if you thought I was completely off my rocker. . . . What did you say?"

"I've been hearing chanting for the past six months. I thought Gigi was into Enigma or one of those other New Age bands. But this makes more sense."

Sam wasn't sure how her Granny being a witch made more sense than her being into New Age music, but she wasn't going to argue. Jake had taken the news much better than she'd anticipated, and he didn't look at her Granny as if she'd grown two heads.

A fact that made her heart swell with love for him, almost as much as the sight of him cuddling Miss Kiss in his big, powerful arms.

Tears burned her eyes, but she blinked them back. She couldn't break down now, she thought, as the cab pulled to a halt outside the fine arts museum where the party was already in full swing. She sniffled and blinked as one of the valets opened her door.

"I guess it's plan B," she told Granny Gigi who'd been leading the sisters in some serious, if fruitless, chanting. "Wish me luck."

"I was starting to get worried." Josie caught her just as she walked in the door. "Where's the doll?"

"Here." She handed over Baby Elizabeth.

"But this isn't Miss Kiss."

"It is for tonight."

The next half hour passed in a blur as the local media got their first glimpse of the coming year's hottest new toy. Much to Sam's relief, everyone was wowed by Baby Elizabeth, including Arthur Kiss who stood near the buffet, a pig-in-a-blanket in each hand and a barebecue-sauce-dotted bib around his neck.

He gave her a huge smile and a thumbs up.

"Looks like you did it," Josie said, catching Sam when she walked off the podium amid a flurry of camera flashes. "A vice presidency, your very own key to the executive washroom and an office with a view."

"Yeah." Yeah? Where was the enthusiastic *yes!* she should be feeling?

"Care to tell me *how* you did it? Namely where this"—she held up the Baby Elizabeth doll—"came from?"

"No."

"I didn't think so. I guess I'll head on over to the lab and see about duplicating this hair color."

"Now? But it's New Year's Eve. Don't you have a date?"

"*Had* a date." She pointed to a nerdy-looking man sniffing a cup of punch. "Www.Doberman.com," she said as if that explained everything. Dober-man moved on to a platter of

Swedish meatballs and leaned down to take several whiffs.

"Why is he sniffing everything?"

"He works with the canine unit of the Chicago police department and, personally, I think he's been around the pooches too long. He sniffed me, the doorman and the cab driver, and I'm ducking out before he cocks his leg."

Sam fielded a few more questions from enthusiastic reporters before she finally made it to the edge of the ballroom. The flurry of activity around her quickly subsided as the press turned to an even more exciting event: ringing in the new year. The band struck up. The champagne flowed. And Sam went in search of Granny Gigi.

"We did it," the old woman said when Sam found her near an ice sculpture of the Three Kisses logo. She handed over the newly restored Miss Kiss. "It was a little cramped in the ladies room, but the acoustics were perfect for chanting."

Sam wasn't prepared for the sudden ache that hit her as she cradled the doll. Just a doll.

"Aren't you happy?" Granny Gigi asked. "We found baby Elizabeth, too, and reversed the spell on her. So all's well that ends well."

Sam sniffled and blinked back a wave of tears. "Sure."

"Good. Then I'll just hold onto this," she

grabbed Miss Kiss, "while you go and say hello to your father."

Her gaze snapped up. "Dad's here?"

"Of course. You invited him, didn't you?"

"Yes, but—"

"You didn't think he would come," Granny Gigi finished for her. "But, then, you never invited him before, did you?"

She hadn't. He'd missed so much while she was growing up, she'd just assumed he didn't want to be a part of her life. And so she didn't invite him to dinners or functions.

But this had been different. She'd wanted him to see her in her moment of glory, and he'd come.

"He's not very demonstrative, but if you gave him half a chance, he just might surprise you," Granny Gigi told her before joining the Spellman sisters who were lined up on the dance floor, ready to do the "Macarena."

The truth hit her as she stared at her father standing near the bar, looking so stiff and remote in his three-piece suit. He was the picture of calm, cool professionalism. So distinguished. So successful. So alone.

She'd spent her entire life trying to please him, to win his approval, to gain his love by being just like him. As a child, she'd eaten his favorite foods, played dress-up with his business suits and pretended to read the *Wall Street Journal*. As a teenager, she'd choosen not to date and go out with friends, but to stay home and study, to make the same grades her father had made, to be valedictorian of her class the way he'd been valedictorian of his. She'd given up an art scholarship to work on a business degree, to turn herself into a cold, career-driven professional with little time or interest in anything other than climbing to the top of the corporate ladder.

A chip off the old block.

And her biggest fear was that she'd turned out more like him than she'd ever intended. Sam didn't fear a marriage and family would interfere with her career. Having it all was difficult, but women juggled both all the time Karen and Marge in R & D were living proof of that. And Josie, when she found the right man, would handle it all, as well. No, what Sam really feared, what had sent her running from Jake that night six months ago, and this morning, was that she was incapable of loving and nurturing someone else. She didn't want to be the same cold, unfeeling person her father had been.

For the first time she noted the sadness in her father's eyes, the loneliness in his stance, and her heart twisted because she realized now that Samuel Skye wasn't a man incapable of feeling, he was a man overwhelmed by it. He felt too much, loved too much, and hurt too much. He *felt*.

And so did she. Feelings swirled inside her—

excitement, anxiety, passion, fear, disappointment and love. . . . most of all, love.

Sam might be a carbon copy of her father, but she wasn't making the same mistakes he'd made. She wasn't cutting herself off, running from her feelings the way he had. Never again.

"Sam." Jake's voice sounded behind her and she turned to see him looking so handsome and sexy and determined. "We need to talk. Look, I know you don't like kids, but—"

She bristled. "Would everybody stop saying that? I like kids. I'm not Mother Goose and I did sort of freak out at first with Miss Kiss, but that doesn't mean I don't *like* kids. I'm just not used to them."

"What are you saying?"

"That maybe I could get used to them. Not a dozen, mind you. Not when one has me feeling like I've just gone eight hours on a Nordic Track. But maybe a few." Her gaze locked with his. "That is, if you love me."

"*If* I love you?" He look was incredulous before he grabbed both her hands and held them in his, his gaze turning intense. "I love you, Sam. I have since the first time I saw you standing on my doorstep with that half-starved dog in your arms. I want you to be my wife. The mother of my children. *Mine*."

"Even though I'm not a witch?"

"What does that have to do with anything?"

"The power skips a generation, which means our children will probably inherit the family gift." She hated to voice the concern, but since Jake was so set on a family and she couldn't give him a traditional one, she had to be sure.

He didn't so much as blink. "If you can get used to playing bridge, I suppose I could get used to the dog meowing."

"Bridge?"

He grinned. "I'll explain later." Then he pulled her into his arms and kissed her, and Sam enjoyed every moment because there was no place else she wanted to be. "I take it you love me, too," he finally murmured.

She pulled away and gazed into his eyes. "I love you," she said, relishing how easy the words slid to her lips. "More than anything." She grabbed his hand. "Which is why I've got someone I want you to meet."

She led him across the room, where she smiled and promptly threw her arms around a very startled-looking Samuel Skye.

After a few frantic heartbeats, her father's arms slid around her for an awkward embrace that sent warmth curling through her.

"Jake," she finally said, pulling away and smiling first at one man, and then the other. "This is my dad. Daddy, this is Jake. We're going to live happily ever after."